# *Murder* AT MOUNT JOY

# Nancy Engle

Published and Distributed By
Maghera Literary Press, LLC
PO BOX 51163
Myrtle Beach, SC 29579

Cover and Interior Design: TWA Solutions
ISBN: 978-0-9904840-0-4

Library of Congress Control Number: 2014911215

First printing May 2014

This is a work of fiction. Names, characters, businesses, places, events and incidents are either the products of the author's imagination or used in a fictitious manner. Any resemblance to actual persons, living or dead, or actual events is purely coincidental.

For inquires, contact the publisher.

*To my husband and daughter for their love and support*

# ACKNOWLEDGMENTS

A very special thanks to my husband Charlie for his love and support; without him this book would not be a reality.

Thank you to everyone who brainstormed ideas and provided feedback. Special thanks to Phyllis Edwards, Judy Meinecke, Cynthia Jeffries, and the Myrtle Beach Writers Group for taking the time to read and comment on my manuscript.

Thank you Max Regan and Lisa Birman for your editing expertise.

Thank you to TWA Solutions for the typesetting and cover design.

# CHAPTER 1

L ogan was trapped. Her breath came in short gasps; her nightshirt was plastered to her cold, drenched body. The more she struggled to free herself, the more trapped she became. She forced herself to take slow, deep breaths to still her pounding heart and shaking body. She was awake, surrounded by darkness. She closed her eyes and opened them again. It was still dark, but now she heard the familiar sound of the rain tapping on the tin roof. Her body relaxed. She was safe in her bed.

Logan was wide awake now and freed herself from the covers that held her hostage, shivering from the damp and cold that permeated the room. She wrapped herself in the thick terrycloth robe that lay across the bottom of her bed.

Her gaze went to the five-by-seven inch photograph of Luke that sat on the nightstand. He was dressed in his standard caving gear—battered yellow caving helmet with headlamp, worn jeans and flannel shirt, and a backpack with a coil of rope attached. His curly black hair was pulled back and fastened into a ponytail at the nape of his neck. The photograph was taken two years ago, the day he disappeared into the crevasse.

She could still see his blue eyes looking at her with horror as his six-foot frame twisted and, arms pinwheeling, he fell backwards into the crevasse. His screams were swallowed up as quickly as his body.

The search and rescue team spent weeks exploring the myriad tunnels, but they were unable to locate any tunnel that would take them closer to the bottom of the crevasse. Search and rescue soon became a recovery operation, which was eventually called off, and Logan was faced with the agonizing truth. Luke was never coming home, dead or alive. She checked out of life, refusing to interact with anyone. Her family, concerned about her well-being, had her admitted to a psychiatric hospital, but that was two years ago.

She sat on the edge of the bed holding the photograph of Luke, running her fingers over his image. Losing Luke was overwhelming. Leaving him in that cave was unfathomable. She had a headstone placed in the family plot, but the grave was as empty as her heart.

She put his photograph back on the nightstand and thought of her journal resting in the drawer. It had been months since she'd written anything. She pulled out the notebook and sat cross-legged on the bed, sketching plans for the visual arts center she dreamed of starting. By the time she finished sketching and writing, she felt lighter and went downstairs to face the day with a new determination.

She stood at the kitchen window watching the male cardinal pecking away at the bird feeder until the final burst of brewed coffee captured her attention; the smell warmed the kitchen against the drizzly, misty chill of April. She took a sip and thought about tonight and how proud Luke would have been to see his work exhibited.

Logan picked up sample prints of the photographs that were going to be displayed and sifted through them, stopping at the photograph of Moses crouched down on the bank of the stream, his cabin behind him. He was running his fingers through the crystal clear water, telling them about the trout fishing. The photograph captured the joy, peace, and contentment on his upturned face.

She swiped at the lone tear making its way down her cheek, and set the pictures down, remembering the day that changed their lives. The exploration of the series of caves, the caves that were on Moses's property, the caves that would claim Luke for their own.

She shook herself out of her reverie and went to get the morning paper, which she hoped rested on her side of the steps she shared with her neighbor, Mrs. Rosen. She opened the door and the chilled air rushed in, causing her to shiver and pull her terrycloth robe tighter against her body. She stood in the doorway for a minute, taking in the 18th century Society Hill Federal style row homes shrouded in a fog that muffled the city sounds. She loved the granite block that paved the streets and the reproduction Franklin lamps strategically placed along the sidewalks. She could almost see and hear the horse drawn carriages traversing the narrow byways.

The house had been in the O'Malley family since Philadelphia's 1950s gentrification project, when Logan's father-in-law, Colin O'Malley, bought and renovated it. It was the house where Luke grew up. When she and Luke got married his mother, Vanessa, gave them the fully decorated house as a wedding gift.

She was bending down to grab her newspaper from Mrs. Rosen's side of the steps, when she heard the click of the front door. A broom emerged, followed by her neighbor.

"I'm sorry," said Logan, looking up at her. "The newspaper boy missed my steps."

"Stay off my property," she shouted in her heavy German accent, waving the broom.

Logan grabbed the paper and ran inside. The woman had never spoken a civil word to her, or to anyone else for that matter.

In the eight years Logan had lived in the house, all she knew about her neighbor was that she spent an inordinate amount of time sweeping and scrubbing her front steps and pavement, waving her broom at anyone who dared to walk on or near her property. It always bothered her that she wasn't on good terms with her neighbor. She had made numerous attempts at polite conversation when she first moved in, but her attempts were met with hostility.

Logan took her newspaper and coffee into the breakfast nook and sat facing the small yard. She could just make out the misty softness of the male cardinal flitting around and grabbed her camera. Unlike Luke, Logan preferred nature shots, but was learning to appreciate the techniques of photographing people, capturing the subtle shifts in lighting and facial features to tell their story.

Luke's work focused on the faces of Americana, the real people that make up America, the invisible people. He saw in their faces their hopes and dreams, their losses and pain, the extraordinary in the ordinary. He wanted people to experience the emotions his subjects were feeling when they looked at his photographs. Luke was photographing the faces of Appalachia, in particular, Moses, who lived in the mountains of Tennessee, when he died. Logan picked up the five-by-seven sample prints again.

She had to limit her choices for the exhibit to thirty-six and decided to take a few from each of three photo shoots which Luke had titled "Appalachia," "Forced Migration," and "Pickers."

Logan had stopped by Rose's gallery last night to see how things were going. The lab had done an extraordinary job printing and framing the photographs. But of course, it was Luke's eye for lighting and body language that made the photos come alive. She ran her fingers over Moses's face and could almost feel the weathered roughness of his skin.

"Luke," she whispered, saddened that he wouldn't be there.

Just then, the front door flew open and slammed shut, causing Logan to jump. Her best friend, Rose, rushed into the kitchen, dictating orders. She was dressed in skintight jeans that barely covered her butt and were tucked into brown suede boots with stiletto heels. The jacket she wore as a blouse needed another couple of inches to fill the gap between the bottom of the jacket and the top of her jeans. She had a Burberry scarf wound around her neck.

"Aren't you a bit chilly?" Logan asked, rolling her eyes.

Rose stopped short. "You're not dressed. What've you been doing? Come on, we have to get going. Big day," she said as she pushed Logan toward the stairs. "Come on, go, go."

"We have plenty of time. Our appointment isn't until nine," Logan said, heading upstairs. "There's a piece of apple cake on the counter," she said over her shoulder. Too late. Rose was chewing and shooing at the same time.

Logan was back a few minutes later, dressed in grey wool slacks, a red cashmere pullover sweater, and her favorite Prada boots. She grabbed her raincoat and followed Rose out into the drizzle.

"I'll drive," Rose announced.

"I can drive," said Logan quickly.

"We have to walk two blocks to the garage just to get your car. Mine's right here," she said, pointing.

"The street parking is for residents only," Logan told her for the thousandth time.

"And you're a resident."

Logan rolled her eyes. Rose always did what she wanted.

They got in the car and passed through the fog shrouded city. The only things visible were disembodied traffic and car lights. The farther they got from the city and away from the rivers, the less dense the fog became.

"Everybody goes there," Rose was saying with pride, bringing Logan back to the present. "Had a heck of a time getting us in."

"You shouldn't have gone to the trouble."

"No trouble. Glad to do it for you."

That wasn't quite what Logan meant, she turned her attention back to the passing countryside. She had to admit it was beautiful out here. The estates and horse farms were all shrouded in mist, giving them an ethereal glow. Logan kicked herself for not remembering her camera as Rose was rushing her out the door.

All the sounds were muffled, adding to the otherworldly feel. These were the kinds of conditions that Logan loved to photograph, again chastising herself for forgetting her camera which usually hung by the door with her purse. Instead it was sitting on the kitchen table where she had set it after photographing the cardinal.

Logan snapped out of her daydream as she felt a change in their speed. She looked up. "That light is turning red," she said.

"No problem. I have plenty of time."

"Maybe you should slow down. The road's wet and you don't want to slam on the brakes and skid."

Instead, Rose sped up. Logan, realizing that she intended to run the light, grabbed the door handle and pressed her foot to the floor. She closed her eyes and said a prayer to St. Christopher, patron saint of travelers in Catholic doctrine. At least, that was until 1969, when the Church wasn't able to find any proof that Christopher was a holy being and decided that he was a legend. They erased him from the list of saints, de-sainted him. Logan was wondering what happened to all of those St. Christopher medals and statues and if her prayer was still valid when she felt the car swerve.

Rose slammed on the brakes. Their car skidded, heading for the edge of the road and the forest of trees that clutched the side of the slope. Logan screamed. The tires hit the gravel and the car began to slide toward the edge. She grabbed the dashboard but the trees continued to get closer. Then suddenly the car stopped. There wasn't any crash or breaking glass. When Logan looked out the window, she saw they were balanced over the edge of the precipice.

The shadowy figures of the trees appeared to move in the swirling fog. Logan's heartbeat pounded in her ears. Her sweaty palms still clung to the dashboard. She saw movement to her left and realized that Rose was shifting in her seat.

"Don't move," said Logan, barely breathing.

"I'm fine," said Rose.

"No, don't move," Logan said, more emphatically this time. "My rear tire. I can see it in my mirror. I think it's hanging over the edge."

"Oh, well I have front wheel drive. No problem," Rose said, moving forward to start the stalled car. Logan grabbed her wrist. The car shifted. Neither one of them moved.

"Can you see your rear tire?" asked Logan.

Rose slowly turned her head so she could look out the side view mirror. "It's close, but I think it's still on the gravel."

An otherworldly glow filled their car just before the state trooper's cruiser, red and blue lights flashing, materialized out of the fog.

"Thank God," said Logan.

They watched the officer walking toward their car while talking into his shoulder radio. Rose slowly moved her arm so she could push the window's down button. The officer's football player size frame filled the opening and he identified himself as Officer Bradley. "A tow truck is on the way," he said. "Just don't move. I'll be right back."

Every so often, a car passed and Logan noticed how the sounds were swallowed up. They sat quietly, barely daring to breathe. After what seemed like a lifetime, the mist in front of them glowed yellow, announcing the approach of a tow truck.

"Finally," whispered Logan. "I hope they hurry."

They watched Officer Bradley direct the truck into position, making sure that he didn't get too close to the edge. The water-logged gravel shoulder began to disintegrate under the truck's weight and gave way, causing the truck to slide sideways down the embankment. Logan and Rose looked on, horrified. The tow truck settled into the ravine, and a minute later the driver emerged and scrambled up the hill. He stood on the road, hands on hips, staring down at his lopsided truck. *Fortunately*, thought Logan, *we weren't hooked up yet*.

They watched Officer Bradley walk over to the driver and heard him inform him that a larger tow truck was on the way. Logan and Rose started laughing. The car shifted.

A couple of small tow trucks passed, blowing their air horns, waving and shouting; these overtures were met with rude gestures from the stranded driver. A larger tow truck emerged from the fog. The new driver spent a few minutes hassling his buddy, then turned his attention to Rose and Logan. He hooked them up, got their car back on terra firma, and completed the paperwork. Rose started the engine.

Office Bradley filled her window. "Not so fast."

"We're okay," said Rose.

"You ran a red light back there."

"Huh?"

"License and registration, please."

Rose just stared at him. Logan wasn't sure she was going to comply, but then she grabbed her purse, flinging receipts, beauty products, cell phone, and other miscellaneous items onto the console before getting to her wallet and producing the asked for papers.

"I told you the light was red," said Logan.

"I had plenty of time."

"Apparently not," Logan said, nodding at the cruiser behind them.

They sat in silence until the officer got back to them with a ticket and a warning. "Slow down," he said. "Your speed contributed to this situation."

"But Officer, someone ran us off the road," protested Rose.

"I didn't see anyone else. What I did see was you driving too fast for conditions and running a red light."

"It was a dark color, and small," she said.

He took out his notebook and began writing. "Not much of a description."

"It came out of that road there." She pointed to the barely visible road on their left. "She was wearing a big hat and driving like a maniac." Logan noticed a slight twitch of the officer's mouth as they both looked at Rose.

"Did you see the car?" he asked Logan.

"I had my eyes closed," Logan said, omitting the part about praying to St. Christopher. "When we skidded I opened them. I might have seen tail lights up ahead, I'm not sure. It all happened so fast."

He finished taking the report, getting as much information as he could, which wasn't much, and told Rose to be more careful.

"Let's just go home," said Logan, leaning her head back and sighing.

"Go home? What are you talking about? We really need that spa treatment now," Rose said, putting the car in gear.

"Really, let's just go home. I wasn't looking forward to it to begin with."

"Nonsense, we're getting the works, pampered and patted." Rose pulled back onto the road, swerving around a slow moving vehicle. "We deserve it. You're too tense. Loosen up."

Logan rolled her eyes. "I don't like being pampered and patted," she said, knowing it was a waste of breath.

"We're almost there. It should be just ahead."

They rounded a bend, and Logan saw a Greek style mansion looming large at the top of the hill. The winding drive was surrounded by misty fields. The parking lot was nowhere in sight.

As if reading Logan's mind, Rose said, "The parking lot's around back."

"I'm rather insulted that we are supposed to enter from the rear," said Logan, as Rose pulled up to the attendant.

"Oh, that's just so people driving by can't see the clients going in or out. Some of them are easily recognizable."

"Valet parking? How much is this going to cost me?" Despite the beautiful house and clothing, Logan didn't have money to burn, and everything she did have was going to the visual arts center.

"My treat." Logan began to protest. Rose put up her hand to forestall any further discussion and got out of the car, giving the attendant a flirty smile. "This is going to be fun."

"I still find it insulting that we have to go in through the back door," Logan said.

Another attendant opened the door and they entered a lobby all done in marble and gold. "Rose, did you check their prices before making reservations?"

"Of course I did. Don't worry about anything. I've got it covered."

They checked in and had a seat in one of the overstuffed leather lounge chairs. Logan filled one of the crystal goblets with the cucumber laced water and took a few sips, surprised at how refreshing it was.

Before she had a chance to take another sip, their personal attendant arrived and introduced herself as Gillian. "I'll be escorting you to each of your appointments. If you have any questions, just let me know."

They followed her to the back, where she got them ready for their massages, followed by manicures and pedicures. Rose chose a blood red polish, while Logan opted for a French manicure. After they were finished, Gillian escorted them to the hair salon and introduced Kate, their stylist.

"Let's have a seat over here," Kate said, directing Logan to the soft leather chair. "Do you mind if I undo your chignon?"

"Go ahead," said Logan, giving Rose a look that said 'I'll get you for this.' Kate undid Logan's hair and let it fall past her shoulders in soft curls, then she ran her fingers through it to get an idea of thickness and texture, while Rose settled herself in the chair next to Logan.

"If we layer it just right, you won't have to do much but blow dry it," she said to Logan, looking at Rose.

"That sounds great," said Rose. "Let's do it."

"Don't I get a say? After all, it is my hair," said Logan, sounding whiney.

"Of course you do," said Kate, patting her shoulder. "Do you have a style in mind?" she asked, looking at Rose.

"I'd like to keep the same style," said Logan. She caught Rose's reflection in the mirror, rolling her eyes at Kate, and Kate's imperceptible nod to Rose.

"But that's so old fashioned," said Rose. "You need an update. Something softer, younger looking."

"But I like this. It's sophisticated."

Rose laughed. "Sophisticated? Logan, you're thirty years old and you look like a schoolmarm."

Logan thought back to all those hairdressing appointments with Luke's mother. Vanessa had used the word sophisticated and made fun of women choosing styles that were much too young for their age and inappropriate for their station in life.

Her mind snapped back to the conversation that was taking place without her.

"Why don't you look through some of these magazines and let me know if you see something you might like?"

"I already know what I like," she snapped, then softened her response with a smile. "I've been doing my hair like this for a few years. It's easy."

"If you're looking for easy, I can give you an updated look that will still be easy to maintain."

"Well, maybe we can trim a little off the bottom," she said, relenting a bit.

Rose spoke up. "Logan, who picked out that style for you?"

"I did," she said with some annoyance.

"Really? Where do you go to get your hair styled?"

Logan didn't answer. She knew what was coming and didn't want to have this conversation again. But Rose plunged right ahead. Either she didn't see Logan's warning look or chose to ignore it. Probably the latter.

"Ellis, that's who." Logan saw Kate's eyebrows raise.

"And who introduced you to Ellis?" asked Rose with a look of satisfaction.

"That has nothing to do with anything," said Logan, but Rose went right on as though she hadn't spoken.

"Your mother-in-law. That's who."

Logan looked over at the stylist, who didn't even pretend she wasn't listening. "She has good taste and always looks impeccable.

Let's get on with my haircut. I'm sure Kate has better things to do than listen to this."

"You've been letting her make your decisions since you met her. Look at your house."

"There's nothing wrong with my house. It's beautiful."

"Yeah, beautiful and stuffy. It's like living in a museum."

"They're valuable antiques."

"Picked out by someone else. Before you married Luke you made your own decisions. Your apartment was funky. It had whimsy."

"Okay, enough. Let's get my hair cut and get out of here." Logan didn't want to have this conversation, particularly about her decorating. Somewhere deep down she knew Rose had a point and it annoyed her. She lived in Society Hill, after all. She was expected to maintain a certain image, and gnome bookends just didn't fit.

Kate interrupted her thoughts. "If we cut some length off and layer it, change it a bit around the face, it will accent the shape and soften it up."

Rose pointed to a photo in the magazine. "This one would look great on you."

"I don't know. It really isn't anything like my current style."

"That's what's so great about it. A new you. It's time."

Logan cast her a scathing look. This time Rose got the message and backed off.

"Why don't we give it a try?" suggested Kate

Rose and Kate looked at her, waiting for an answer. "Well," she said slowly, "I guess that would be okay." An unbidden thought popped into her head. *What would Vanessa say?*

"Now, how about some highlights to bring out the natural highlights in your hair?"

"No, I don't want to be bothered having to do touch ups."

"Let's do it," said Rose.

Logan sighed, knowing that she'd lost the battle. But she determined that she and Rose would have a long talk once the exhibition was over.

When Kate was finished, Logan admired her new look. She hadn't realized how severe the other style was and how much older it made her look.

It was still misting when they left, and Logan's hand went to her hair, trying to protect it.

"It looks great," said Rose. "You look twenty years younger."

Logan stopped in her tracks and gave Rose a wide-eyed look.

"Well, maybe not twenty years," said Rose, "but you do look younger."

Logan had to admit that she felt good, actually attractive. "Thank you for doing this," said Logan, patting her hair.

"You're welcome. There's nothing wrong with change. It doesn't mean you're being disloyal to anyone."

"I don't want to talk about it."

"I'm just saying…"

"Rose." It came out sharper than Logan had intended. She put her hand on Rose's arm. "I really do appreciate everything," giving her a smile.

She barely noticed the countryside whizzing by. The fog had lifted and it looked as though the sun was trying to break through the thick grey clouds.

"You're awfully quiet. Are you okay?" asked Rose.

Logan didn't know what she was feeling. She was relaxed after all the pampering. She felt good. But tonight was going to be emotionally draining. She wasn't sure she was up to seeing Luke's work everywhere she looked.

Everyone would be asking her about the photographs. They'd want to know about the people in them, but most of all they'd want to know how she was doing, and all of them would be wondering what had happened that day. Logan never talked about it. Their friends only knew the barest of details, and she knew they were curious. They never asked her outright, but always tried to steer the conversation in that direction. She was well practiced at diverting their attention. This would be the first time they'd all be together since Luke's memorial service.

"I'm okay," said Logan. "Just tired."

"We have some time before the exhibit. Maybe you should take a nap."

"That sounds good, but I always feel groggy instead of refreshed after a nap."

They rode the rest of the way in silence and before she knew it they were back in the city, stopping and starting, horns honking, sirens blaring, and she found herself wishing for the earlier quiet.

They pulled up to Logan's house and Rose left her, saying she would be back in two hours in a tone that didn't leave Logan any room for argument. Actually, she was pleased that Rose was picking her up. It was going to be a difficult evening and she could use the moral support. Her body tensed with anticipation, nervousness, and excitement.

She made herself a cup of tea and a sandwich, not because she was hungry, but because she thought she should eat something. She packed up her camera and put it by the door. She probably wouldn't need it though. Rose had hired a photographer for the evening.

She went upstairs to get ready, stopping in her office to answer some e-mails. When she got to her bedroom she turned and studied herself in the mirror and had to admit the new hairstyle was flattering. She laid out her gown and accessories. The gown's emerald green material shimmered, and she knew it would complement her fair skin and green eyes. Her jewelry consisted of an emerald and diamond necklace with matching earrings and cocktail ring, all compliments of Vanessa. Not something she would want to own, but she would enjoy wearing them.

She freshened her makeup with the products she had purchased from the spa. Everything was new, hair, makeup, dress. It had been a long time since she'd changed anything and she was feeling some guilt. Luke liked her hair long, and Vanessa had helped pick her hairstyle as well as her makeup.

She studied herself in the full-length mirror before going downstairs, and was pleased with the results. She did look younger, and realized she felt younger. Halfway down the stairs, she heard Rose pull up and blow the horn. *My neighbors will love that*, she thought, *especially Mrs. Rosen*. She hoped she wasn't lurking outside because a quick getaway would be impossible in a gown and heels. *Well, here goes*, she thought, stepping outside and looking around. No Mrs. Rosen.

# CHAPTER 2

The rain had stopped by the time they arrived at The Gallery, the name Rose came up with when she couldn't think of a name. She rented the space for an exorbitant price because of the location, but Logan knew that she wasn't sure if she would be able to stay once her lease was up in August, not unless business picked up. Summer was their busy season and Rose had several exhibits planned. Logan hoped it would be enough.

The Gallery occupied two row houses that were renovated years ago and converted into a single dwelling. A front porch spanned the width of both buildings. The original entrance on the left was replaced by a large triple window. The entrance on the right was widened and replaced with French doors. Visitors walked into a large, softly lit reception area containing permanent pieces of art, but the main exhibits were through the archway on the left. That was where Luke's photographs were. Rose had also insisted on including some of Logan's prints. At first Logan had disagreed, stating that this was Luke's night. After much coaxing and prodding, she reluctantly agreed, but insisted that her prints be displayed in a smaller area, a request that Rose ignored.

Rose's gown was a black satin sheath with spaghetti straps and a back that dipped to just below her waist. The side slit ended just inches from her hip. She wore a single teardrop cut diamond that dangled from a silver chain, and silver tiered earrings. Considering Rose's penchant for unusual haute couture, this was boring.

They walked up to the front porch, which was lit up like Christmas, and Logan's heartbeat quickened. They went into the large open reception room, heels clicking on the polished oak floors, and directly into the exhibition room. The lighting was soft and shone at an angle that brought out the minutest details of each photograph.

She turned to Rose. "It's beautiful. Everything is just perfect." The black and white prints were arranged by cultural subject, "Forced Migration," "Pickers," and "Appalachia." Some of the prints contained a single object that Luke had hand-colored before he died, and these were interspersed with the black and white prints. Logan's favorite picture was of the little Navajo girl playing in the rain. The unpaved road was a quagmire. She was bending over, the tips of her braids dipping into the mud. She was barefoot. Her yellow sundress had little red flowers around the neck and hem. Luke had painstakingly hand-colored the dress and each small flower. Logan turned to Rose and hugged her. "Thank you."

Rose's smile lit her face. "I loved putting it together."

"Well, you've outdone yourself. It's just spectacular."

Rose was grinning from ear to ear. "Trish will handle the donations and sales," she said as they made their way down the hall to Trish's office. Trish was Rose's part-time assistant, working her way through Temple University, studying Fine Arts. Trish was tall and thin as a rail, which appeared to be genetic rather than an eating disorder. Her long blond hair hung in a single loose braid, tendrils of curls escaping here and there. She was wearing a plain black floor length knit dress. Around her neck hung a silver chain with a three-inch filigree silver owl with huge turquoise eyes that matched Trish's own eyes.

"We have you scheduled to give a talk around nine o'clock," said Trish. "That'll give everyone a chance to get here, have some champagne and hors d'oeuvres and view the exhibit."

Logan started to say something, but Rose held up her hand in a stop motion. "Not to worry," said Rose, "you'll be fine."

"You know how I hate talking in front of crowds."

Rose smiled at her. "Trish made up cue cards. It'll be easy to keep your thoughts in order."

"Thank you, Trish. You're a lifesaver."

"You'll do fine. The cards are here," she said, pointing to the top drawer. "I took the highlights from the speech you wrote. When you're ready, we can take a few minutes to go over them."

Rose took Logan's arm. "Let's check out the kitchen, see what the caterers are up to." They walked down the hall to the back of the gallery, where the kitchen ran the width of the combined houses. It appeared to be in chaos, shouted orders, timers dinging, people moving about. A collision looked imminent. But as Logan watched she realized that it was really well choreographed. The counters held trays of picture perfect canapés. She couldn't resist trying one of the crab canapés, which was wonderful. Wine was breathing, wine was chilling, the bar was set up. Everything looked to be in order.

The buzzer alerted them that someone had come into the gallery, so they headed up front to greet their guests. Ran and Michael had just arrived. Kingston Ranford, everyone called him Ran, and his brother Michael Ranford, Monsignor Ranford. They were Logan's paternal uncles. Her father, William, had passed away six years ago from lung cancer, the result of years of working in the Naval Shipyard and smoking. Ran and Michael were her only remaining family. The brothers shared the same six-one height, but that was where the resemblance ended.

Logan and Rose hugged each of Logan's uncles. Ran was pulling at his tie and readjusting the jacket over his slight paunch. His wiry, shoulder-length grey hair, flecked with the black of his youth, was sticking out from under one of his many signature berets, the color of which was determined by his mood. Tonight he had chosen a black and red tartan plaid. *He must be going for the formal effect*, she thought, smiling. The huge cigar clamped between his teeth completed the picture.

Rose leaned in and whispered to Logan, "He can't smoke in here."

"Not to worry, it's not lit."

"Just make sure he knows not to light it."

"I heard that." His voice was gravelly and slightly admonishing, but his azure blue eyes twinkled.

Ran lived alone on his mother's estate, Mount Joy, located in Fairmount Park, Philadelphia. The property sat atop a knoll with a commanding view of the Schuylkill River, complete with its own dilapidated dock. The estate was comprised of seventy-five acres, a mansion, caretaker's cottage, and various outbuildings, all of which suffered from her uncle's neglect. All, that is, except for the six bay garage he had built to restore his antique cars. Developers were falling all over each other trying to get their hands on this prime piece of real estate, but her uncle ran them off at regular intervals.

Michael, on the other hand, looked dashing in his tux, and completely at ease. His dark wavy hair, which Logan suspected he touched up, was perfectly cut and coiffed, and the fit of the tux emphasized his well maintained body. Michael ran at least five miles a day and was careful about his diet.

He was the Monsignor of St. Bernadette's Roman Catholic Church, a Romanesque structure which was completed in 1828, and resided in the adjacent priest house. Michael, Logan knew, aspired to become Archbishop of the Philadelphia Diocese.

"You've outdone yourself, Rose," said Michael. He wandered around, hands behind his back, nodding. "Excellent selections, Logan."

Logan's eyes misted. "Luke would've been proud. I…" Her voice choked.

Michael put his arm over her shoulder. "I know. I wouldn't be surprised if you make more than enough money to satisfy the bank's conditions for a loan for the visual arts center."

"I would've given you the money," said Ran. "You didn't have to go to all this trouble."

Logan shook her head and smiled at him. "It won't hurt you to get dressed up and get out once in a while. You spend every minute with your head under the hood of one of your cars."

"Ran was always a loner. Growing up he spent all his time tinkering with whatever he could get his hands on," said Michael.

Rose laughed and patted Ran on the back. "There's lots of food and drink. Enjoy your night out."

"You have any beer?" he asked.

"Just for you." She winked at Logan and Michael, and took Ran's arm, leading him into the kitchen. Logan heard him say something about real food, not those wimpy sandwiches.

"You changed your hair," said Michael. "Very becoming." Michael always noticed things like that, unlike Ran. She could've walked in with tattoos up her arm and Ran probably wouldn't notice.

"Thank you," she said, smiling. "I'm liking it too. Rose talked me into the change."

"Well, she was right. It's striking."

The front door buzzer sounded again, and Logan turned to see who had come in. "I'll go turn off the buzzer for the evening," said Michael, walking toward the back.

"Jane," Logan said under her breath. Jane was a pear shaped five foot two inches. Her medium brown hair was cut short and she wore it spiked, like the kids Logan had seen hanging around on the street corners. Jane mostly wore t-shirts and baggy jeans, making it difficult to determine gender. Tonight, however, she had traded her usual attire for a black sack-looking dress and low heels that she was clearly uncomfortable wearing. Logan walked over to Jane and greeted her with a flat voice that Jane didn't seem to notice.

"Welcome," said Logan, almost choking on the word. Jane was the last person Logan would have invited, but somehow she had managed to get Trish to add her to the guest list. Trish couldn't be blamed though. She didn't know their history.

Just then, Michael came back in. He looked at Logan with raised eyebrows.

"Michael, this is Jane."

"Nice to meet you, Jane," he said. "Will you excuse us, Logan needs to attend to something," he said, taking Logan's arm and leading her into the exhibition gallery.

"So what's the story?" he whispered.

"What story?"

"Jane?" he asked, lifting his eyebrows.

"It's a long one and now isn't the place to tell it."

"So should I keep an eye on you two? Play peacemaker?" Logan rolled her eyes and gave a hint of a smile. "That's better," he said. "Now, this is your evening. Enjoy it."

Ran came in from the kitchen carrying a can of beer. "What's she doing here?" he asked in a voice loud enough for Jane to hear, nodding in her direction.

"Shush," said Logan, steering him away from her. "Don't antagonize her. Maybe she'll leave early."

"You know her?" asked Michael, looking at his brother.

"Had the dubious pleasure of meeting her at Luke's memorial service. You were officiating so didn't get to meet her."

"Looks like I missed something," commented Michael, eyebrows raised.

"You didn't miss a thing. She's a mean one," said Ran.

"She's coming this way," said Logan under her breath.

Ran stepped forward. "Come to spread more venom?"

Logan sighed. "Ran…" She took his arm and tried to lead him away.

Michael stepped between them and Jane. "So, Jane. What do you think of the exhibit?" he asked, nudging her in the opposite direction from Ran and Logan.

Logan let out her breath. "Ran, what's wrong with you?"

He looked at her rather sheepishly. "Sorry."

She took his arm. "Just do me a favor and promise me you'll stay away from her. Please?"

"I promise."

"I mean it."

"I promise," he said again, more emphatically.

"Okay. Now, enjoy yourself, and stay out of trouble. I have to see to my guests."

More guests arrived and Logan greeted each one of them. These were not the elite of Society Hill, whose tastes ran toward original canvas and paint artists selling for exorbitant amounts of money. Photographs did not fall into their definition of art. These were Luke's and Logan's friends and business associates, and they appreciated eclectic works of art.

Logan watched the caterers moving among the guests, offering food and drink. She noticed that Michael was talking to Jane, who was looking up at him like a wide-eyed school girl. "You know

Luke and I were very close in college," Logan heard her saying as she passed them. Logan caught Michael's eye, smiled and just shook her head. He was getting Jane's perspective on their history.

Rose came up to Logan, noticed where her attention was focused, and also shook her head. "She's telling the story about her and Luke, right?"

"How did you know?"

"Just look at her face, how animated it is. She only looks like that when she's talking about Luke."

"The sad thing is that she really thinks I stole him away from her. She really believes that Luke was interested."

"I felt sorry for her, watching her throw herself at Luke when he only had eyes for you."

"Something about her is different since Luke died. Nothing I can put my finger on, but lately she's been giving me the creeps."

Rose took Logan's elbow and led her away. "Ignore her. Tonight is your and Luke's night."

"He would've been proud," she said, unable to keep the sadness from her voice.

Rose squeezed her arm. "I know." She smiled, and in a cheerful voice asked, "Have you noticed that we've already sold several photos?"

"Really," said Logan. "That's wonderful. Which ones?"

"Come on, I'll show you," she said, leading her into the exhibition room. "You're going to have that visual arts center before you know it."

"And you can exhibit all the students' works, as only you can," said Logan, then caught the sadness that passed over Rose's face. "You'll have your gallery. If it's not here, then somewhere better."

"I will," she said, smiling, "but for tonight, let's focus on you."

Logan looked around. "I am blessed to have so many good friends. Now, I'd better go mingle with those friends." She gave Rose a hug and headed toward a group of women who were admiring the little Navajo girl. Logan told them about the girl's family and the problems of poverty, and drug and alcohol addiction facing the Navajo nation.

A short time later, she excused herself and continued to move around the room chatting with her other guests. Michael and Ran were standing by the window about ten feet from her. Michael was standing straight and smiling at Ran. Ran was leaning into him with his index finger just inches from Michael's chest. Rose joined Logan and they started toward them. They caught a few words of their conversation.

"… last time," Ran was saying to Michael. Michael tipped his champagne glass toward Ran and smiled.

"Hmm, I wonder what that's about," whispered Rose.

"Who knows. They're always bickering about something, usually religion or politics. I think Ran just makes absurd statements that he knows are in opposition to Michael's beliefs, just to get him going. Sometimes it's funny, but it does get on my nerves after a while."

Michael turned to them and smiled. "So, ladies, I noticed some sold signs. It looks like you're on the road to success," he said, eyes twinkling.

"We won't know for a couple of days," said Rose, smiling, "but indications are that we may exceed our expectations."

"Have you picked a site?" Michael asked Logan.

"Not yet. I need to raise at least one hundred thousand dollars before the bank will even talk to me. I have some ideas, though."

"How about Mount Joy?" asked Ran.

"What about Mount Joy?" asked Logan, momentarily distracted by Jane who was headed toward the offices. "Excuse me while I see what she's up to."

"Stay here. I'll check," Rose said, following Jane down the hall.

Michael looked at Ran. "Mount Joy?"he asked, bringing Logan's attention back to the conversation.

Ran turned to Logan and winked. He had a mischievous twinkle in his eyes. "I have a plan."

"I'm sorry," said Logan. "What were you saying about Mount Joy?"

"I was saying that I have a plan."

"A plan? A plan to do what?" she asked.

Ran draped his arm across her shoulders and smiled down at her. Just then it dawned on her what he was saying.

"Wait a minute. Mount Joy? You can't be serious!" said Logan. "You can't do that. It's your home. Besides, I have my eye on a couple of other sites."

Ran ignored her and went right on talking. "I still have some details to work out with my lawyer, but we can make it work. When everything's in place, then I'll let you know. It'll work out. You'll see," he said, patting her on the arm.

Logan was dumbfounded. This was the first she'd heard about using Mount Joy for her visual arts center, and she wasn't sure how she felt about it, although it did have merit. "But it's your home," said Logan.

"Now, don't you worry about anything," he said, patting her again and looking at Michael. "I have a plan." He winked. "Let's go look at some of the exhibits," he said, giving them a Cheshire cat smile. He took pleasure in getting in the last word where Michael was concerned. They went into the exhibition room and he spent all of five seconds looking at the photos. "I think I'll go check on things in the kitchen."

"Ran." Logan hugged him. "Thank you."

"For what?"

"For coming. I know this isn't your thing," she said, patting the lapels of his tux. "Black tie. All the people. Thank you for making the sacrifice."

"You know I'd do anything for you."

"I know. Now, go on into the kitchen."

Logan scanned the room and saw Michael deep in conversation with C.J. Forster, Carly Jo. C.J. was average height and a little on the bulky side, but it was her short, auburn curly hair that people noticed. She was an only child, and she began using the non-gender specific initials C.J. when she inherited her father's builder/developer business five years ago. She found it easier to work in the male dominated building trade when people assumed C.J. was a male.

Logan was aware that C.J. had approached Ran more than once about selling his property. She had recently heard that the company was struggling financially and snagging a deal like the development that was being proposed would turn things around for her and her husband, Sam.

At one time, C.J. and Sam were Luke's and Logan's best friends, and they had both been with them in the cave that day. But Logan hadn't seen much of them lately. The length of time between their visits expanded as time went on. Logan supposed that was the natural progression of things. She had noticed C.J. and Sam's discomfort the few times they got together. Logan was surprised to realize that she had some resentment toward them. Sam was standing next to Luke when he lost his balance. Why didn't he grab him? She wondered if C.J. might have sensed her unasked question.

"It's a beautiful shot."

Logan jumped and turned to see her neighbor, Irma Morgenstern. She was referring to the photograph of Moses kneeling by the stream, his home to the left and slightly behind him. Moses wore coveralls that were worn and patched, but scrubbed clean to within an inch of their life. His grey flecked hair was brushed and hung to his shoulders. He was wearing a battered hat and heavy boots with no laces.

He was a proud man and had taken great pleasure showing them the log cabin he'd built. It sat alone in a clearing surrounded by hundreds of thousands of acres of National Park Service land. She studied the photograph. The hand-made porch chairs stood like sentinels on either side of the front door. Inside, the cabin was one large room, everything neat as a pin. The outhouse was barely visible nestled in the small clearing surrounded by trees. She could almost hear the sound of the creek that skirted the western side of the cabin, and then she remembered the invitation to explore a cave on his property. The invitation that ended Luke's life, and changed hers forever. Tears dampened her eyes.

"Irma, how are you?" she asked, blinking back tears.

"I'm fine, dear." Irma took Logan's hands in hers and stood back. "You look beautiful. That color suits you. And your hair. Turn around. It makes you…" she hesitated.

"It's okay, Rose already informed me that it makes me look years younger." They both laughed.

"That Rose," Irma laughed, shaking her head. "So, how are you doing?" She reached up and brushed an errant tear off Logan's cheek. "Luke was very talented," said Irma, squeezing her hands.

"Yes, he was," said Logan, closing her eyes to block the flow of tears that was waiting.

Irma was somewhere in her late seventies, by Logan's estimation. She couldn't be sure because she would never reveal her age. She was a widow and lived down the street from Logan. When Luke was alive he had helped her with the occasional lifting or moving of heavy pieces of furniture.

"What is the man's name?" she asked, Logan interrupting her thoughts.

Logan smiled. "Moses," she said, "just Moses," she added before Irma could press her for a surname she didn't have.

Irma stood quietly and just stared at the photograph. After several minutes she turned to Logan and said, "I feel like I know him. I can see his soul. Look at his eyes. He is a kind and proud man."

"Yes, he is."

"I'd like to buy this one." Before Logan had a chance to respond, she said, "I'll give you twenty-thousand dollars."

"Ir... Irma," she stammered. "That's very generous, but we're not asking anywhere near that amount.

"I know, consider it a contribution to your very worthwhile enterprise."

"Are you sure?"

"My dear, I'm old, not senile." Logan laughed. "That's better," she said, patting her arm. "I'll just go and find Trish and settle up. Then I'll be on my way. I need my beauty rest."

"Thank you, Irma," she said, giving her a hug.

"I know that school of yours will be very successful." They hugged again and Logan watched through dampened lashes as Irma made her way to Trish's office to complete the sale.

Ran came up and put his arm across her shoulders and hugged her. She looked at him and smiled.

"I know," he said. "I know how hard this has been for you, but I also know how proud Luke would have been. Maybe selling some of his work will help you move forward, one photograph at a time."

She stiffened slightly. "I don't want to let him go."

Michael came up behind them. "What do you two have your heads together about?"

"Just admiring Luke's work," said Ran.

"Ran, can I see you for a second?"

Logan looked at him. "Everything okay?" she asked.

"Of course," said Michael. "I just want to introduce him to someone."

She put her hand on Ran's arm. "Go ahead, I'll be fine. I'm going to find Rose."

"You're sure?"

"Absolutely. Go," she said, giving him a slight nudge.

She watched them head into the reception room, then heard her name and turned to see Jane talking to C.J., rather loudly. "Well, I think exhibiting her own photographs beside Luke's was in poor taste. Her pictures are mediocre at best. The lighting's wrong, the framing's off..."

"If you'll excuse me," said C.J., and she turned to greet someone she recognized. Jane scanned the room looking for someone else she might engage in some gossip.

"Jane."

She turned to face Logan, wearing the ever present just-sucked-a-lemon face. Logan wanted to ask her to leave, but knew Jane would make a scene and ruin the evening. Instead she offered to show her the exhibits.

"No, thanks. I've seen all I need to see."

"Excuse me then," Logan said, heading toward Rose and a group of guests gathered around the "Forced Migration" exhibit. Suddenly she was so overwhelmed and tired that she changed direction, making her way through the reception room to the front porch for a bit of fresh air. Ran and Michael were at the far end and appeared to be in an intense discussion. Weary and tired of their constant bickering, she turned to go back inside when she heard Michael say "It's the least you can do." Ran backed away. As he did, he saw her and came toward her.

"What was that about?" Logan asked.

"Oh, nothing important."

Michael passed them and smiled. "Just give some thought to my proposal," he said to Ran.

"What proposal?"

"You know Michael. He's always got something going on and thinks I should jump on board."

"Well, you know he tries to help everyone and sometimes gets in over his head. But he has good intentions."

"Yeah, let's go inside. It's chilly out here."

Ran turned to greet some friends from his antique car club, and Logan was going to check on things in the kitchen, when she noticed for the second time tonight that Michael and C.J. had their heads together. Curious, she walked behind a group of guests, putting them between Michael and herself, and slipped behind the pillar. She heard C.J. pitching her development idea and the money that they could all make if Michael could get Ran to sell the estate.

"What exactly would you do with the property?" Michael asked.

"Well, my plan is to create a gated community with town homes, single family homes, and condos close to the river. The rest of the development would consist of stores, some restaurants overlooking the river, movie theaters, a performing arts theater, etc."

"Sounds pretty ambitious."

"It is, but its success is a matter of knowing the right people in charge of development. And we have some top notch marketing people waiting for the go ahead."

C.J. and Michael saw Ran approaching. Logan was furious because Ran had told C.J. more than once that he wasn't interested in selling, and now here she was trying to get Michael to change Ran's mind.

"What are you two talking about?" Ran asked.

C.J. jumped in. "Nothing important. Small talk."

"This better not be about selling the estate."

"We all know how you feel about that," said C.J.

Logan stepped from behind the pillar and smiled at them. C.J. eyed her suspiciously then excused herself.

Ran turned to Michael. "Was she talking to you about the estate?"

"Don't worry about her."

"Okay you two, no more talk about the estate."

Logan saw Millicent come in and waved her over. Logan hugged her and told her how lovely she looked. Millicent was a healthy looking sixty-two year old woman, who most often wore tailored slacks and a sweater or plain blouse. She worked at the Preservation Society and was helping Ran restore the property and have it designated as a historical landmark. Tonight, however, she deviated radically from her tailored look and was wearing a lavender gown with spaghetti straps and sequined bodice. The skirt was floor length layers of chiffon that fell from just below the breasts.

"You really look beautiful," said Logan. "That color is perfect for you."

"Thank you. And you look beautiful too. Turn around. I love the new look."

Logan was smiling. "I do too. I wasn't sure about it when Rose dragged me off to the stylist, but it turned out great."

Millicent smiled and looked even younger than her sixty-two years.

"I'm glad I have you all together," she said, looking at Logan, Ran, and Michael.

"Is everything going okay?" asked Logan.

"Oh, yes. I just wanted to tell you that while I was researching the history of the estate, I found the original blueprints for Mount Joy. They were packed away in a box in our archives."

"Really? That's wonderful. I can't wait to see them. Have there been many changes since it was built?" asked Logan.

"Actually, there's something really interesting on the plans."

"Are these the actual working plans or just ideas?" asked Michael.

"That I'm not sure about. I'll bring them by tomorrow and we can explore and compare."

"Give us a hint," said Logan.

"Nope, I want you to see it and tell me what you think before I tell you my thoughts."

"What are we looking for?" asked Logan.

Millicent just smiled. "Let's wait until tomorrow."

"Do you have them with you?" asked Ran.

"I do, but you'll have to wait until tomorrow. Until then my lips are sealed," she said, winking at them.

"You're being very mysterious," laughed Logan.

"I'm not saying another word until tomorrow. Now, let me have a look at the exhibit. I see some beautiful photographs here," she said as she broke from the group and headed into the exhibit area.

Before they could say anything else, Logan sensed movement just to her left on the other side of the pillar and stepped aside to see who was back there.

"Jane. Did you hear everything you wanted to hear?" asked Logan.

"Jane, I didn't know you'd be here," said Millicent.

"You two know each other?" asked Logan.

"Jane started working at the Preservation Society a few months ago."

"Oh," was all Logan could manage.

Jane looked at Logan and hissed, "You think you're so special that you should get everything you want."

"Look, this isn't the time or place. Whatever you think I've done to you..." Logan shook her head. *Why am I trying to reason with her?* she thought. *She's nuts.* Logan took a closer look at her. *And drunk.* She turned to walk away but Jane grabbed her arm. They were face to face. Logan shook her arm free, looking at it as though it needed a good cleansing, and walked away.

"Don't walk away from me while I'm talking!" Jane yelled, and several people turned their heads to see what was happening. Michael took Jane's elbow and gently ushered her toward the door, whispering something in her ear. She stiffened. "This isn't over," she said. They were the last words Logan heard before Jane broke free of Michael's grip and started to walk away. Her gait was slightly off balance. She turned and faced Logan and the look on her face turned Logan's blood cold. "You know, Luke's dead because of you," she shouted, storming through the front door, slamming it.

There was a collective intake of breath and complete silence. The color drained from Logan's face. Rose took one arm, and Ran and Michael followed them to her office.

"I've been watching her," said Rose. "She's drunk. Don't listen to her."

"No," said Logan. "She only said what I've said to myself a thousand times. What if..."

"She's wrong," Rose insisted.

"You don't know that. We weren't tethered."

"There was no need for you to be tethered. You weren't climbing or descending."

"We were in a cave. We should've been."

"And you had the equipment if you needed it. There's nothing you could have done differently." Rose took Logan's hand. "There was nothing anyone could have done," she said firmly, looking straight into Logan's eyes.

"She's wrong," said Ran. "Now, no second guessing that day."

"It wasn't your fault," said Michael.

"Listen to him," said Ran, nodding toward his brother. They chatted for a few minutes, then Michael said he should check on Jane.

"I'll get her a cab," he said, leaving the office. "Don't worry about her."

They followed Michael out. Logan watched as he went outside, presumably in search of Jane, then turned her attention back to her guests. She answered questions about the exhibit and avoided any questions about the incident. When things calmed down, she excused herself and went in search of Ran.

She spotted him going into the kitchen, but he was nowhere in sight when she got there. One of the staff thought they saw him go out back. *Most likely to smoke*, she thought. The lights illuminated two figures arguing by the corner of the house. She could hear their raised voices but not what they were arguing about. One of the men was Ran. She didn't recognize the other man, but when he raised his left hand, jabbing Ran in the chest to emphasize his words, she saw that he was missing his ring and pinkie fingers. Ran smacked his hand away, but before the man could react, Logan coughed and both of them turned toward her.

"You just remember what I said," Ran told him, walking toward Logan. "Look at you, you're shivering. It's too cold to be out here without a coat," he said, hustling her inside.

"Who was that?"

"Oh, not to worry. Just business."

"It didn't sound like business to me. You were arguing. What kind of business anyway?"

"Nothing for you to worry about," he said, steering her back inside.

# CHAPTER 3

"I need a minute alone," she told him, slipping into Rose's office. She stood gazing out the window, taking some time to regain her equilibrium. She heard the soft rustle of clothing before she smelled the heavy musky perfume that threatened to choke her. Logan recognized the scent and braced herself. The intruder tapped her on the shoulder.

"Excuse me," she said as Logan turned to face her. "I'm looking for Logan O'..." She stopped and stared.

*Well here goes*, thought Logan.

The woman was a stately five foot seven and stood ramrod straight. Her greying hair was perfectly coiffed in a chignon. In that moment, Logan realized that she had allowed the woman to turn her into a younger version of herself. She took a deep breath. "Vanessa, I'm so glad you could make it," she said, giving her a hug. "Have you seen the exhibit yet?" She was hoping to distract Vanessa, but no such luck.

"What have you done to your hair?" Vanessa wailed.

Logan tried once again to distract her. "Let me show you the exhibits. Rose has outdone herself."

"What have you done? Ellis is going to hear about this. What was he thinking?"

"Vanessa," she said.

"What have you done?" she screeched. "Look at that mess! What's wrong with Ellis?"

"Vanessa!" Logan said sharply. This time Vanessa stopped talking and looked at Logan in shock. "Vanessa," Logan said more softly. "Sit down."

"I don't want to sit down."

Logan took a deep breath. "Look, Vanessa, I really appreciate everything you've done for me."

Vanessa's mouth became a thin straight line. Her ice blue eyes were glacial. "So, you're saying you don't need me anymore."

"No, of course not."

"Now that Luke's gone…"

Logan saw that her eyes misted and waited for her to compose herself before continuing.

"Vanessa, I value your opinion." Okay, so maybe that was a bit of a stretch, but she did care about Vanessa and she learned a lot from her. "I just felt like I needed a change."

"Well, Ellis had no business doing this without talking to me first."

"Well, actually…"

"What kind of grammar is that? You sound like a child who just got caught eating cookies before dinner."

*Here goes.* "Vanessa, I didn't go to Ellis. Rose made appointments for us at…"

"Oh, her. I might have known she was involved. The girl has no concept of appropriate decorum."

Logan took a deep breath and willed herself to speak calmly. "She's an artist and she expresses herself differently. And she's my best friend."

"You need to be making friends in our circle. I've tried to introduce you to young people who would be appropriate friends. You spend too much time with that Rose."

It took every ounce of will power for Logan to keep her voice level. "Vanessa, Rose and I have been friends since first grade and I'm not going to dump her for people in 'our circle,'" Logan used her index and middle fingers to put quotes around the words.

"Well, of course I'm not suggesting any such thing. I'm merely suggesting that you expand your circle. You spend all of your time with that girl or your uncles. You need to associate with others." Her voice perked up as an idea occurred to her. "I'm having a dinner party next week. I'll have the car pick you up at seven sharp on Saturday."

"But…"

"Now, no excuses. I'll have a dress sent over tomorrow so there will be plenty of time for alterations. You go see Ellis on Monday. No, that won't do. They're closed on Monday. I'll call him personally and ask him to see you. I just hope he will be able to do something."

In that moment, Logan saw Vanessa in a whole new light. She was seeing her the way Rose saw her, and the reality hit her hard. "Vanessa, I appreciate everything, but I like my new hairdo. I don't want to change it back."

Vanessa was shocked. "Well, I guess if my opinion isn't important."

"No, it isn't that," said Logan, placing her hand on Vanessa's arm. "I wanted something different."

Vanessa stepped back from Logan, effectively disconnecting the physical contact. "Well, it's your hair. I wanted to help you fit in."

Logan stood where she was, but put her hands out toward Vanessa, palms up. "I know, and I appreciate it, but it was time for a change."

"Well, if that's the way you feel, I won't give you any more advice."

Logan sighed. "It doesn't mean that I don't value your advice and help. I do. And my hair's still long enough to pull back," she demonstrated, hoping Vanessa didn't notice the curls springing free of her hand. "And I'll be at your dinner party next week," she said. Logan watched Vanessa transform from victim to her old take charge self, secure in the knowledge that she would be bringing Logan back into the fold. Logan was shocked at how easily Vanessa made the switch. *That's how she keeps people in line and gets what she wants*, thought Logan. She'd never paid attention to Vanessa's manipulations before now.

Logan brought her attention back to the conversation. "I'll see that you are included in all of the upcoming gatherings," Vanessa was saying.

Logan groaned, but thankfully Vanessa didn't hear her; she was busy ticking off the various invitations she knew were coming. Logan knew that she wasn't going to go to these affairs, but decided to tell Vanessa later, when they could be alone.

Rose appeared in the doorway. "Logan, sorry to interrupt."

*Thank God*, thought Logan. "You're not interrupting. What can I do for you?"

"We're having a private conversation here," said Vanessa.

Rose raised her eyebrows at Logan.

"What can I do for you?" asked Logan again.

"It's almost nine. I thought we could spend a few minutes going over the cue cards."

"Absolutely, we're through here," she said. "Vanessa, we'll talk later."

With her obvious dismissal, Vanessa walked out of the office, back straight, chin up, without looking back.

"Well," said Rose, "she wasn't happy."

"She's never happy these days. But enough of her, let's see the cards," she said, taking them from Rose. "I really don't want to do this, but I know it's important."

"You'll be fine. It's short and to the point. All you have to do is thank everyone for coming. Talk for a few minutes about Luke's work and the significance of the exhibits. Then remind everyone why they're here: To get out those check books," said Rose, laughing. Logan shuffled through the cards as Rose highlighted the main points. "Talk about Luke's and your dream of opening a visual arts center, and your desire to honor that dream and make it come true. Thank everyone for their generosity."

"I know what I want to say, it's just my mind goes blank when I get in front of a crowd."

"That's why you have the cards. You can improvise some, but the cards will help you make sure you cover the important points."

Logan hugged her. "I know, I'll be fine. Thank Trish for these," she said, waving the cards. "I'd better get out there."

She walked up onto the small stage and took her place behind the podium. After adjusting the microphone, she thanked everyone for coming. When she looked out at the audience, the only person she could see was Jane. Maybe that was because she continued to talk to someone Logan recognized as a friend of Rose's. Apparently Michael hadn't been successful at getting her into a cab and away from here. Several people turned to give Jane dirty looks, but either she didn't notice or, more likely, chose to ignore them. Out of the corner of her eye, she saw Michael heading in Jane's direction. He casually walked up to her, whispered something, then took her elbow and guided her out the door, all before Jane knew what was happening, Logan was sure. She'd seen Michael in action before. He was smooth. With Jane safely removed, for the second time tonight, she continued her speech. She described the three themes of the exhibit and gave a brief history about the people and locations.

"Luke recognized that the disenfranchised young people we see every day, hanging on Market Street and various other corners throughout the city, see the world from a unique perspective that he was confident would translate into unique images." She noticed heads bobbing assent and knew that they understood her and Luke's vision. Once she began talking about Luke's work, all her nervousness disappeared. A few patrons asked questions and she thanked everyone for their generosity.

By the end of the evening, Logan realized that all of the prints had sold, including her own. She didn't have a final total yet because many people wrote checks for more than the listed price. It was well after midnight when the last guest left and they locked the doors.

"That was a huge success," said Rose, leaning against the closed doors. "You can go talk to the bank now."

"Are you sure?" asked Logan. "They told me I needed to have a minimum of one hundred thousand dollars before they would talk to me."

"Like I said, you can go talk to the bank."

"I can't believe it. I thought this would just be a start toward getting the money. I never dreamed I would raise it all with one exhibit."

"You look exhausted," said Michael, putting his arm across her shoulder. "Let's get you home."

"I have to help Rose clean up."

"All taken care of," said Rose. "The caterers finished their work and I have someone coming in the morning to take care of the rest. Michael's right. Go home. We'll talk in the morning."

"Well, if you're sure. Where's Ran?"

"In the kitchen. I'll get him," said Rose.

Ran and Michael dropped her off at home. Logan was physically and emotionally exhausted. She dragged herself up to her bedroom. She left her clothes lying on the chair and got into bed, hoping that tonight she would be tired enough to sleep through until morning.

But again, Logan's sleep was disrupted by images of Luke disappearing into blackness, this time with Jane's accusations incorporated. The image of Luke twisting to regain his balance. His black curly hair. His blue eyes. The look of anguish as he fell backwards into the crevasse.

She checked the clock each time she jerked awake. It seemed like she was waking every two hours. This last time, she sat on the edge of the bed looking out the window at the pre-dawn grey. Her thoughts ran back to last night's event and the overwhelming generosity of her friends and neighbors. She needed to get busy with her plans to get the center up and running. Things were moving faster than she'd anticipated and there was a lot to do.

She got up, anxious to get started, something she hadn't experienced since Luke's death. Coffee and the paper were what she needed first. The paper boy didn't pay much attention to where he threw it as long as it was in the general vicinity of the customer's address, and, of course, it on Mrs. Rosen's step again. *Great*, she thought, scooting surreptitiously toward it, hoping Mrs. Rosen wouldn't see her. As luck would have it, just as she grabbed the paper and prepared to leap back onto her own steps, Mrs. Rosen appeared with broom in hand, dressed in her usual uniform:

starched white long-sleeved blouse, mid-calf black pleated skirt, nylons and sensible black shoes. *Who starches their clothes and where does one find pleated skirts?* Logan wondered as she scooted back to her own steps.

Mrs. Rosen waved the broom and yelled at her to get off her property. It wouldn't do any good to explain that she was just getting her paper. Mrs. Rosen wouldn't listen. Within seconds she was furiously sweeping the spot the errant newspaper and Logan had just vacated, all the while keeping a close eye on Logan's movements. Logan opened the paper and perused the front page. Not because the news was captivating, but because she knew it annoyed Mrs. Rosen, who once told her that she considered reading the paper dangerous. Logan never figured out exactly what that meant. 'Litter,' she had called it, saying there should be a law against just throwing paper all over the neighborhood.

The headline "FIREY CRASH TAKES LIFE" caught Logan's attention. The photograph below showed a car embedded in a tree. She began to read the article. "The late model Toyota Prius crashed on Kelly Drive just north of the Art Museum."

Logan was familiar with that stretch of the road. She read further, "The police believe speed, wet roads, and possibly alcohol were responsible for the crash." She scanned the article looking for the name of the driver. No name. "The driver's name is being withheld pending notification of next of kin."

Logan left Mrs. Rosen furiously sweeping. She and Ran were meeting Millicent at Mount Joy at ten o'clock to see what she had found in the Preservation Society's archives, but Logan planned to get there early. She and Ran were going to start bringing down boxes from the attic to sort through them.

On her way to Ran's, she stopped for pastries at Mrs. Sabatino's, the best in town. She headed over to Mount Joy driving the restored vintage 1968 Mustang convertible that Ran had given her for her graduation from college. She pulled up to the iron gates, which lay wide open.

She knew they were supposed to be closed, not necessarily to keep anyone out, because they didn't lock. More as a deterrent. Thick shrubbery claimed the fencing on either side of the gates. As she drove through, she thought she saw movement out of the corner of her eye and swung her head around just as a fox shot across the path.

The driveway was approximately a quarter of a mile of rutted gravel and was shaded on both sides by virgin forest. She drove five miles per hour, zigzagging around potholes and debris. At one point she had to remove a fallen tree limb, annoyed because Ran paid Jimmy Donahue to do general maintenance.

Logan knew Jimmy from high school. He was three years older than her, but he had been left back a couple of times. She remembered that he had spent most of his time in the alley behind the school, smoking pot with his friends, and couldn't remember if he ever actually graduated. But Ran felt sorry for him and, at the request of Michael, whose housekeeper was Jimmy's mother, gave him the cottage to live in. In return, Jimmy was supposed to do odd jobs around the estate.

Logan made the last turn and stopped to admire the Federal style house built somewhere in the early to mid-1800s. Two wings and a large front porch were added sometime later. The outside paint on the house was peeling and there were cracks in the foundation, but Millicent assured them that she could recommend people who would work miracles. The various outbuildings, including an outhouse, were barely visible through the thick vegetation that ran wild. In a clearing to the left of the house sat Ran's carefully maintained garage. All of the bay doors were closed, but his fully restored mint green 1932 Ford Roadster convertible sat just outside of the sixth bay. He'd had the block garage built to house the vintage cars that were in various stages of restoration. It started out as a hobby, but his expertise and reputation quickly spread, bringing him more business than he could possibly handle. She knew owners sometimes waited as long as a year for Ran to get to them.

He loved transforming old rusted wrecks of cars into pristine, showroom condition. Unlike Michael, Ran had no time for all the shiny new plastic cars that manufacturers were spitting out at lightning speed. He said they all looked alike, like clones, no character at all.

Behind the garage was an old clapboard shed covered in vines which, Logan noticed, were interspersed with poison ivy. A tree leaned against one corner of the partially crushed roof. The door hung at an angle, but Logan could see that it was crammed full of old machinery and wondered if Ran even knew what was in there.

She looked around at what were once the formal gardens, which had all but disappeared into the encroaching brambles. She noticed that wildflowers were sprouting up among the weeds, recognizing the phlox and bluebells. The various statuary were felled and some were damaged, but Logan hoped, not beyond repair.

Logan stood looking up at the house, remembering the first time she had returned. It had been five years after the day her mother had disappeared when she was twelve years old. Logan had been told by her uncle, Michael, that her mother had left her and her father. After that, Logan's father had cut off all contact with family and friends and she hadn't seen her uncles since then. But she had wanted to reconnect with the two family members she had left, Ran and Michael, so she contacted them when she started her freshman year at Temple University.

Her uncles had welcomed her and invited her out to the estate. She remembered having a hard time finding the dirt road that led up to the house. Everything was even more overgrown back then. She had picked her way around potholes the size of small craters and rounded the bend. The dilapidated house stood straight ahead. What shutters were still attached barely clung to the sides of the windows like drunken sentries.

Some improvements had been made by now, but they had a long way to go. The once elegant foyer still had its original decorative plaster ceiling. On a sunny day, the second floor landing would be full of rainbows cast by the large flora and fauna style stained glass window. Logan was looking forward to the restoration of the once beautiful home. She passed the stairs on her left and headed to the kitchen in back, calling for Ran.

"Up here. Be right down."

"No problem. I'll get coffee started." She laid out the pastries while the coffee was brewing, and heard him thumping down the stairs.

"Look what I found," he said, hefting a large sagging box onto the red striped porcelain kitchen table. "I was rummaging around in the attic and found this box of pictures."

"Our family?" she asked, excited.

"I think so. I just glanced through them and recognized some of the people."

"Let's see," she said, pulling out a handful of pictures and sifting through them. She separated one picture from the bunch. The woman was stout and dressed in a housedress. There was no hint of a smile on her face or twinkle in her eyes. "Who is this?" she asked, holding out the picture so that Ran could see.

He looked at it and smiled. "That's your great-grandmother. She's the one who came here from Ireland with her husband and their two sons. She had three more children here in the States. One of them was your grandfather." He shook his head. "She was a hard woman. Refused to learn English. Made everyone in the house speak Gaelic. And she was quick with the switch too."

She held the photograph to her chest. "I don't have a lot of information about our family, our ancestors. I always wanted to know more about them, but dad changed the subject whenever it came up. Then after mom..." She looked down at the photo strewn table.

"It wasn't right what she did, running off and leaving you behind."

She didn't want to hear about her mother running off. "In fact," she said, changing the subject, "you and Michael haven't told me much either. So tell me all the family secrets. Where are the skeletons hidden?" she asked teasingly.

He looked at her. "I don't know about any family secrets or skeletons. Now, how's that coffee coming? Millicent should be here soon."

"Just about ready." Logan's interest was peaked. His response, or lack of one, alerted her to the fact that he was hiding something. After all, every family has secrets. "So, let's see what else is in this box," she said, reaching in.

"Why don't we wait until later," said Ran.

Michael strode into the room, looking around. His eyes stopped at the box. "What have we here?" he asked, moving toward it.

"Just some pictures and stuff I found in the attic," said Ran, moving it off the table. "I'll put this in the dining room out of the way until after Millicent leaves."

"Any idea what she found?" asked Michael.

"None. Just what she said last night," said Ran.

They looked at Logan. She shrugged her shoulders. "She didn't tell me anything. Not even a hint. She did seem pretty excited, but I couldn't get anything out of her. I guess we'll know soon," she said, looking at the wall clock.

They had some coffee and chatted while they waited. Finally, Logan spoke up. "I wonder where she is. Millicent's usually very prompt."

Ran shrugged. "Maybe something came up."

"It's not like her to be late without calling. She's a stickler for promptness."

"Yeah," Ran laughed. "She read me the riot act the last time I went to see her. There was an accident on Market Street and I was trapped."

"And, of course, you didn't have your cell phone."

He shrugged and rolled his eyes at her.

"I'll give her a call," she said, picking up the phone and speed dialing. "It went right to voicemail."

"I'm sure she's on her way," said Michael.

"Let's dig into that box while we're waiting," she said, going into the dining room. "There are a lot of papers mixed in with the pictures. Maybe we should sort them into piles so we know what's here." She pulled out a handful of papers. "Michael, you haven't said a word since you got here. Is everything okay?"

"Yes, of course. There are some parish things that need attention."

"And?" said Ran. He knew his brother well enough to know that he had something else on his mind.

"I'm worried about you."

"No need. I don't plan to kick the bucket just yet," he said, reaching into the box and taking out a handful of papers.

"You did have that heart attack last year," said Logan, lightly touching his arm.

"It wasn't a heart attack, just angina," he said, waving the paper at them.

"Oh, well," said Logan, not bothering to hide the sarcasm.

"I agree with Logan," said Michael. "I'm worried that you're taking on too much with this project. It's going to be very disruptive; people wandering all over the property, digging holes all over the place."

"They won't be digging holes all over the place," laughed Logan. "Archaeologists are going to select a few places that might contain artifacts and excavate. It'll be very systematic. I'm excited about it. I'm especially looking forward to their excavation of the outhouse."

"Why in the world would they want to dig up an outhouse?"

"Because early settlers dumped garbage, broken glassware, animal bones, and other unusable items into the pit. We can learn a lot about how the people lived, what they ate, etc."

"My main concern is Ran and his health. I don't want all this activity to impact him."

"I think you're more worried about the financial cost than my health," said Ran, picking up a handful of pictures.

"The doctor said you need to minimize stress, and this project is bound to create stress."

"I have everything all worked out. The Preservation Society will take the lead with the excavation, and I know how much it's going to cost to convert this place into an arts center. As for the stress, I think I might enjoy watching the restoration."

"These things always end up costing a lot more than the initial estimate. You're only fifty-six. You have a lot of good years ahead of you, and you'll want to be financially secure."

Ran laughed. "And what would you recommend be done with the property?"

"I don't recommend anything. I just think there are options that you should explore before settling on the restoration."

"Such as?" Ran seemed to be pushing Michael for a specific response.

"What about development? Logan's friend, C.J., was telling me about her ideas. There are seventy-five acres of waterfront property. I'll bet any developer would jump at the chance to buy it. Then you'd be set for life."

"And so would you," said Ran.

"I'm a priest. Vow of poverty?" he said with a touch of sarcasm.

"Yeah, but as long as I live on the estate I can do what I want with it. If I sell it then all the proceeds are divided equally between us. So there's something in it for you."

"Not for me, Ran. Anything I have goes to the church." His voice was weary and Logan knew they'd had this argument before.

"The proceeds would go a long way toward securing that Archbishop position you covet."

"You know I don't need money to gain that position."

"Yeah, but it wouldn't hurt, now would it?"

"Stop, both of you."

Both men snapped their heads toward Logan. They were so engrossed in their bickering, they had forgotten she was there.

"Sorry," said Ran. "I'll go up and bring down some more boxes and stack them in the dining room. We can use the table."

"I'll do it," said Michael. "Don't exert yourself."

Michael brought down boxes, and they began to separate the papers from the photos. Logan looked up. "Michael, what are you staring at?"

He jerked his head up. "Oh, it's just my Baptismal Certificate."

"Let me see," she said, reaching for it.

They heard a car door slam and footsteps on the porch.

"Here she is and only four hours late," said Ran. "I can't wait to see what she found."

# CHAPTER 4

When Ran opened the door, all three of them stood staring, not at Millicent, but two men. Finally, Ran spoke up. "If you're developers you can get off my property right now," and he closed the door in their faces. They knocked again and Logan answered.

The men took out their badges and identified themselves as police detectives before anyone could close the door on them.

"I'm Detective Frank Costello and this is my partner Detective Doug Beatty."

"Sorry, I thought you were someone else. What can we do for you?" asked Ran.

The younger one, Costello, looked to be in his early thirties and pretty fit. His blond hair was cut military style and his suit was perfectly pressed. Beatty, on the other hand, was closer to fifty, and didn't look like he could chase a toddler let alone a criminal. He had a two inch wide bald strip from his forehead to his crown. The brown hair on either side was wiry and thick. He reminded her of a clown and she coughed to hide the giggle.

"May we come in?" asked Costello. Ran stepped aside.

"Are you Kingston Ranford?" asked Beatty. Logan noticed a distinct difference in their tones. While Costello's was almost apologetic, Beatty's was confrontational.

"I am," he said, offering his hand. "This is my brother, Michael Ranford, and our niece Logan O'Malley."

Ran took them into the living room and offered them a seat. Costello sat, but Beatty remained standing. The room was neat, but the fabric on the sofa and two side chairs was threadbare on the armrests and cushion edges. The pine tables were scratched and decorated with years of water rings. Ran, Michael, and Logan followed Costello and sat. "What can I do for you?" asked Ran.

"Tell us what you know about Millicent Hamilton," said Beatty, looking down at them.

"Is she okay? She was supposed to be here hours ago," said Ran.

Logan shivered, apprehension building.

Beatty ignored Ran's question and instead asked, "What's your relationship to her?"

"She works for the Preservation Society. I've been working with her to have this property listed as a historical landmark."

Logan watched Beatty survey the room as if they had to be kidding. She didn't bother to explain the history of the estate. After less than a minute in his presence, she decided that she didn't like him.

"When was the last time you saw her?" asked Beatty.

"We all saw her last night at The Gallery. There was a photograph exhibit featuring Logan's husband's work. Is she okay?" asked Ran again, standing to face Beatty.

His question was ignored again. "Was she drinking?" Beatty asked.

"I think she had some champagne, but I wasn't really paying any attention," said Logan. "What's happened?"

"Was she upset about anything?" asked Beatty, continuing to ignore their questions.

"No, in fact, just the opposite. She was excited," said Logan, standing next to Ran. She was trying to be helpful to the detectives, but had to restrain herself from screaming at Beatty.

Michael noticed her agitation and stood up. "Look, Officers, Millicent is a friend. Now, are you going to tell us what's going on?"

Logan noticed that Michael downgraded them from detectives to officers and so, she thought, did Beatty.

"We'll ask the questions," Beatty snapped. "What was she excited about?"

"We asked you a question," said Ran. "If you're not going to answer it, then you can leave."

Costello cleared his throat. "I'm sorry. We're investigating a car accident."

"Millicent? Is she okay?" asked Logan.

Costello continued. "The car caught fire. I'm afraid she didn't make it."

"No, that can't be! There must be some mistake!" she said, looking from Costello to her uncles. She sat down hard on the chair, color draining from her face. Her hands began to tremble.

Ran took a step backwards, mouth agape.

"Are you sure it was her?" asked Michael, clenching his jaw.

"We're positive. The car was registered to her and we found her identification," said Costello.

Michael blessed himself and said a short prayer.

Beatty snorted and everyone looked at him. "I don't think prayers are going to help her now," he said disdainfully.

Michael gave him a scorching look. "I pray for all souls."

Logan realized that Michael was dressed in khakis and a knit golf shirt. The gold cross around his neck was the only indication of religious belief. They didn't know he was a priest. "Michael is the Monsignor at St. Bernadette's Catholic Church," Logan announced, and noticed a kaleidoscope of emotions pass over Beatty's face all in a split second. She wondered what that was all about.

Michael pretended not to notice the snub. Ran picked up a cigar, lit it and paced back and forth, then he took a drag and blew the smoke directly at Beatty, who stepped aside quickly enough to avoid being completely immersed in smoke.

"You're as pale as a ghost," said Michael, looking at Logan in concern. He walked quickly toward the hall.

"Just where do you think you're going?" asked Beatty.

"I'm getting my niece some water. In case you hadn't noticed, she's had a shock," he threw over his shoulder as he continued down the hall.

"I still can't believe it. She was fine last night," said Logan.

Michael came back and handed Logan the glass of water. She sipped it and looked at the detectives.

Costello sat down across from her and leaned forward. "What was she wearing?" he asked, his tone gentle.

Logan described her gown, ignoring Beatty's sneer. Her brow furrowed, then she remembered. "The accident in today's paper. Was that Millicent?" Ran and Michael looked at her. She told them about the article.

"We're not next of kin. Why are you here?" asked Michael.

Beatty spoke up. "Your name was on her calendar for this morning. Just following up."

Looking at his notes, Costello asked, "You said she was excited. What about?"

"She found the original blueprints for this house," said Ran.

"Why would that cause her to be excited?" asked Costello in that low, mellow voice.

"Because of the landmark designation," said Logan. "Any original documentation supporting the application is exciting. And there was something on the blueprints she wanted us to see."

"What was that?" asked Costello.

"We don't know. She wouldn't say. She wanted to show us. That's why she was coming here today," said Ran.

"Where are these papers she was going to show you?" asked Costello.

"We don't know. Last night she said they were in her car," said Michael.

"You people don't know a lot," commented Beatty, just loud enough that they heard him.

"What time did she leave?" asked Costello, ignoring Beatty's comment.

"I didn't notice," said Logan. She glanced at Beatty to see his reaction, caught a look of disgust, then looked at Michael and Ran. "Did either of you?" They both shook their heads. "What happened?" Her voice was shaky, and she took another sip of water.

"We're still investigating," said Costello.

"Is there any family?" asked Michael.

"We're still checking. Do you know if she had any family?" asked Costello.

"She never mentioned anyone," said Logan. "You could check where she works. They might have next of kin listed in her personnel records."

"I thought you said she was a friend. You don't know a whole lot about her."

"She was a very private person. Like I said, check with her employer."

"I think we know how to follow leads," said Beatty.

"There's no need to talk to her like that," said Ran, blowing a stream of cigar smoke right in Beatty's face.

"Is there anything I can do?" asked Michael, hoping to diffuse the situation. "She wasn't a member of our parish, but I'd like to help if I can."

"What will happen if there's no family?" asked Logan.

"The city will bury her," said Costello.

"No," said Logan. She looked at her uncles. "Ran, Michael? Please, we can't let that happen."

"Don't worry," said Ran. "We'll see that she gets a proper burial."

Logan looked at her uncles and breathed a sigh of relief. "Thank you."

"That's a very generous offer," said Beatty, "for someone you didn't know that well".

Logan could hear the skepticism in his voice. For some reason he was closely watching them.

"I've been working with her for a few months," said Ran.

"But I've known her for years," said Logan. "I've had some dealings with the Preservation Society over the years and Millicent has always been helpful. We go out to lunch or dinner on occasion."

Costello coughed. "Thank you for your time." He handed each of them his card. "If you think of anything else give me a call." Ran walked them to the front door.

"Poor Millicent," said Logan after they shut the front door. Her voice was shaky. She didn't try to hide the tears that formed.

Michael put his arm around her shoulders. "I'm sorry. I know you liked her."

"This is such a shame," said Ran.

"I don't understand. Millicent was never a drinker. But they insinuated that she drank too much, and somehow we might be responsible," said Logan.

"Not they, just that Beatty fellow. The other one seemed pleasant enough," said Ran.

"Well, you didn't help matters any by blowing cigar smoke all over the place when you could see that it bothered him."

"It did? I didn't notice," he said, feigning innocence.

"Right," said Logan.

"Let me make some tea," suggested Michael. They sat around the kitchen table and discussed the accident. Logan relayed as much as she could remember from the article.

"When did you see her last?" Logan asked, looking at each of her uncles.

"I saw her during your speech," said Ran.

"I saw her then too, and I'm pretty sure I saw her after you finished your speech," said Michael. "But I don't remember what time it was, and I didn't notice her leave."

"I was thinking about that," said Logan. "Do either of you think it odd that she left without saying goodbye?"

"Now that you mention it," said Ran, "yeah."

"Maybe you were busy," said Michael, "and she didn't want to disturb you. She probably figured she'd see you in the morning."

"I suppose," she said, taking the empty cups to the sink and blinking back tears. "I can't believe she's gone. I think I'm going to head home. I'd like to be alone."

"Why don't you stay for a while longer? You've had a shock," said Ran.

She smiled at him. "Thanks anyway, but I'd like some time alone. I'll call you later." She hugged them and drove home. Wondering. Trying to remember everything that had happened last night. She didn't really see Millicent much after they'd talked about the documents she'd found. Michael and Ran both saw her during the speech, and Michael saw her once after that.

She started for home, then made the decision to go to the accident site. She didn't know why or what she might find, if anything, but she needed to understand what had happened. She knew Millicent was a careful driver, but the roads had been wet from the recent rains. And it wasn't unusual for a deer to run across the road.

She found the site and pulled over onto the shoulder as far as she could without risking slipping down the incline. The churned up soil showed Logan the path that Millicent had taken to her death. Up ahead, the charred tree stood out like a beacon. She slipped on the boots that she always kept in her trunk, and walked the perimeter of the crime scene tape. She took a moment to say a prayer for her friend, then brought her focus back to the accident scene and walked to the backside of the tree that had stopped Millicent's car. She ran her hand over the scorched bark and shuddered. *At least the rain prevented the woods from catching fire,* she thought. Tears blurred her vision. "Millicent, what happened?" she asked aloud.

She thought about what the police had told them. 'The car exploded on impact and she most likely died instantly,' Costello had said. A screech of brakes and a horn blaring caused her to jump and made her aware of the traffic whizzing by. The area was littered with debris and she noted pieces of Millicent's car strewn among the beer bottles, cans, and general litter. There were some papers lodged against the trees just outside the perimeter and Logan stepped over some fallen branches to retrieve them, wondering if they might have come from Millicent's car.

It was a soggy mess of paper stuck together, but Logan saw the faint image of the Preservation Society logo bleeding through the top sheet. She took a final look around and went back to the car with the papers in hand and headed home.

She took her blow dryer and began peeling the pages apart as they dried, nine pages in all. She placed each sheet between glass and photographed the images, which gave her the flexibility of zooming in on specific areas to make them more readable. She downloaded the images to her computer, and was able to decipher enough to know that these papers were about Ran's property.

One page was a summary of the history of the ownership of the property. Another sheet was a detailed description of the materials and labor used to build the house. The owner at that time was Duncan Armstrong, who also owned a publishing house in Philadelphia. The Armstrong family owned the house for twenty-two years, but bad business decisions caused the fledgling publishing company to go bankrupt. The next page was missing a substantial amount of text, but seemed to chronicle the changes that were made to the property when ownership changed to the Ranford family.

She couldn't wait to share what she had found with her uncles and called Ran. No answer. No surprise there. He was probably in his garage and didn't have a phone there, even though both Logan and Michael had encouraged him on numerous occasions to get one. Michael, on the other hand, answered on the first ring.

"Michael, you'll never guess what I found." She was so excited that her words were tripping over one another.

"Whoa, slow down."

"Papers. I found papers about the estate."

"Really? What kind of papers? Where did you find them?" She told him about going to the crash site. "You went there? Whatever possessed you to do that?"

"Michael, calm down. I needed to see where it happened. Anyway, I found some papers and they talk about the original house and changes our family made." There was silence on the other end of the phone. "Michael, are you there? Did you hear me?"

"Oh, I'm sorry. I got distracted for a second. Well, that does sound exciting. I can't wait to see them."

"I can e-mail the file to you."

"File?"

"Yes," she laughed. "Weren't you paying attention? I made digital copies. I'm sending them now."

"I'm sorry. You caught me. Mrs. Donahue came in with some phone message slips and I wasn't giving you my full attention."

Logan heard a ping on Michael's end. "Sounds like the file just arrived."

"I'll check it out. By the way, where are the originals?"

"In my office."

"Do you think you should have removed them? I mean, there is a police investigation."

"Michael," she said, like she was talking to a small child. "It's an accident scene, not a crime scene."

"You're right. But still...I have to return some calls, but I'll check out the file in a bit. In the meantime, no more snooping, you hear. Leave the investigating to the police." Logan remained silent. "Millicent is dead," he reminded her.

"You don't have to remind me of that," she snapped.

"I don't want you snooping around."

Logan still didn't reply. She knew she couldn't promise him anything, so she compromised. "I'll be careful." She heard him sigh.

"Keep your cell phone with you at all times. And charged," he added.

She could picture him smiling and rolling his eyes, just like her father. *That is, before my mother left*, she thought. After that Logan couldn't remember him smiling again. "I will. I'm going to take a bike ride and do some shooting in the park. So much has happened this weekend. I just need to clear my head. I'll call you when I get back."

"You be careful. We'll talk later."

She got out her new Valkyrie touring bike, and headed to her favorite hiking trail at the park. Her uncles didn't like her to ride her bike in the city. They said drivers were too careless and didn't pay attention to bikers. Some drivers even resented bikers taking space on the streets.

She noticed a few cars scattered throughout the lot when she arrived. Most people didn't venture into the park after days of rain. There was only so much they were willing to endure in the name of nature. She locked her bike, hoisted her specially padded camera backpack onto her back, and walked along the path, breathing deeply, feeling the cool air fill her lungs. She loved the smell of the woods after a rain, the smell of damp earth, that 'woodsy smell' was what she called it when she was little.

Her mother had always laughed at her description. Her mother, the woman who walked out of their lives. The woman who supposedly loved her. A pang of grief struck her, then anger at her mother for leaving her, anger at her father for not stopping her. She wanted to know why. Why did she just walk away? It still hurt all these years later. She wondered where her mother was now, and what she was doing. Did she have another family? Logan wasn't sure what she would say or do if she ever saw her again, but a part of her longed to have her back.

Putting all thoughts of her mother out of her mind, she shifted her focus to her surroundings. An occasional drop of rain slid from its leafy perch and fell gently on her head. The ground was spongy and muddy in some places, but she ignored it. She was always in search of something beautiful. In her mind, some of the most beautiful images were of the rain dappled flora sparkling like gems in the emerging sun.

She stooped to examine a perfect spider web dotted with drops of mist as fragile as the web itself. The web stood out against the dark green ferns that held it in place. She set up her tripod and attached her digital camera. Someone brushed past her and she had to grab the tripod for support as she teetered.

She was always extremely careful to disturb as little as possible of the biota, the ecology of the geological organisms. She was aware of the precarious balance and the subtle changes even a small disturbance could set in motion. It angered her to think of the lack of consideration visitors had toward the fragile ecosystem.

She focused on her photography, checking all of the settings, then studied the spider web from various angles and took some light readings from her hand-held light meter. She positioned everything with care. Logan had learned that it paid off to be methodical up front. It saved time later. Some professionals thought all this extra care wasn't necessary. They argued that all of the new software and technology changes made cleanup after the fact easy, but she knew from experience that some things couldn't be corrected without changing the integrity of the shot. She preferred that her shots be as close to nature's creations as possible. She didn't believe anyone could improve on nature's perfection and she didn't intend to try.

She took a dozen or so shots and viewed the results, then took some more, changing angles slightly and bracketing each shot. As the sun filtered through and began to dry the leaves, she sprayed a fine mist of water from a bottle she always carried with her.

She loved this solitary work, at one with the flora and fauna. Occasionally, someone would come along and slow or stop to watch her. This was a small snag. She loved talking to others about her work, but sometimes she just wanted solitude. That was what she was after today. She was emotionally drained from the exhibit, Jane's hostility, and now, Millicent's death. She needed to recharge.

Just as she was ready to shoot, she felt a prickle on the back of her neck. Someone was watching her. Not unusual, she told herself. But this felt different. Invasive. She turned but didn't see anyone on the path. As she turned back to her camera, she caught movement to her right and jumped up. What she saw was a fifteen or sixteen year old girl, dressed in camouflage. At least she thought it was a girl. Shoulder length straight black hair, olive complexion, almond shaped eyes. Very exotic but with a hard edged, street smart look. Logan realized she recognized her. She'd seen her hanging around Market Street with some rather disreputable looking young people, smoking cigarettes and who knows what else, hassling passersby for money. Logan scanned the vicinity but didn't see any of the girl's friends and wondered what she was doing there.

"Can I help you?" asked Logan.

The girl leaned against the tree, arms folded across her chest. "No."

Logan glanced at her setup and considered leaving, wondering if this girl was going to rob her. She'd been in these woods hundreds of times and never felt threatened. But this girl with her piercing stare unnerved her. She tried again. "What's your name?"

The girl took so long to answer that Logan thought she was going to refuse to tell her. Then finally she said, "Jewel."

"Well, Jewel. Do you come out here often?"

She answered a litter quicker this time. "Sometimes."

"I've never seen you here, but don't you hang out around Market Street?"

Jewel shifted from one foot to another, but never looked away from Logan, even as Logan took a couple of steps toward her. Jewel stood her ground.

"I love coming to the woods, especially after a rain. Everything's fresh and clean," said Logan. "How about you?"

Jewel shrugged. "Rain can't wash away anything," she said quietly while continuing to stare at Logan, not moving.

Logan wasn't feeling as threatened as she was a minute ago. However, she didn't let down her guard. Luke, on the other hand, wouldn't have given a second thought to Jewel's presence, she told herself. The longer they faced each other, the more Logan relaxed.

"Well, I need to get back to work. You can watch if you'd like," Logan said, turning back to her equipment. She spent the next half-hour shooting and could feel Jewel watching, but the girl never said a word. Jewel seemed wary and so was Logan, but she didn't want to scare her off if she was interested.

Logan wandered around and spotted another spider web, this one complete with fly and spider. The breaking sun filtered through the trees and caused the rain drops to glisten on the beautifully intricate design. Logan began to set up her equipment. She could feel Jewel inching closer but didn't say anything to her. She'd let her make the first move. She began to shoot. By this time Jewel was less than two feet from her. Logan looked up and smiled. Logan sensed that Jewel was very attuned to the world around her. Hypersensitive. She saw everything from her life experiences. Logan had a thought.

"Would you look at these spider web shots and tell me what you see?" she asked, handing her the digital camera. "Just push this button to scroll through them."

Jewel took the camera without saying anything. She stood there for a long time just looking at the shots. Then she handed it back to Logan.

"Well?" asked Logan. "Any suggestions?"

She shrugged her shoulders. "They're okay," she said.

"I'm open to another point of view."

"They're boring." Logan was taken aback by her bluntness, but she laughed. Jewel eyed her warily. "You making fun of me?"

Logan was confused and immediately felt guilty. She saw the hurt in Jewel's eyes, quickly replaced by defiance. "No, not at all. I was laughing because most people wouldn't have the courage to tell someone their work is 'boring,' as you put it." Jewel continued to watch her, but didn't say anything. Logan could see that Jewel wasn't sure if she was telling her the truth, so she tried another approach. "So, can you tell me why they're boring?"

Jewel didn't hold anything back, and Logan was amazed at her insight. "Anybody can take pictures of spider webs."

"You're right. So how can we make these better?"

She nodded toward the one Logan was setting up. "The fly is trapped. The spider is getting closer. He's going to kill the fly and eat it."

Logan gasped. She was pretty sure that was how Jewel viewed herself and the world around her, and her heart constricted. She instinctively knew that Jewel had a unique perspective to offer, but she was stunned. Jewel had a good eye for composing a shot to tell a story. Not necessarily a pretty one. Just like Luke.

She gave Jewel a few lessons on using the digital camera and let her photograph the fly and spider sequence as the spider drew closer to his prey. Logan thought that it wasn't just Jewel who felt that way, but probably all those children who were litter on the streets, thrown away like trash. The thought of someone not wanting their child broke her heart, and she knew how it felt too. Her mother had thrown her away. She shook her head and refocused on Jewel, who was completely engrossed in the project.

She was excited because Jewel showed her that she and others like her could tell their stories through art. The visual arts center that Logan was in the process of creating would be the perfect venue for them.

Logan reached into her camera bag and took out her backup Nikon. "Jewel, would you like to use this camera?" she asked, holding it out to her. "Shoot whatever interests you or catches your eye. You have an unusual perspective. I'd like to see what you come up with."

Jewel took the camera and they spent the rest of the afternoon shooting, holding conversation to a minimum. They seemed to be able to sense each other's thoughts. Logan had never worked with anyone as easily as she did with Jewel. *Not even Luke*, she thought sadly. Logan incorporated Jewel's suggestions and was amazed at how her shots came alive. She couldn't wait to get home to download and print them.

Logan glanced at her cell phone and was shocked to see that it was almost four o'clock. "It's time I head home," she said. "Where do you live? I'll see that you get home okay."

"I'll be fine."

"It's no problem. Where do you live?" Logan asked again. She wanted to know more about this girl. Logan could see that she had a thirst for learning and an extraordinary eye when it came to creating a shot. She knew she had something special. *That's what Luke would have said*, she thought. "I want to give you copies of the photographs you took."

Jewel hesitated, then said they could meet back here on Saturday, about the same time, and off she went before Logan could protest.

She was on her way home when it suddenly dawned on her that she'd promised Vanessa she would go to her dinner party on

Saturday. Great. How would she explain canceling to Vanessa? She couldn't tell her the truth. She'd have to think of some excuse that would satisfy her because there was no way she would disappoint Jewel.

She brought her attention back to the traffic and put out her right hand to signal a turn. Just as she started into the turn, the car behind her clipped the rear of her bike. She lost control, hit a parked car, and then the street. She felt her head hit the road and it hurt despite the helmet. She skidded along, taking skin off her left side from face to foot, tearing up her bike shorts and top. Someone blew their horn and swerved around her. She heard a screech of brakes and held her breath, waiting for the impact. When it didn't happen, she slowly let out her breath, then tried to get up.

"Don't try to move," a man's voice said.

She tested her limbs and everything seemed to be in working order. "I'm fine," she said, trying to get up again, but the world spun and went fuzzy.

"You really shouldn't get up. The ambulance will be here in a minute." She tried to see who was talking to her, but everything was fuzzy and she felt woozy. Her brain was having trouble comprehending his words. She shook her head to clear her thoughts and her world started to spin.

"Lay back. You shouldn't sit up. The ambulance is on its way."

She did as she was told, then one word broke through the haze. *Ambulance.* "No. I'm fine. Really. I don't need an ambulance." Her voice squeaked and she could feel the hysteria rise from within. Then she heard the sirens and was transported back to Appalachia and the cave. The beauty of the stalactites and stalagmites. The crystal room. And then the horror. Luke disappearing into nothingness and the arrival of police and ambulances. Search and rescue teams.

She was brought back to the present by the arrival of the police and ambulance, sirens blaring. Her mother had always told her to say a prayer when she saw an ambulance or funeral. Her mother, also missing. "Please, I really don't need an ambulance. I'm fine." Here she was lying on the road, people standing around staring. She had a new appreciation for the feelings of the zoo animals.

The paramedics stooped down on either side of her and began poking and prodding. "Doesn't look like anything's broken," said one of them. "Mostly bumps and bruises. Possible concussion. We'll take you to the hospital so they can check you out and clean up those wounds."

"I'm fine. I only live a couple of blocks away. I just want to get home." She blinked to prevent the tears from coming. When they couldn't convince her to go to the hospital, the paramedic gave her a 'Refusal to be Transported" form to sign and they packed up.

She heard a man conferring with them and heard him say he would see that she got home okay. Logan panicked. She didn't want this stranger to know where she lived. She hadn't even seen his face. Maybe the hospital would be better. She called out to the paramedics, but it was too late. They had closed up shop and were leaving. She was getting up to leave before the stranger got back to her, but he picked up her bike.

"My car is over there."

Car? She can't get in his car. "I'll walk," she said to his back. He turned around and she gasped. It was the detective from this morning. The good looking one. "It's you."

He smiled. "Who did you think it was?"

"I...I didn't know. I didn't recognize you." What was she going to tell him, that she thought he was a serial killer going to lure her into his car and she'd never be seen again? "It was a little confusing."

"And the paramedics said you probably have a mild concussion."

"Yeah, that too."

"Come on, we'll get you home. What's your address?"

She felt rather than saw someone watching her. She turned and saw Jewel standing apart from the crowd. "Jewel?" she said.

"What's that?"

She blinked and looked again, the spot where she thought she saw Jewel was now empty. "I thought I saw someone."

He cocked his head and watched her move toward his car. "You should go to the hospital. Let me drive you there."

"No, really. I'll be fine. I just want to go home."

He shook his head and asked again for her address. She told him and he loaded her into the car, then went back for her bike and camera bag. They rode the few blocks in silence.

Logan let herself into the house with Costello right behind her. She leaned down to pick up the mail and swayed as the room started to spin.

"You go sit down."

"I'm fine, really. Just a little woozy."

He scooped up the mail. "At least let me clean up those scrapes for you." She started to protest, but he asked where her bathroom was. Good thing she listened to Vanessa, who always said 'Your home should be ready to receive guests at anytime.' She directed him to the powder room just off the kitchen. "You go get those things off and we'll have you cleaned up in no time."

She showered and came back down wearing a pair of baggy shorts and an extra large t-shirt, feeling a bit sore, but much better.

"Nice outfit," he said, looking her up and down. She shifted, uncomfortable with his attention while enjoying it at the same time. He cleaned and bandaged her various cuts and scrapes. His hands were gentle. Her mind began to drift. "All finished," he said.

"Oh," she realized she was disappointed, but immediately told herself she was being silly. He was a police officer. He probably bandaged victims on a regular basis. "Do you think you'll catch the guy who hit me?"

"Did you see who it was?"

"No. I was hit from behind."

"Then how do you know it was a guy?" he asked, trying not to smirk.

His question annoyed her. "Because it probably was a man."

"We probably won't catch him, unless someone comes forward with information."

"You mean you aren't going to look for *him?*" she said, emphasizing the him.

This time he didn't try to hide the smirk, but laughed out loud. He had a genuinely handsome face, especially when he laughed. "There are officers questioning the people who were at the scene. Unless we can get a lead from one of them…" he shrugged. "But, we'll give it our best."

She didn't say anything for a minute, until the silence became uncomfortable. "Well, I have work to do," she said, heading to the front door. "Thank you for your help."

"I'll get your bike and backpack from the car."

"Oh, right. Thank you." She'd forgotten all about them. "How bad is it?"

"Scratched up, but it doesn't look too bad. That's a pretty fancy bike."

"It was a gift to myself."

He brought her things into the house. He was right, the bike only had minor scratches. She took the backpack. It was scraped and one corner had a small tear. She set the bag on the kitchen table, opened it, and lifted out each of the cameras and lenses to examine them. Then she took both cameras and photographed the birds at the feeder, trying different settings, all the while feeling Costello's gaze.

"Is everything working?"

"I think so," she said, scrolling through the shots. "I guess the bag lived up to its claims. It's supposed to absorb shock."

"Looks like you might need a new one."

"Cheaper than replacing the cameras. Well, thank you for everything. I appreciate your help."

"No problem. I was glad to do it. You get some rest. You'll probably be a little sore for a few days."

She remembered the papers she had picked up from the scene of Millicent's accident and wondered if she should say something. Maybe she shouldn't have taken them. She also realized that she enjoyed his company. His hand reached for the door and she stopped him.

"Do you know what caused Millicent's accident?"

He turned toward her. "I can't discuss an open investigation."

"Oh. It's just that she was a friend." She thought again about the papers and wondered if she should tell him. He turned to the door again, then turned back to face her. His look had softened some.

"Look, we're still investigating." He hesitated and Logan thought that there was something he hadn't told her.

"What haven't you told me?"

"I can't discuss it."

"Then there is something," she said, looking him right in the eye. She wasn't going to be the one to blink first. She could tell he was struggling.

"This is between us," he said, and she assured him it wouldn't go any further. "A witness came forward. He said that it looked like someone ran her off the road. He couldn't say if it was deliberate, and he was too far back to give us any information about the car. All he knew was that it was a late model dark SUV and that he thought the driver was a woman."

Logan was too stunned to speak for several minutes. Costello led her into the living room. "I knew something happened. Millicent wasn't a drinker and she was a good driver."

"The crime scene team is out there now."

Logan gasped and thought about tramping around the scene. At least she hadn't crossed the tape. And the papers. She should tell him. Can he arrest her? She didn't think so. After all, as far as she knew, it was an accident.

"Let me get you some water," said Costello. He came back and handed the glass to her. "You really should go to the hospital. You have a head injury and you're white as a sheet."

"I'm okay." She took a deep breath. "I think I need to tell you something."

He immediately shifted to police mode. She was amazed at how it happened. He had his notebook and pen poised. Waiting. Logan shifted uncomfortably under his stare.

"I went there." There, she said it. Not all of it, yet. See how he reacts.

"There? The crime scene?"

She noticed that he referred to is as a crime scene. "Yeah, but I didn't know it was a crime scene and I stayed outside the tape. I thought it was an accident. That's what you told us." She glared at him.

"It is still a police investigation and you had no business out there."

"I had every right to be there. My friend died there," she shouted. She was barely able to control the crack in her voice or the tears that threatened.

"I know." His voice softened just a bit, but still retained the authority indicative of his position. "Look, I can see this has been hard for you."

"I don't understand. Why would someone want to hurt her?"

"We're looking into that. We still don't know if it was deliberate or an accident. It could have been a drunk driver." His phone rang. "Costello." Logan watched him pacing and listening. When he finished, he turned to her. "I have to go. I'll be in touch. If you think of anything, let me know." She still didn't tell him about the papers.

# CHAPTER 5

She watched him until he turned the corner, then closed the door and walked upstairs to her office. Soreness was beginning to settle into her muscles; her movements were slower, more deliberate. She had been looking forward to getting home and downloading and printing Jewel's pictures, excited to see what she had captured. That was, until some lunatic mowed her down. For now, she would download them, make her customary two backups, and print them after a good night's sleep. She was feeling some stiffness from the accident and got up to stretch. Fortunately, she was in good shape and thought the soreness would be minimal.

She went down to the kitchen and put on the tea kettle while she rifled through the mail. Junk. A couple of bills. A plain white envelope addressed to her. No stamp, no return address. She opened the envelope and found a single sheet of white paper. She unfolded it, read the words that were pasted in the center, and watched it flutter to the floor. She dropped into the chair and sat there for a long time, just staring at that single piece of paper.

The tea kettle whistle jerked her back. She turned off the burner, not bothering to make the tea, and forced her shaking body to lean down and pick up the note. She put it on the table, where it lay like a neon light signaling for attention, but she refused to look at it, focusing instead on taking a long slow breath in and letting it out with the same slow rhythm.

Now seemed like a good time to clean out her junk drawer. She busied herself tossing out junk and rearranging what was left, making a heroic effort to ignore the note. *I read it wrong,* she told herself. *It's a mistake.*

But she knew what she'd read and she forced herself to read it again. The ring of the phone pierced through the fear and disbelief. She ignored it, hoping the caller would go away. She didn't want to talk to anyone. The ringing stopped but immediately began again and she stole a look at the caller ID. Rose.

She grabbed the receiver and shouted, "Rose, get over here right now," and hung up. She went into the living room and paced by the front window, waiting for Rose and trying not to think about the note which was still lying on the kitchen table.

She looked out to the street and saw Mrs. Rosen heading her way. *No, I can't deal with her.* The doorbell rang, followed by pounding. Logan didn't move, hoping that if she ignored her she would just go away, but no such luck. Ignoring her only added to her resolve. Logan threw open the front door and glared at her. Mrs. Rosen took a step back and, for the first time, seemed at a loss for words. Rose screeched to a halt in front of the house, front tire straddling the curb. She jumped out of the car and came running up behind Mrs. Rosen.

"Logan, are you okay?" she said, breathless. "You look terrible. What happened?"

Without saying a word, Logan grabbed Rose's arm and dragged her inside, slamming the door in Mrs. Rosen's face.

"What did that witch do now?" asked Rose.

Logan shook her head. "Not her," she said, barely able to get the words out.

Rose followed her into the kitchen. "You're all scraped up. And you're black and blue."

Logan looked down at her arms. She had completely forgotten about her accident. "It's a long story. That's not why you're here."

"Then what?"

Logan thrust the note at Rose.

In the center of the paper in large red letters were the words "A CAR ACCIDENT CAN HAPPEN ANYTIME, ANYPLACE."

After a few seconds Logan plopped down in the kitchen chair. "My God," said Rose, pacing around and waving the paper. "Does this say what I think it says?"

"What do you think it says?" asked Logan, her arms hugging her body, trying to suppress the trembling.

Rose stopped pacing and faced her. "That someone is threatening you?" she asked in a low voice, dropping into the chair opposite Logan.

"That's how I read it," said Logan. Although she had hoped Rose would have another explanation. Something less sinister.

"Where did this come from?" asked Rose, waving the note at Logan.

"It was with my mail, plain white envelope," said Logan, handing the envelope to her.

"Someone put this in your mailbox?"

Logan was bent forward, her elbows on her thighs, hands covering her face. "It looks that way."

"But, why?" asked Rose. "I don't understand. Why is someone threatening you?" She turned and looked at Logan. "Is that what happened to you? Were you in an accident?

"Yes, but not a car accident. I was on my bike," she started to explain. Then looked up at Rose, a stricken look on her face.

Rose took Logan's shaking hands into her own. "You're white as a ghost."

"I thought it was just a miscalculation. But, now," she said, gesturing to the letter. "Maybe…"

"Maybe what?"

"Well, someone clipped the back of my bike when I was turning the corner. The police don't know who did it and I figured that maybe the driver didn't realize he hit me."

"You think it might not have been an accident? That the note is a warning? But why would someone threaten you?"

It only took a second to realize that Rose didn't know what had happened. She took her copy of the newspaper from the counter and opened it up to show the headline. "I think this is why," she said as Rose skimmed the article. When Rose looked up from reading, Logan said, "The unidentified person was Millicent."

Rose looked at her, her face white with shock. "Millicent? Our Millicent?"

"Yeah. Our Millicent."

"How did you find out it was Millicent?"

"Two detectives came to Ran's this morning and asked us a lot of questions. They told us what happened."

Neither one said anything for the next couple of minutes. Finally, Rose spoke up. "Why did they come to your uncle's?"

"They said they found his name on her calendar. They wanted to know why he was meeting her; when we last saw her. Things like that."

Rose got up and stared out the back door window. She watched the birds at the feeder then turned to face Logan. "What I don't understand, is why they were asking questions if this was a simple car accident."

"I don't know. I didn't really think about it."

"Well, if you ask me, there's more to this than we know. And now this note," she emphasized by waving it in Logan's face. "But why threaten you?"

"I don't know. I went to the crash site, but just to see where it happened."

"Have you been asking questions, snooping?"

"No, all I did was go to see where it happened," she said, sounding defensive. "She was a friend. I wanted to know what happened and why. I didn't know it was anything more than a terrible accident."

"Sometimes an accident is just that, an accident," said Rose. "But this," she said, tapping the note, "this looks like you made someone nervous." She sat back down at the table. "The police. We have to call them," she said, picking up the phone.

"Wait," said Logan. "That detective gave me his card. It's upstairs. In the pocket of my jeans."

"I'll get it," said Rose. "Where are the jeans?"

"On the bed," she shouted after Rose, who was running up the steps.

She was back in record time, waving the card. "Here it is," she said, grabbing the phone. When Costello answered she explained who she was and what she needed, then hung up. "They'll be here in a few minutes, and he said not to handle it. They want to try to get prints."

"Well, it's a bit late for that, don't you think?" asked Logan.

"Now, while we're waiting for them to get here maybe you'll tell me what happened to you."

"Here, I'll make us some tea while we wait," said Logan, needing to do something. She looked down at her scraped body. Dark purple bruises were beginning to color her skin. She sighed and gave Rose a condensed version of the accident.

"Another accident. That's three in two days. I think that goes beyond coincidence."

Logan looked over at her. "Three? Where did you get three from?"

"Have you forgotten what happened to us on the way to the spa?"

Logan laughed. "I don't think that counts. That was poor driving skills."

"No, don't you remember? I told you someone tried to run me off the road."

"That's what you said, but I didn't see anyone force us off the road."

"Well, I did, whether you believe me or not. I think something's going on."

"Okay, but what do we have to do with what happened to Millicent? And if someone," Logan raised her hand to stop Rose, "and I stress *if*. If someone was after us, then why hurt Millicent? It doesn't make any sense. And why would anyone want to hurt us?"

Rose cocked her head and countered with a question of her own. "If someone knows you went to the crash site, then how did they know?"

Logan thought for a minute. "Maybe somebody saw my car there."

"Or, maybe they followed you."

"Don't be absurd. I'd know if someone were following me."

Rose cocked one eyebrow. "Would you? We live in the city. Everywhere you go there are cars behind you. How would you know?"

Logan shrugged, conceding that she probably wouldn't. "But it doesn't make sense to follow me. No one would have any reason to think I would go to the accident scene. It's more likely that someone saw my car there."

"Didn't you say the police were asking a lot of questions this morning."

"Yeah, why?"

"Well, I'm thinking that if it were a simple accident then they wouldn't be asking questions. Maybe there's more to it."

Logan fidgeted, and saw Rose's antenna going up. Rose knew her so well. But she promised Costello she wouldn't say anything. She loved Rose, but knew she couldn't keep a secret. Thankfully, the shrill whistle of the tea kettle interrupted any further discussion.

"If that's the case then this note might be useful," continued Rose.

While Logan busied herself making a pot of tea, they discussed Millicent's accident. "I don't understand why anyone would want to hurt her," said Logan

"Millicent dies in a car accident. You go to the scene. Someone hits you while you're riding your bike. You get a note threatening you."

"When you put it like that, it does seem a little too coincidental. But why?" asked Logan again. "It doesn't make sense," she said, pouring the tea and placing the mugs on the table. "After all, she worked at the Preservation Society. Not what I would consider a high risk job."

"What about her personal life?" asked Rose.

"I don't know much about her personal life, but if it were personal, why target me? I know we were friends, but she didn't share much. I think she spent most of her time doing research." Logan got up and grabbed the lavender legal pad from beside the phone and sat at the table facing Rose. Together they made a detailed chronological list of the incidents, including the one on the way to the spa. On a new page she listed what they knew about Millicent, both personal and professional. "I don't ever remember her mentioning anything about family," said Logan.

"That doesn't mean she doesn't have any. Maybe they're estranged for some reason. Is she from Philly, or somewhere else?" asked Rose.

Logan sat back and thought about Millicent and what she really knew about her, which sadly, wasn't much. "I'm not sure where she's from. You know," she said, tapping the pen on the notepad, "I've known her for about seven years, we've gone out to lunch and dinner, but I don't know anything about her personal life. I never realized that until now."

"Well, I think we should just let the police handle this when they get here," said Rose.

Logan looked up at her. "Someone threatened me. I take that very personally. I'm not about to let that idiot Beatty blow me off and then when I get killed he's all surprised."

Rose laughed. "Not your favorite person I see."

"Just wait until you meet him. You should have seen the way he treated us when he questioned us about Millicent. And the way he treated Michael. Like he was Satan himself. Clearly he has some issues regarding the Catholic Church."

"Maybe he was an altar boy and something happened."

"Not every altar boy was molested. Besides, I can't picture him as an altar boy. Wait until you meet him. He's just plain mean."

"Well, you do have a bit of a bias yourself, when it comes to the police."

Logan glared at her. "My mother has nothing to do with this."

Rose got up and stood by the kitchen door, looking out, then turned and faced her, hands on hips. "You never believed she ran off. You've always blamed the police for not taking her disappearance seriously. I'd say you have some issues with the police."

"They wouldn't even take a report," Logan argued, slapping the palm of her hand on the table. The mugs rattled and tea sloshed over the edges. "They said she had to be missing for at least twenty-four hours before they would consider her missing. They just didn't want to be bothered."

"Calm down," said Rose, grabbing some paper towels to mop up the puddles. "Even your father told the police that she left on her own," she said, her voice barely above a whisper.

Logan threw down the pen and got up. "I'm not discussing my mother with you."

"Okay, okay," said Rose, throwing her hands up in a back off gesture.

The doorbell rang several times, followed by knocking.

"Mrs. Rosen," they said together.

"I've had enough of this," said Logan, stomping to the front door, trying to ignore the soreness. She threw it open. "Now, look..." Costello and Beatty stood staring at her. "Oh, sorry," said Logan. "I thought you were someone else."

The corners of Costello's mouth twitched a bit. Beatty's dark personality shone through the glare he gave her. "You people have an interesting way of answering the door," said Costello, referring to Ran slamming the door in their faces. Logan laughed at the image of them standing on the doorstep and Ran thinking they were developers.

"Yeah, come in," she said, stepping aside. "We're in the kitchen."

They followed her down the short hall to the back of the house. Costello was perusing the framed photographs that lined the walls. "These are wonderful," he said. "Are you the photographer?"

"These are mostly my husband's work," she said.

"Oh," he said.

Logan thought she detected disappointment in his voice. "My husband died two years ago."

"Where's this letter?" asked Beatty, rolling his eyes.

"Right," said Logan as she led them into the kitchen. "This is my best friend, Rose Parker. This is Detective Frank Costello and Detective Doug Beatty."

Rose looked them up and down. Costello was wearing a black suit that Logan recognized as Armani, a crisp white shirt and red tie, and spit-shined tasseled loafers. His blond military style hair was perfectly coiffed and his blue eyes held a twinkle.

Beatty, on the other hand, was wearing a brown tweed sport coat with some fraying around the cuffs. His tan shirt was open at the collar and in desperate need of an iron. His brown pants were baggy at the knees. His suede shoes were run over on the outsides, a result of his duck feet. His muddy-brown eyes held not a twinkle, sparkle, or anything else. Just darkness. It was the clown hairdo that caused Rose to turn toward the sink, but not before Logan caught a smirk.

"Can I get you something to drink?" asked Logan.

"Just show us the note," said Beatty. She glanced at Costello, who raised his eyebrows at her, and retrieved the note and envelope from the counter. "I guess there's no point in dusting for prints," said Beatty sarcastically, handling it by the corners as he put it into a plastic bag.

"As you can see, it looks like Millicent was killed. And now the killer is threatening me," said Logan.

Beatty gave her a look that could turn glass back to sand. "I wasn't aware that you were a detective."

Costello broke in. "Let me see what we've got," he said, holding out his hand. Beatty passed the note and envelope to him, which he read before flipping it over. "When did you get this?"

"It was mixed in with my mail." She stopped and looked at Costello. "Come to think of it, your prints might be on the envelope." Beatty snapped his head around and Costello rolled his eyes. He filled him in on Logan's bike accident.

"That's two accidents in two days and now this letter. Kind of coincidental don't you think?" asked Rose, her tone mimicking Beatty's earlier sarcasm.

Logan coughed to keep from laughing.

Costello handed it back to Beatty. "We'll check with the neighbors to see if anyone saw anything." They stood to leave.

"That's it?" asked Logan.

"We'll be in touch if we find anything," Costello said. Logan saw Beatty shoot him a disgusted look. Costello pretended he didn't notice but she saw just a flicker of amusement in his eyes.

Mrs. Rosen was still sweeping when they stepped outside, so they decided to talk to her first. Logan stood in the doorway watching. She wanted to see what Beatty would do when she ordered him off her property and waved her broom at him.

Beatty flashed his badge and Mrs. Rosen turned sickly grey. What happened next left Logan speechless. Mrs. Rosen raised her broom and began beating Beatty. He stumbled backwards down the steps. trying to get away from her and her broom. Mrs. Rosen fled into the house. Logan just stood, mouth agape. Beatty was apoplectic. His veins were popping. Logan, afraid he was going to have a stroke, rushed out.

Beatty started up the steps, but Costello stopped him. "That woman is headed to jail."

"Let it be," said Costello.

"I am going to have her charged with assaulting an officer."

"Beatty, let it go. Couldn't you see that the woman was terrified." Costello turned to Logan. "What do you know about your neighbor?"

"Nothing, only that she's always cleaning and throws a fit if anyone walks on her property. She's never said a civil thing to me."

Costello stood looking up at the house, assessing the situation. He turned back to her and asked if she knew the woman's name or where she came from.

"I know her name's Mrs. Rosen, but nothing else. Why?"

"The minute Beatty showed his badge, she reacted. She was terrified."

"Her reaction was a bit over the top," said Logan.

"I noticed something."

Logan watched him, waiting for more. Beatty, who had been standing apart from them, moved closer. Logan could still see the veins in his neck, but his color was better. "So, what's your diagnosis, doctor?" he asked, his voice thick with sarcasm.

Logan looked over at Costello. "Doctor?"

Costello glared at Beatty, who ignored him. "He analyzes the perps," Beatty said. "Has to understand why they do what they do." His color was rising again and the veins began to bulge a bit more. "I should arrest that old bat for assaulting a police officer!"

Costello continued to talk to Beatty in his calm voice. "I would just leave it," he said. "I believe that woman has been through enough."

"What do you mean?" asked Logan, her brows drawn together.

"Haven't you ever noticed her wrist?" he asked, looking at Logan.

"No, she always wears long sleeves." No one said anything, then Logan spoke up. "You mean, she tried to commit suicide?"

"No, it's worse."

"Well, here it comes. His analysis," said Beatty.

Costello ignored him and continued. "When she raised her arms, I saw the black tattoo." Logan still wasn't sure what he was saying. "She's a Holocaust survivor," he said.

With that statement, all of the pieces fell into place. Her obsessive behavior with cleanliness, people encroaching on her property, her disconnection with others. Logan had seen photographs of the horrific conditions Holocaust survivors endured during their internment in the concentration camps. "Oh, that poor woman."

Rose popped her head out. "What's going..." Her words drifted away when she saw the expressions on everyone's faces.

"I'll fill you in later."

"We'll talk to some of your other neighbors. Maybe they saw something," said Costello.

She watched them walk to the house on her other side, but her mind kept going back to the stricken look on Mrs. Rosen's face when Beatty flashed his badge. She felt so guilty for all the mean things she'd said about her, never realizing that there might be a reason for her hostility. She considered knocking on her door but thought it would be better to approach her when she saw her outside. She wanted to explain what Detective Beatty wanted and to assure her that they meant no harm.

They went back into the kitchen and Rose brewed some fresh tea. They sat at the table. Logan wrapped her hands around the mug while she explained what happened. "Oh," was all Rose said. They finished their tea in silence.

"I feel so bad for her," said Logan, taking the cups to the sink.

"Yeah," was all Rose could manage.

"I'm going back."

"Back? Back where?"

Logan was standing with her back to the sink, her hands on her hips. She didn't have to answer Rose. She saw comprehension wash across her face. She said it anyway. "I'm going back to the accident site." Rose started to say something, but Logan held her hands up, palms out, to stop her.

Rose glared at her. "Are you out of your mind. You can't go back there. Someone just threatened you. And the police aren't going to let you walk all over the site. And what do you expect to see that you didn't see the first time?"

Logan gasped. She had completely forgotten about the pages she had found.

"What's wrong?"

"Nothing, just something I forgot to tell the police."

"Forgot?"

Logan glared at her. "Yeah, I really did forget."

"So, what did you forget?"

Logan sighed. There was no point in trying to evade the question. Rose would just hound her. "When I was out there earlier I found some papers. They were wet and some of the print was washed away, but they were from the Preservation Society, so I picked them up."

"Where are they?"

Logan couldn't help but notice the excitement in her voice and rolled her eyes. "In my office. They're on the work table. You can go get them."

"Then that's good reason not to go back out there."

"No, that's a good reason to go back out there. If, as you said earlier, my bike accident is related to Millicent's accident, then I want to know why." Rose gave her the 'I told you so look,' glad that Logan was thinking the two incidents might be related.

"That doesn't mean I agree with you, but after getting that note, let's just say I'm open. The note was a threat. I'm not about to back off. Before this I was looking at Millicent's death as a terrible traffic accident. I don't believe that now and neither do you. Something is going on and I'm going to find out what it is. You can lock up and set the alarm when you leave," she said, struggling to put on her boots and grabbing her jacket.

Rose sighed. "Wait for me, I'm going with you," the rescued papers forgotten by both of them.

98 | Nancy Engle

"Not necessary."

"I'll go. Someone's got to make sure you don't get into trouble."

Fifteen minutes later Logan and Rose approached the accident site, but there were police and crime scene people milling about, so they kept going.

"Let's eat," said Rose.

"We might as well. You pick."

Logan's cell phone rang. Rose listened to her side of the conversation. "Really?" she asked. "That's great. I'll be right over."

"You'll be right over where?" asked Rose, rolling her eyes. "I guess this means we don't get to eat."

"It's Ran," she said. "He found something in the attic. He sounded excited. Let's swing by. We'll eat…"

"Don't say that we'll eat at Ran's. We'd be lucky to find a moldy piece of cheese in the refrigerator," said Rose. "Call him back and tell him you'll be over later."

"This won't take long."

Rose sighed. "Can we at least pick up a pizza on the way?"

"Sure."

They got to Mount Joy an hour later, pizza in hand, and found Ran coming down from the attic, carrying two medium sized boxes. The tape that sealed them was yellowed and brittle. Logan ran to relieve him of them while Rose headed to the kitchen with the pizza.

"You know you're not supposed to be carrying this stuff down. I told you to wait for me."

"I'm fine. You worry too much."

Logan set the boxes down.

"Is that pizza I smell?" he asked, heading toward the kitchen. "I'll get…" He stopped and looked at Logan. "What happened to you?"

"Just a little accident." She didn't want to go into the fact that she was riding her bike. Ran hated her riding a bike in the city. "Nothing to worry about. It looks worse than it is."

Rose came in from the kitchen. "A *little* accident?" said Rose. "Someone tried to kill her."

Ran's face went as grey as the old white paint on the baseboards. Logan ran to him. "Here, sit down." She gave Rose a scathing look and was gratified to see Rose repentant as she tried to backtrack.

"Someone hit her."

"I'm okay," said Logan. "I look worse than I feel. Are you okay?"

"I'm okay. Just a shock hearing that someone tried to kill you."

"No one tried to kill me. It was an accident. Now, let's eat," she said, changing the subject. "Rose is probably starving, as usual."

"I am. I'll set everything out in the kitchen."

Ran attempted to pry more details out of them while they ate, but Logan was deliberately evasive. "So, tell us what you found in the attic."

# CHAPTER 6

"You won't believe this," he said, walking toward the dining room. "I was moving some furniture and bumped against the wall."

"What are you doing moving that stuff around? Next time, call and we'll help you," said Logan, following him.

"Yeah, yeah," he said, waving his hand in dismissal.

"I mean it. You had that heart problem last year, and don't roll your eyes at me," she said to his back.

"So, tell us about the wall," interrupted Rose.

"It sounded different when I hit it, plus, it was paneled. It's the only part of the attic that isn't bare plaster. So I knocked on the wall all around the area and heard the same hollow sound. I went down to get my flashlight and looked at it more closely. You know how dark that attic is."

"Another reason for you to wait until someone can help you." A thought occurred to her. "Call Jimmy to help you. He doesn't do anything else."

He ignored her. "Anyway, there was a seam where two pieces of paneling butted together. I had to get my tools to pry it open. When I finally got one piece of the paneling down I found a space about the size of a small closet."

"A hidden room? You're kidding? I thought you only found things like that in gothic novels," said Rose.

"Who built it, do you know?" asked Logan.

"Don't know. But these boxes were hidden in there," he said, pointing to the medium sized sealed boxes that sat on the dining room table amidst other boxes, papers, and photographs.

"Hmm. Sealed room. Sealed boxes. I knew there were family secrets. Skeletons in the closet."

"Skeletons? What skeletons?" asked Rose.

"I was trying to get Ran to tell me some of the family secrets the other day, but he tells me there aren't any."

"Of course, there are," said Rose. "Every family has them."

"Let's see what's in them," said Ran. "I haven't opened them yet. I thought we could look together," he said, ripping off the yellowed, brittle tape, sneezing from the dust.

"You know, we haven't even touched the surface of the stuff in the attic," said Logan. "We need to get the furniture down. I noticed some pieces that we can use to decorate after the restoration's completed. If there's anything you don't need or want, maybe we could have an auction."

"We'll see," he said. Logan didn't press. The idea of a large gathering of people was off-putting to Ran, but the seed was planted.

Logan's phone rang. She looked at the caller ID. "Costello." She pushed answer. "Hello?" Rose moved closer so she could hear Costello. "Right now?" Logan asked. "Yeah, she's right here. We'll be there shortly," and hung up.

"What was that all about?" asked Ran.

"Costello. Wants to fingerprint us so they can eliminate..." Rose had a sudden coughing fit and Logan began smacking her on the back. She'd have to thank Rose later for her quick thinking. The last thing Ran needed to hear was that someone most assuredly murdered Millicent, and sent her a threatening note.

"We'd better get going," said Logan. "The boxes will have to wait until we come back."

"We'll be back later," said Rose, shoving Logan out the door, leaving Ran standing there open-mouthed.

"That was close," said Logan. "I almost told him about the note. Quick thinking."

"Glad it worked."

"For now, but he knew something was up. He isn't as clueless as he pretends to be."

Rose laughed. "Yeah. You're going to have to do some fancy footwork to get out of this one."

"Let's get this over with," said Logan when they got in the car. "I want to see if Costello has any updates." She was hoping to see him alone. She knew Beatty wouldn't tell her anything, but Costello might.

They found a parking place three blocks away. Logan didn't mind the walk, especially when the weather cooperated. She looked up at the square brick building that was built somewhere around the turn of the 20th century. She'd read somewhere that the building was originally a feed supply warehouse. She could see where some of the original windows and doors had been removed and re-bricked.

They walked up the old, cracked concrete steps to the generic glass doors and pulled them open. Just inside the lobby on their right was a conveyer belt with an officer on the other side.

"Put your purses down here," he said, indicating the belt, "then walk through the metal detector."

Logan walked through without a problem. When Rose started through it beeped. Logan looked down at Rose's feet. She was wearing cowboy boots and the toes were decorated with gold fleur-de-lis metal tabs.

"Take them off and put 'em up here," said the officer, looking as bored as anyone Logan had ever seen.

"I'll tell them to let Costello know we're here," Logan said, pointing to the visitor window.

Logan took one of the two seats in the waiting area and watched Rose walking toward her, boots in hand.

"He didn't have to make me take these off," she complained as she struggled to get them back on. "He could see they had metal."

"Maybe he thought you were concealing a weapon in them," Logan said, rolling her eyes.

"Don't be ridiculous."

"Well, Mrs. O'Malley, Miss Parker. That was quick," he said, shaking Logan's hand, holding onto it a few seconds longer than necessary. He looked down at Rose fighting with her boot, the corners of his mouth curving up.

"We were at my uncle's when you called," said Logan, explaining the reason for their quick arrival. She felt her cheeks warm.

"Mrs. O'Malley, Miss Parker, would you follow me?"

"Call me Logan. Mrs. O'Malley sounds so matronly." Rose coughed and Logan caught a glimpse of a snicker.

"Okay, Logan. Let's get you two printed. It'll only take a few minutes. It's all digital now. No black ink on your fingers."

"Why are we being printed?" asked Rose.

"We found some prints on the letter and need to eliminate both of you and see what's left."

"Let's get this over with," said Logan. "I want to know who's doing this and why, and the sooner the better."

He led them into an alcove where the machine stood. Rose went first. It was all done in a matter of minutes. Logan was impressed.

"Your turn," said Costello, turning to Logan.

She stepped up, placed her fingers where she was told. He punched some buttons and frowned.

"What's wrong?"

"The machine's having trouble reading your prints. Let's try it again." After several more tries it was clear to all of them that the machine wasn't going to get anything from Logan. Costello took her hands in his and examined her fingertips. The warmth from his hands permeated her whole body. "Well, I see the problem." His smile lit his entire face. Then he started laughing.

"What?"

"You don't have good definition. I'm afraid we're going to have to do this the old fashioned way," he said, bringing out the ink pad and card.

"Great."

He inked her fingers one by one and pressed them on the card. Logan saw what looked like ten oval black blobs. "These don't look like anything to me."

"The definition is very faint, but it's there."

"Hey, this could work out for you." Logan gave Rose a scathing look but she kept talking. "You know. If you decide to change career fields."

Logan rolled her eyes. "I think this is the best we can do," said Costello, handing her a towelette.

"Am I finished?" asked Rose.

"You're both free to go."

"I'd like to talk to you for a minute, if you have time," said Logan.

"I have to make some phone calls," said Rose. "I'll see you outside."

"Come on back to my office," he said with a smile in his voice. Logan followed him down the dreary, poorly lit hall. The parquet tiles were worn and chipped. The beige walls, she guessed, were an attempt to brighten the place, but the color had a greyish tint that clashed with the floor.

He stepped aside and gestured her into his office. She stopped just inside the doorway, not sure where to go. The office looked like a converted broom closet, the worn grey metal desk taking up most of the floor space. The florescents were the only source of light and they gave everything a greenish tinge. He offered her one of the brown, wooden straight-back chairs. They were scuffed and scarred and piled with folders. He cleaned off the closest chair then took his seat behind his desk.

"Do you know what happened to Millicent?" she asked without preamble.

"We're still looking into it, but I can't discuss an ongoing investigation." She noticed the smile was gone from his voice after he answered her question. All business.

She cleared her throat. "I just don't understand why someone would hurt her."

"Do you have any ideas?" he asked twirling his pencil between his thumb and forefinger. *A lefty*, she thought. *What were the odds that we'd both be left handed?* He continued to hold her gaze, waiting.

"She was a nice person. She worked at the Preservation Society and was helping my uncle get landmark designation for Mount Joy. She said she found something interesting and had the papers in her car the night of the exhibit, and that she would bring them by the next day."

"Do you know what these papers were?" They'd covered this ground just this morning. *Was that just this morning?* she thought. It seemed so long ago.

"Like we said this morning, she was very mysterious about what she found. She said she wanted to come out to Mount Joy and check some things before telling us what she was thinking." He didn't respond, and looked like he was debating whether or not to share something. "Did you find anything in the car? Any papers I mean?" she asked.

He shook his head. "Most of them were burned." He saw her flinch. "I'm sorry. We're looking at everything that survived to see if there is anything that might point to a reason someone wanted her out of the way." She experienced a tinge of guilt as she thought of the copies sitting in her office, wrestling with whether or not to tell him.

Then she realized what he had just said. *So*, she thought, *some of the papers did survive*. She was about to ask if she could see them when the door burst open, almost plastering her to the wall. If her arm hadn't been on her lap she might have lost it. "Beatty," she muttered under her breath.

"That's Detective Beatty," he said, glaring at her. *He must have hyper-sensitive hearing*, she thought, refusing to break eye contact. He folded first. She glanced at Costello just as the smirk left his face. "I see you found her," he said, jerking his head toward Logan.

"Found me?" she asked Costello.

"The fingerprints," he said.

She shifted in her chair, attempting to put some distance between Beatty and herself. No easy feat. It didn't work anyway. He took one step forward and was right in her face.

"Would you mind telling me what you were doing at the accident scene?" She saw Costello jerk his head up and she wondered how Beatty knew.

Costello came around to her side of the desk and perched himself on the corner. One foot was planted firmly on the floor just inches from her feet. If she moved they'd be playing footsies. He was looking down at her. "Yes, I'd like to know the answer to that question too."

"I...I just wanted to see where it happened," she stammered, partly because she was feeling intimidated with both detectives staring down at her waiting for an explanation, and partly because of Costello's close proximity.

"Rather morbid, or did you want to make sure there wasn't anything incriminating?" demanded Beatty, leaning in.

Logan jumped up from her chair stepping on Costello's foot as she did so. Her face was red and her fists clenched. "Incriminating? What are you talking about? Millicent was my friend."

"Funny, not what I heard. You two barely spoke. You bullied her into working on the landmark papers when she didn't think the property qualified."

"What are you talking about? She approached us. Numerous times, actually, before my uncle would agree to even discuss it. I don't know who you've been talking to, but she was excited about the project." Logan realized that she was beginning to ramble and shut her mouth, and it suddenly dawned on her the tone of the investigation had changed. Beatty, while normally unpleasant, was downright hostile. Logan looked at Costello for help, but all she got from him was a slight shrug.

He looked over at Beatty before saying, "Mrs. O'Malley, thank you for coming by." She didn't think this was the time to remind him to call her Logan. "I'll be right back," he said to Beatty.

"Before you go," said Beatty. He took out a paper from his inside jacket pocket, took his time unfolding and perusing it. Logan stood just outside the door, half-turned. "Oh, here it is," he said. "What's your relationship with C.J. Forster?"

"C.J.?" She looked from Costello to Beatty, not understanding, then settled her gaze on Costello. If Beatty was trying to keep her off balance, he had achieved his goal. She hesitated, then said, "What does she have to do with Millicent?"

"Just answer the question," barked Beatty.

She flinched. "She and her husband, Sam, are friends of mine."

Costello rubbed his chin, but didn't say anything. "You can go now, but…"

She finished the sentence for him. "I know, don't leave town." Probably not the smartest retort, but she couldn't resist.

Costello walked her out. When they were out of earshot, or maybe not, since Beatty seemed to have extraordinary hearing, she asked Costello what was going on.

He ignored her question and asked one of his own. "How close are you and C.J. Forster?"

"Why all the questions about her? We've been friends for years. What's going on?"

"I can't comment on an ongoing investigation."

"Why was Beatty so hostile? It almost sounded like he thought I had something to do with Millicent's accident. He shouldn't be a detective."

"He solves cases. He gets results."

"By badgering and bullying. I wonder how many false confessions he's beat out of people."

Costello sighed. "He doesn't beat suspects, but he's good at what he does. He has great instincts."

"Not so great from where I stand. He's acting like I'm a suspect. I had no reason to hurt Millicent. She was my friend," said Logan again, emphasizing every word. "And I have a hundred people who can tell you where I was that night."

They reached the front door and he held it open for her. "Thanks again for coming."

"Will you let me know about the papers?"

"We'll see." He turned and she watched him walk back down the hall before heading to the parking lot.

"How'd it go?"

"Don't ask," she said, walking so fast that Rose had to run to keep up with her.

"Uh oh. What happened?"

"Beatty came in and practically accused me of running Millicent off the road."

"That's absurd. You were at The Gallery all night."

"Just what I told them." Her hands were shaking. Beatty's interrogation had rattled her. She wasn't sure what was going on, but she was more determined than ever to find out what had happened to Millicent. Beatty was treating her like a suspect and she wasn't going to sit still and let him railroad her. It was clear that he had already formed an opinion, and that opinion was that Logan knew something.

"Let's go to the Preservation Society," said Logan.

"Why there?"

"Beatty seemed to think that Millicent was working on Ran's landmark designation under protest."

"I wonder where he got that idea?"

"We're going to find out right now."

Luck was with them. There was a parking spot out front. The clock on the dashboard told them they were getting ready to close.

"I'll be right back."

She went up the worn marble steps, pushed open the ornately carved oak door, and came face to face with Jane. Logan stiffened. Jane's face registered surprise, then amusement.

"Sorry, we're closed," she said, attempting to push the door closed on her.

Logan stuck her foot in the door. The sharp edge stung and she winced. She pushed it open and walked into the glass enclosed vestibule, noticing that the marble floor was just as worn as the front steps.

"I told you we're closed," Jane's grating voice jerked her back to the reason she was there. "If you don't leave now, I'll call security."

"I just want to talk to the person who is going to handle Millicent's work."

"The poor woman isn't cold, but you don't care about that. You just want what you want." Jane was virtually shouting now.

Logan opened her mouth to protest, but stopped. The security guard was approaching from behind Jane. "Is there a problem, Miss Jane?"

Jane smirked at Logan just before turning to face the guard. Her voice was all innocence. "Oh, Mr. Singer. Thank you for coming."

"What's the problem."

"No problem," said Logan.

"I told her we were closed, but she forced her way in." Her voice virtually gushed. Logan wanted to gag.

Mr. Singer approached Logan. "You'll have to leave."

"But…"

"Now," he said, taking her elbow.

"I'll be back in the morning," she threw over her shoulder. She heard Jane praising Mr. Singer for his quick thinking as the door slammed behind her. *What's her problem?* Logan wondered. Now she'd have to wait until tomorrow. She was getting into the car when she heard the Society door open. She turned and saw Jane emerge, literally dancing down the steps. "Great."

In a voice as sweet as saccharine, she said, "Don't bother coming back tomorrow, or any other day. I won't have time to meet you anytime in the near future."

Logan opened her mouth to say something, but Jane was already several doors down the street. *What was that all about?* she wondered. She got into the car. "You heard?"

"Yeah," was all Rose said, at a loss for words.

Rose dropped Logan at home and she watched her drive off. The street was quiet, she noticed while she rummaged for her keys. Logan saw a slow moving car coming toward her. The windows were tinted so she couldn't see who was inside. She balanced her purse on her knee, tossing the contents about trying to find her keys. This is one time when she would welcome Mrs. Rosen's presence. She laughed. *I must really be spooked if Mrs. Rosen is looking good.* "Finally," she said, shoving the key into the lock as the car pulled alongside her. She ran inside and locked the door, leaning against it and listening. Everything was quiet. Logan turned to switch the alarm from Away to Home when she realized it wasn't set. Thinking back, she couldn't remember if she had set it when she left. With all the craziness, she had probably overlooked it.

She set it to Home and went to the kitchen to make a cup of tea, all the while listening, feeling edgy. She checked all of the windows and doors to make sure everything was secure. Tea in hand, she went up to her bedroom and peeked out the window. The car was sitting outside her house. She grabbed her cell phone to call Costello, but the car moved on before she finished dialing. *No need to disturb him,* she thought. It was probably a tourist. It wasn't unusual for cars to drive by slowly or even stop to do some sightseeing and take pictures. Anyway, what would she tell him? There was a car parked on her street? He'd ask her for details, such as make and model of the car, tag number, etc., none of which she could give him. She had been too rattled at the time to think of getting any information.

Her nerves were on edge from everything that was happening. She told herself she was overreacting. Millicent was dead and the police seem to have made her their number one suspect. *No,* she thought, *to be fair, Beatty seems to be the one focusing on me.* She wasn't sure about Costello.

She looked out the window. The car wasn't anywhere on the street. Maybe if she took a hot bath she'd be able to relax. She filled the tub and sank her sore, tired body into the hot lavender scented water and tried to relax, ignoring the stinging from her wounds, but her mind wouldn't shut down. The events of the last two days played over and over, and didn't make any sense. After a futile attempt at relaxation she gave up and crawled into bed, hoping that exhaustion would overtake her.

# CHAPTER 7

The next morning she woke from a restless sleep, still exhausted. A chilly breeze blew through the open window. Shivering, she grabbed her robe, made her way to the kitchen, chose a bold blend, and got the coffee going. She stood by the window watching the birds flit here and there, busy building their nests. She took the bag of seed outside and replenished the bird feeder before getting her newspaper.

She hesitated before opening the front door, peeking through the front window to make sure Mrs. Rosen wasn't lurking about. No sign of her. Logan stepped outside to fetch the paper, which, as usual, was partially on Mrs. Rosen's property. She glanced around, grabbed the paper, and had just reached her door when she heard Mrs. Rosen's door open. Now was as good a time as any to try a different approach, so she turned and faced her, smiled and wished her a nice day, then went in. Her last vision of Mrs. Rosen was of her standing in her doorway, mouth open. She hoped that someday soon they could at least say good morning without any hostility. Logan briefly wondered if she had family and where they were. Sadly, she thought, it was more likely that they were separated or killed in the Holocaust. Too many lives were torn apart.

She took her coffee upstairs and set it on the large ornate antique dresser, careful to use a coaster, and looked at herself in the wavy mirror. It was always a bit disconcerting to see her distorted image, but today it felt somehow different and she wasn't sure why. She could see the bed in the mirror, the bed she had shared with Luke, and felt the emptiness creep into her heart and tears moisten her eyes. Then the anger crawled in. At first, it was a fleeting thought, then it grew and began to consume her. Her jaw tightened. Her body tensed. Luke was careless. He was an experienced caver. He didn't have to die.

She shook her head to clear the angry thoughts and focused on taking deep breaths to relax her body, the way they had taught her in the hospital. She moved to the bed and pulled and straightened until it was shipshape. Her mother-in-law's voice invaded her conscience, telling her to remember that her home should always be ready to receive guests.

Logan punched the pillows, then grabbed them and threw them across the room and turned toward the bathroom. Her whole body was trembling. She lay down on the bed in fetal position, and cried until there weren't any more tears. She took herself into the bathroom to attend to her red, puffy eyes. On her way out of the bedroom she bent and straightened the covers and placed the pillows in their correct place.

She headed down the hall to her office to sort through her bills, which she'd let pile up. She flipped on the light switch. Her antique mahogany desk reflected prisms of light on the polished surface. The top was clear of papers. Her in/out trays were stored away in the matching credenza. On the far wall was a utilitarian work table that held her laptop, printer and works in progress. She stood in front of it. Something was different, but try as she might she couldn't put her finger on it. Maybe it was her imagination working overtime. The recent events had unnerved her.

The phone rang and she jumped, snatching it up without checking caller ID.

"Hello."

"It's me, Ran. I found something else really interesting. Something in the attic, hidden in the drawer of an old desk."

She focused her attention on the conversation. "That attic is probably full of interesting finds. We still have to go through those boxes you found yesterday. So, tell me, what did you find this time?" she asked, excited.

"Come on over."

"I can't right now. I was just getting ready to pay some bills."

He laughed. "Believe me, this is far better than paying bills. They'll still be there when you get back." Her uncle wasn't one to waste time on such mundane things as bill paying, she thought, smiling.

She laughed. "Okay, I'll be over soon. I want to see what was in those boxes too."

"Hurry now."

He sounded like a little kid and it was catching. She was curious and excited, leaving her office without even looking at her bills. Like he said, they'd still be there when she got back. *Oh, God,* she thought, *I'm starting to think like him.*

It was a sunny but chilly morning, so she decided to ride her bike. It wouldn't take much longer than walking the two blocks to get her car from the garage and driving over. Aside from a few scratches, it appeared to be in good working order. This would be the first time she had ridden since the accident, then realized it was only yesterday. She was a bit sore, but there wasn't any reason she couldn't ride her bike. In fact, a leisurely ride along the river path would do her good. Ran thought that riding in a car was dangerous enough in the city, let alone riding a bike. Of course, no one was safe if he was behind the wheel. She smiled, thinking about his last escapade when he sideswiped a parked car and argued with the police officer and the owner of the damaged vehicle that he was in the right. The car was parked too far from the curb, he told them. Mention driving in the city and he still complains about the unfairness of the situation.

She took a quick shower and decided to wear jeans and a long sleeved shirt instead of her biking clothes. She packed her camera and jacket, and carried her bike down the four front steps. The morning mist was beginning to burn off. She looked up to admire the emerging buds along the tree-lined brick sidewalks, one tree for every couple of houses.

She maneuvered her bike between the parked cars and onto the cobblestoned street that was barely wide enough for cars, especially if there were cars parked on both sides. The uneven cobblestones made balancing on a bike an art. On top of that, they were wet from the morning dew. At the first break, she merged into the line of cars and headed northwest to her uncle's estate. A horn honked somewhere behind her and she risked a quick glance. The driver was waving his hands about and yelling something unintelligible. Logan moved closer to the parked cars, waved and continued down the street, passing all the drivers who were inching their way to some destination, giving her commute her full attention.

Even at ten in the morning the streets were as congested as rush hour. There were delivery trucks, buses, commuters, and residents all spewing toxic fumes into the air. Despite the grit and fumes mixed with the inattentive drivers, Logan still preferred riding her bike in the city. She headed west toward the Schuylkill River and the bike path that would take her north to Mount Joy.

She stopped by the corner market for some lunchmeat, rolls, and Pepsi. She didn't know how long she would be at Mount Joy and it was always prudent to come with food if she planned to eat.

It was an enjoyable twenty minute bike ride to Mount Joy. The path ran along the river from Philadelphia to Valley Forge. Heading from home, she passed from comfort and affluence to hopelessness by merely crossing the street.

When she got to Market Street, a group of teens dressed in low slung jeans and hoodies were spread out across the sidewalk, making it difficult for people to get to their destinations. Most of the teens looked as though their clothes and persons hadn't seen soap and water in recent times. Cigarettes dangled from their lips. Each face had the same hard look. Logan noticed the young girl, too old for her age, standing just a bit apart from the others. Their eyes locked for an instant before the girl looked away. She recognized Jewel and knew that Jewel recognized her. She felt bad that things had gotten so hectic. Today, she promised herself, she would make the prints.

Logan tried to catch the girl's eye again but she was giving all of her attention to the young man who looked like he might be the leader. He was taller than the rest and better groomed. He pointed toward the river, using a cane with a silver skull handle. He was speaking and everyone seemed engrossed in what he was saying.

Logan debated whether to approach her, but continued on toward the river trail. The cool breeze of the city streets turned into a cold breeze that ruffled the lingering mist coming off the river. The sun was breaking through, promising to warm things up as the day went on. The flowers and trees were just beginning to bloom, introducing the promise of new beginnings.

When she got to the river, she took pictures of the barely visible rowers moving in and out of the morning mist before continuing on to her destination. The fog was thicker here than it was in the city. The trail was muddy and littered with debris from all the rain. She pedaled carefully to avoid skidding, while admiring the small boats dotting the river's surface, stopping periodically to take more shots.

A trail that led from the river to the estate was just ahead on her right, but virtually invisible to someone who didn't know it was there. It was a narrow, untended path, if one could call it a path, that ran about one hundred yards from the riverbank through the woods to the clearing. She could lift her bike over some of the fallen branches, but was forced to move larger ones out of the way. Tangled brambles grabbed at her legs, tearing at her jeans. She mumbled about Jimmy's irresponsibility as she struggled up the path, and wondered why her uncle was paying him money to maintain the property. It was a rare day she even saw him, let alone witnessed any kind of maintenance happening. She had only gone a few feet when she heard rustling on her left. She stopped and peered through the dense growth and heard a branch crack.

"Who's there?" Silence. Not even the birds were chirping. Another rustle. She tightened her grip on her bike and took a few more steps. She could sense rather than see that something or someone was keeping pace with her, and stopped again.

"Who's there?" she demanded.

She continued to move toward the house as fast as the bike and trail would allow, noting that whatever was in the woods was keeping pace with her. She stopped and moved to the other side of the bike, putting it between herself and whatever was stalking her, and quickened her pace. A cloud overhead obscured the sun, throwing the woods into darkness. Another rustling, and a second later a man rushed out of the woods and landed in front of her. Logan screamed and pushed the bike toward him, then realized it was Jimmy.

"What do you think you're doing?" she screamed at him. "What's the matter with you?"

He stood there. She could see he needed a bath and a shave. His clothes were disheveled and there were dark stains on the front of his shirt. She took a step backwards. Jimmy still hadn't said a word.

"Aren't you supposed to be doing something constructive?" Logan demanded. His cell phone rang and he turned and ran past her into the woods, away from the house. Logan heard him shout "What?" into the phone as she continued to walk up the path to the garden wall in the clearing, sitting down to dislodge the burrs digging through her pants legs, scratching her skin. Logan shook her head, vowing to speak to Ran about him again. If that didn't work, she'd talk to Michael.

She stood looking up at the house. Shrouded in the early morning mist, it looked even more broken and forlorn. It saddened her to see it in such disrepair. The paint was peeling, shutters hung drunkenly or were missing altogether. The front porch roof sagged and the porch itself was rotted in spots. She took out her camera and stepped back to take a few shots.

Her great-grandparents had purchased the estate and operated a working farm until her grandmother passed away, long before she was born. She had no idea when she died or where she was buried, and made a mental note to ask Ran.

The property was overgrown and the outbuildings were barely standing. She'd peeked into some of them a few months ago when she was giving Millicent a brief tour and found they were full of stuff. She had asked Ran if he knew what was stored in there, but he had no idea. Just stuff that they weren't using, he'd told her. Logan had tried to find an inventory among her grandmother's papers in the library, but so far nothing had turned up.

She gathered the lunchmeat and rolls, slung her camera bag over her shoulder, and headed for the front door, being careful not to step on any rotting wood. She knocked and opened the door, calling for Ran. It bothered her that he never locked the doors. He said he didn't see the need for locks way out here, which was precisely why Logan thought he should be more careful. The property was isolated and approachable from the river. She knew there were valuable antiques, not only in the house and attic, but she suspected in the outbuildings.

She let herself into the two story foyer. The flocked wallpaper was faded and peeling in some areas. The marble floor was dull from decades of neglect. She called out, but didn't get an answer, which wasn't unusual. She hung her bag on the coat rack with her jacket and called out to Ran again, stumbling through the dimly lit hallway on her way to the kitchen. After she divested herself of the food, she went in search of him, flipping on lights and opening drapes as she went. She continued calling, but got no response. She wondered if he had run over to the rectory and was just about to call Michael when she heard a noise overhead and rolled her eyes. He was up there rummaging around, totally oblivious of her arrival.

She went up the stairs to the second floor, being careful not to snag her foot on the frayed stair runner. At the top she turned to the right and saw the dim attic light bleeding through the partially opened door. She called his name again and heard a light scraping as she reached the top of the stairs. The single bare bulb illuminated a small circle just below it. Some ambient light filtered through the grime covered windows. The rest of the attic was nestled in darkness. She took in the disarray and called out to Ran again. No answer. She moved toward an area in the back that looked like someone had recently been moving things about. There on the floor lay her uncle. She ran to him, calling his name.

"Ran, Ran." She felt for a pulse. It was faint. When she took her hand away it felt warm and sticky. She stared down at it. Blood. She needed to get help. What was it they taught her in CPR training? Think. Call 911 first, then attend to the injured person, but she didn't want to leave him. She had to force herself to go down to call for help, cursing herself for leaving her cell phone in her camera bag.

"Hang on, Ran. I'll be right back." *Oh, God, please don't let him die,* she prayed, running down the stairs to the phone in his bedroom. She gave the information to the operator, grabbed some towels from the bathroom and a spread from the bed, and rushed back up to the attic. She covered him and pressed the towels to the wound on the side of his head.

"Please, Ran, hold on. Help's coming. Oh, please, be okay." She heard a noise behind her and froze. She half-turned and saw someone standing at the top of the stairs in the shadows.

"What's going on?"

She breathed a sigh of relief. "Michael. Help me. Ran's been hurt."

In an instant Michael was kneeling beside her. "What happened?"

"I don't know. I found him like this. I think he fell."

Michael pressed his fingers to the side of Ran's neck. "There's a faint pulse."

"The ambulance is on the way," said Logan.

"Go let them in," said Michael.

"Please, I can't leave him," she said. "Please don't make me leave him."

"Someone has to show them where Ran is."

"No, I won't leave him," she said, pulling away from him and turning back toward Ran and kneeling beside him. "He's hurt. We have to help him." Her voice betrayed the hysterics she was feeling.

He tried again to lead her from the attic, but she refused to budge. He knelt down beside her and turned her so they were face to face. "Logan, you need to go down so you can show them where he is. They'll be here in a few minutes."

"No," she shouted. "You go. I'm not leaving him."

His voice was low and soft. His hand rested gently on her shoulder. He turned her head to look at him. "I can't go."

She looked at him, tears streaming down her face. Neither moved. He didn't need to tell her that he wanted to administer the last rites. She couldn't think about that, wouldn't think about that. It was too final. It meant that Ran wasn't going to make it.

"No. No, no, no" she said, sobbing, beating her fists on Michael's chest.

He took her hands. "Logan, it doesn't mean he's going to die, but he would want to be prepared if he does. I have to do this." He held her for a minute. "Let me do my job. You go down and show them where we are."

Then a thought hit Logan. "Call Jimmy. He can let them in." Michael began to protest. "Please Michael. I can't leave him."

He pulled out his cell phone and made the call. "Where is he?" he mumbled, pacing. "Finally," he shouted into the phone. "Where've you been? Listen to me. Go down to the gates and show the EMTs and police to the house. Ran's been hurt. He's in the attic." He continued to pace. Logan couldn't ever remember seeing him so agitated. "Don't argue. Just do it." He pressed end, leaving Jimmy no option but to obey, then turned back to Logan who was kneeling beside Ran.

"He's trying to say something." She pressed her ear close to his mouth. "What happened?" she asked. His voice was barely a whisper and she couldn't make out the words. "Hang on. The ambulance is on the way. Michael's here too."

Michael moved closer to Ran. Ran's eyes fluttered and he gasped, and Michael began to give him the last rites.

Logan was holding Ran's hand and sobbing. "Stay with us. Don't leave. Come on Ran, hang in there. I can hear the sirens. Help will be here in a minute." She kept talking and Michael prayed. The sirens got closer. "Help's here. Stay with us," she kept saying.

Michael patted her arm. "Try not to worry." Empty words that didn't make her feel better.

Logan heard the ambulance doors slam, men shouting orders, EMTs coming through the front door. Heavy running footsteps, and then they burst through the attic door with their equipment. Logan stepped back, but never took her eyes off Ran.

"Will he be okay?" The EMTs were taking vitals and inserting an intravenous line. "He's still alive," she whispered, and grabbed Michael's arm. "Please God, don't take him. Please let him be okay."

Once they finished their preliminary exam, they stabilized him and lifted him onto the stretcher. The narrow attic stairway presented a challenge, and Logan found she was holding her breath until they reached the second floor. She ran right behind them, followed by Michael.

"I'm going to ride with him," said Logan.

"I'm sorry," said one of the paramedics, "you'll have to follow us. We're taking him to University of Pennsylvania Hospital. You can meet us there."

She started to protest but Michael took her arm and steered her toward his car. "I'll drive," he said, heading back to the house.

"Where are you going?" her voice raised in panic.

"We have to get his wallet, his insurance information."

"Hurry," she said, pacing by the front steps.

"Go get in the car, I'll be right there." She got into his black Acura MDX SUV. "Hurry Michael," she whispered. After what seemed like forever, he emerged from the house, locked the front door, and got into the car. They moved slowly, too slowly for Logan, toward the road, avoiding potholes and fallen debris.

"Michael?"

"He's in good hands. All we can do now is pray. Ran's tough. If anyone can make it through he can."

They wove their way through center city traffic to the hospital. "Can't you get around this traffic?"

"Priests don't get special driving privileges. We're almost there." Within minutes they pulled up to the emergency entrance. "You go on in. I'll park. Here's his information," he said, handing her Ran's wallet.

Logan grabbed it, jumped from the car and ran into the Emergency Room. The guard directed her to an admissions clerk. "I'm looking for my uncle. They just brought him in. His name is Kingston Ranford. Can you tell me where he is?"

"Have a seat."

"I just want to know where he is." Her voice was almost hysterical. She was pacing in front of the window.

"I need you to fill out some paperwork first. Please have a seat," she said, indicating the chairs in front of the window.

"No," she shouted, leaning into the desk area. "I need to see him. Where is he?"

"Ma'am, please sit down. We'll get this done as quickly as we can."

"Why can't I see him?" she asked, tears forming. She swiped at them, willing herself not to cry. She turned to look for Michael, and saw that the guard was looking in her direction, ready to move in if he had to. Michael came in, saw her and headed over. "They won't let me see him."

"Sir, I was just explaining to her that we need to get his information so we can register him."

He touched Logan lightly on the shoulder. "It's okay. They need to register him," he said, repeating what the clerk had just told her. The clerk's shoulders relaxed and she smiled a thank you at Michael.

He guided her into the chair and they made it through the admissions process. The clerk directed them to have a seat in the waiting room. "The doctor will be out shortly," she assured them.

"Why can't we see him?" Logan asked.

Michael directed her toward a chair in the waiting room. "They're working on him," he said. "We'll have to wait until someone comes out. They'll let us know what's going on as soon as they can."

A short time later, the doctor came out to the waiting room. "There's extensive head trauma. There's swelling of the brain and some bleeding. They're prepping him for surgery. We'll insert a shunt to help drain the fluid."

"Will he be okay?" asked Logan.

"I don't know. First, we have to get him into surgery. After that, we'll just have to wait."

"How long will it take?"

"The surgery will probably take a few hours. I'll come out and talk with you as soon as we're done."

"Thank you," said Michael.

Logan paced in front of the plate glass windows, watching people come and go. When Michael's gentle prodding failed to persuade her to go with him to the cafeteria, he went alone and brought tea and a sandwich for her, which sat untouched. After waiting for over five hours, a doctor finally came through the doors and called for Kingston Ranford's family members. His face was expressionless as he shook their hands and escorted them through the doors into a small room that consisted of a hospital issue couch, battered end tables, and a couple of worn chairs. Dark stains dotted the carpet. *The room where they give you bad news,* Logan thought. He offered them a seat, but they declined.

"I'm Dr. Lawrence," he said, reaching out to shake Michael's hand.

"I'm Father Ranford, Kingston's brother, and this is Logan O'Malley, our niece."

"How is he?" Logan asked.

Dr. Lawrence stretched his hand toward the couch, indicating for them to have a seat. *He wants us to sit down before he tells us that Ran didn't make it,* she thought. She was close to throwing up. She followed the doctor's direction and sat, but couldn't control her shaking. Michael took her hand.

Dr. Lawrence started without preamble. "He had extensive bleeding in the brain, as well as swelling. We had to insert a shunt to drain the fluid and relieve the pressure. Right now he's in a drug induced coma." Logan's hands flew to her mouth and she let out a strangled cry. Dr. Lawrence reached out to calm her. "This is a common procedure," he assured her. "We need to keep him quiet to give the brain time to begin the healing process."

"Is he going to be okay?"

"We don't know that yet. Right now it's touch and go."

"Can we see him?" asked Michael.

"You can go in, but only for a minute. Please be careful what you say to him. We aren't sure just how much he can hear. You need to be positive and speak very quietly."

Logan nodded her head in agreement.

"Follow me."

They wound down the corridors, passing visitors and medical personnel, all speaking in hushed tones. Monitors were clicking and pinging. Family members hovered in doorways, looking at each other with blank expressions, unable to comprehend what was happening to their loved ones. Dr. Lawrence stopped. "You can go in one at a time, but only for a minute."

Michael leaned down to Logan. "You go in first."

She started to protest but he ushered her through the doorway. She stood, afraid to move. The room was dimly lit and it took a few seconds for her eyes to adjust. Then she saw Ran, his head swathed in bandages, needles and tubes protruding from various points on his body. Monitors registered numbers that meant nothing to her. A machine was breathing for him. She walked slowly, carefully, toward his bed, not making a sound. She took his cold, limp hand in hers, and spoke quietly. "Ran, I'm here. Please get better. I love you."

She sensed movement and turned. Dr. Lawrence stood in the doorway and motioned her out. She gave Ran's hand a squeeze, kissed him and left.

Out in the hallway Michael took her in his arms. "Oh, Michael. He's so cold and still."

Dr. Lawrence spoke. "That's to be expected. We're watching him very closely and he has a trauma nurse assigned to him." He turned to Michael. "You can go in, but just for a minute." She could hear him talking to Ran, but couldn't make out his words. She was sure he was praying. Logan tried to read his expression when he emerged, but Michael was good at keeping his face blank, just like Dr. Lawrence. The nurse passed them, crepe soled shoes squishing on the tile floor, and went into Ran's room.

# CHAPTER 8

L et's get you home," said Michael.

"No, I think I'll just stay here. Can I see him again later?" she asked the doctor.

"No more visits tonight. He needs to rest."

"Well, I'll just wait here in case there's any change."

"Logan, you need to get some rest. I'll take you home. We can come back first thing in the morning."

"If there's any change we'll call you," Dr. Lawrence assured her. "We have both of your phone numbers."

There was no use arguing, so Logan allowed Michael to lead her through the deserted corridors and out to the parking lot. "He's in good hands," he assured her. "He's tough. I won't tell you not to worry, because I know you will. The best you can do now is pray. I'll take you home. Do you want me to stay with you?"

"No, I'll be fine." Her hand flew to her mouth. "Oh, no."

"What's wrong?" asked Michael, concern and urgency in his voice.

"My bag. It's at Ran's."

"We can get it tomorrow."

"I need it now; my house keys are in it."

"It's okay. Remember, you gave me a key for emergencies?

Come on, I'll take you home and I promise to come back for you first thing in the morning. If I hear anything, I'll call you right away."

There wasn't anything she could do but follow Michael's suggestions, although she knew she wouldn't be getting much sleep.

The house was pitch black when they got there. *Empty and lonely*, she thought, flicking on the foyer light.

"Here, sit down," he said, leading her into the living room. "I'll make you some tea and something to eat. You haven't eaten all day."

"Don't bother. I'm not hungry."

"It's no trouble, and we can't have you getting sick." She sat where he told her and could hear him in the kitchen. Water running, refrigerator door opening, silverware being placed on the counter. The tea kettle whistled, making her jump. Michael brought in the tray and set it on the coffee table. He handed her a mug of tea, her favorite mug, made by one of the Navajo women, but she just held it.

"Drink it," he said, "you need something in your stomach."

She put the cup to her lips and the memories of that awful day two years ago leaped into her consciousness. The mug slipped from her shaking hands, hit the coffee table, and shattered. She didn't move, just stared at the mess.

"Come on. You're going to stay at the rectory tonight. I'll have Mrs. Donahue freshen up the guest room," he said, taking out his cell.

"No, I'll be okay. I was remembering someone handing me a cup of tea and urging me to drink it that horrible day Luke disappeared. I just need to be alone," she said, scooping the shattered mug onto the tray, thinking that Luke's mother would be very upset by the tea stains on the carpet and furniture.

"I'll stay in your guest room."

"No, really, you go on back to the rectory. I'd like some time alone."

"I don't want to leave you alone."

"You don't have to worry about me. I'll be okay."

"I am worried. I will worry."

"I'm going to take a hot bath and go to bed. I'm exhausted." *I doubt if I'll be able to sleep though*, she thought. "Every time I close my eyes I see him lying on the floor all crumpled up, blood everywhere," she said.

"I know," he said, patting her hand.

"I don't understand what happened."

"Try not to think about that tonight," he said. "Drink this," he said, handing her his own untouched cup, "then I'll leave you to get some rest."

"But I don't understand it. There was so much blood. How did he fall?"

"I don't know." He shook his head and looked at her. "Right now, we need to take care of you. Ran's in good hands."

"You don't have to babysit me. I'll drink this and go to bed," she said smiling a weak smile. "You look like you could use some sleep too. Dark circles under your eyes."

"I am a bit ragged. Get some sleep."

"I will. You too."

Satisfied, Michael hugged her, bid her good night, and left. She locked the door behind him and ran a bath.

An hour later, Logan climbed between the crisp cotton sheets and closed her eyes, but all she saw were alternating scenes of her uncle lying on the attic floor and Luke disappearing into the darkness. She tossed and turned, dozed off for a while then woke. 1:30 a.m.

She listened to the occasional car pass by. Then she heard it. A scratching sound coming from downstairs. She lay there, summoning the courage to investigate. It took every ounce of nerve to pull the comforter back and slip from the bed, careful not to make a sound. She crept into the hallway, checking her surroundings as she went. From the top of the stairs she could see into a corner of the living room, and thought she saw movement. Her heart was pounding. Sweaty palms held the banister as she moved quietly down one step at a time, stopping on each step to listen. The scratching sound was coming from the back of the house, the kitchen. She hesitated, wanting to go back upstairs, but crept down the narrow hall toward the kitchen. A board creaked. She froze, then lifted her foot carefully. The board creaked again, but not as loud. She listened and crept closer. Then she saw it. The small Japanese maple tree outside her kitchen window. The wind was rustling the branches and one of them was scratching the window. "Oh, my God," she said, putting her hand over her wildly beating heart. She sat at the table, watching the tree until her heart went back to a more normal pace. She thought she might as well check on Ran to see if there had been any change. She picked up the phone and dialed the hospital.

"Intensive Care nursing station, please."

"Nurses' station. This is Zoe."

"Hello, Zoe. This is Logan O'Malley. I'm calling to check on my uncle's condition, Kingston Ranford."

She heard keyboard clicking. "There's no change. He's stable."

"Okay. Thank you."

She dragged her exhausted body back to bed, but her mind refused to shut down, rehashing everything that had happened in the last couple of days. Nothing made sense. The key to solving the puzzle was to find the common denominator, which seemed to be the estate. Ran wanted to have the estate designated as a historic landmark. Millicent was doing the research to make that happen. C.J. wanted Ran to sell her the property so she could develop it. Michael was concerned that the property was too much for Ran to maintain. The only person who didn't fit into the equation was herself. She wasn't a threat to any decision. She was missing some piece of the puzzle.

She shifted her thinking to the attic and Ran. There was an antique oak dresser, some cane chairs stacked beside the dresser, boxes, an old wardrobe. She couldn't remember seeing anything that might have fallen on him. There was something she had noticed, but whatever it was eluded her at the moment. She thought back to their phone conversation. He'd said he had found something really interesting. He was excited, even pleased with himself. She tried to remember if there were any open boxes by him, but couldn't. She was exhausted; her brain was fuzzy.

Eventually, with those thoughts running through her head, sleep overtook her. The room was bright with sunlight when she opened her eyes and looked over at the clock. "Eight thirty," she exclaimed, jumping out of bed.

Michael, he was supposed to pick her up. She grabbed the phone. He answered on the first ring.

"Where are you?"

"Calm down. I was getting ready to call you. I'll be over around nine. Will that be okay?"

"I'll be ready. Thanks."

She rushed through her morning routine and was just about finished when Michael pulled up and she ran out to meet him, anxious to get back to the hospital. Mrs. Rosen stuck her nose out the door and appeared to be saying something as Logan slammed the car door shut.

"I think your neighbor wanted to talk to you."

Logan rolled her eyes. "Yeah, I'm sure she did, but I didn't want to talk to her. Oh, did you get my bag?"

"Your bag...Oh, Logan, I'm sorry, I completely forgot. We'll stop on the way home."

"It's chilly. Let me have your key. I need to grab a jacket." Michael separated her key and handed it to her. "Be right back," she said.

"Let's go," she said, as she slid back into the car. "Did you call the hospital this morning?"

"Just before I left. They said Ran is resting comfortably."

"That's what they told me when I called a little while ago."

The morning rush was in full swing and they inched along toward the hospital. Delivery trucks were double parked here and there on various streets, only making a bad situation worse.

"I don't know how people do this every day," exclaimed Logan. "Dealing with this could make a person homicidal. Can't you get around it somehow? After all, you're a priest. What if you had to give someone last rites?"

"We'll be there in a few minutes."

They rode the rest of the way in silence. When they finally reached the hospital, Michael dropped her at the entrance while he parked. "I'll meet you at his room."

"Okay, thanks."

She hurried through the hallways, now bustling with activity. Food carts were parked outside rooms. The odors mixed with antiseptic and other hospital smells made her nauseous. She tried not to think about it. She rounded the corner and saw a small congregation outside Ran's room and ran the rest of the way. "What's happened? Is he okay?"

The nurse she spoke to yesterday separated herself from the others. "He's fine."

"Well, what's going on?" she asked, looking at the people assembled at Ran's door. One of the men who was standing in the doorway turned around and came over to her. The other man followed. Beatty and Costello.

"Ms. O'Malley," said Beatty.

"That's Mrs. O'Malley."

"*Mrs.* O'Malley. Why don't we step over here," he said, indicating a small room next to the nurses' station.

"This'll have to wait," she said. "I'm here to see my uncle. He had an accident yesterday."

"We're well aware of your uncle's 'accident.' Now come with us. We can do this here or at the station. Your choice."

"I don't know anything more about Millicent's accident. If I did I would tell you. I want to know what happened to her as much as you do."

"What were you doing at your uncle's yesterday?" asked Beatty, standing in her personal space, feet apart, hands on hips. He didn't bother to hide his derision.

The question confused her, took her off balance. "What? I was visiting him. He's my uncle."

"Why were you there?" Beatty asked again.

She looked over at Costello, who was quietly watching. "What is this all about?"

Costello stepped forward. "Your uncle didn't have an accident," he said.

She plopped down onto the sofa, mouth open and silent. He gave her a few seconds to process the information.

Beatty spoke again. "It seems someone bashed in his head," he said, not even bothering to soften the news.

"No, that can't be. He fell. I was there." Beatty fixed his glare on her, willing her to say more. "I mean, not when he fell. Afterwards. I found him lying on the floor. He was hurt. I called the ambulance."

"Mrs. O'Malley," said Costello. "We need to know what happened. Did you two argue?"

"Argue? No, we didn't argue. What are you talking about? I love my uncle. I would never hurt him." She caught sight of Michael passing the nurses' station and called out to him. As Michael came toward the room, Beatty closed the door on him.

"He'll have a chance to give his side of the story after we're finished with you."

The door opened, and in strode Michael. He saw the stricken look on her face and turned to Beatty. "What's going on here? Logan, don't say another word to these men. What are you doing to her?"

"We're questioning her, which we have every right to do. It seems your brother got his head bashed in. We're just wondering why."

"Bashed in? What are you talking about? It was an accident. He fell."

"We're investigating a crime."

"And you think Logan did it? You're crazy. She wouldn't hurt a fly. If he was attacked, then you'd better do your job and find out who did do it, but it wasn't Logan."

"That remains to be seen." Beatty turned to Logan. "You need to come with us."

"My brother's lying in a coma and you're saying he was attacked. And you're wasting your time questioning Logan instead of tracking down the person who did it."

"I'm not leaving the hospital," said Logan. "I have to see my uncle."

Beatty grabbed her arm. Logan shook him off and headed for the door. "You're not going anywhere except down to the station with us," he said, stepping between her and the door.

Michael stepped over to Logan and pulled her close. "Logan, I'm afraid you're going to have to go with them."

"Very sensible advice," sneered Beatty. "You'd be wise to listen." He looked at Logan, willing her to defy him.

Michael ignored Beatty's interruption. "Don't say a word. I'll call Mr. Jacoby and have him recommend a good criminal attorney."

"Do I have to go?" she asked Michael. "Can't you come with me?" Then the full impact of Michael's words 'criminal attorney' hit her.

Before Michael had a chance to answer, Beatty responded. "Yes, you have to go."

"Remember," said Michael, "don't say a word until someone gets there. I'm calling him right now," he said, taking out his phone. "Not a word," he repeated as Beatty and Costello escorted her down the hall.

Logan sat hunched down in the back seat of the unmarked car with her eyes closed, ignoring Beatty's attempts to rile her, to try to get her to say something stupid, something he could use against her. When they arrived, she was placed into an interrogation room, alone. The furnishings consisted of a table bolted to the floor and three chairs. She looked at the mirror on the facing wall and knew they were in the other room watching her every move. She was afraid to move a muscle for fear it would be misinterpreted. For the life of her she couldn't figure out why they thought she would hurt Ran. She didn't even know what had happened, only that someone had hit him on the head. Why would they think she would do something that despicable? This whole thing was crazy. She stood and turned away from the window, not sure that it did any good. She was sure the room was full of cameras and they could view her from any angle. Would pacing make her look guilty? Would just standing still make her look like she didn't care? She didn't know what to do or how to act. Where was the lawyer Michael promised her? Shouldn't he be here by now? *What time is it?* she wondered. How long had she been here? She knew they wanted to stress her out, make her act like she had something to hide. Tears formed. *A sign of weakness,* she thought. She can't show weakness. They'll use it against her. She straightened her spine and lifted her chin slightly. A sign of defiance? She wanted to feel defiant. She thought of Rose and what a ruckus she'd be making just about now, demanding her rights, and smiled, then quickly replaced the smile with a blank stare, or what she hoped was a blank stare. They could turn a smile into guilt.

She sat and went over and over what happened just before and when she found Ran. She thought she had the details firmly in her mind, but something was missing. There was something just on the periphery; something she couldn't put her finger on. Just as despair was setting in, the door swung open and in walked Beatty and Costello, followed by another man. He walked over to her and put out his hand.

"I'm Mr. Jacoby. Your uncle called me."

Mr. Jacoby was in his fifties and just over six foot tall, with the body of someone who worked out on a regular basis. She could tell his tan was naturally acquired, not the orangey fake tan so many people think looked good. He was impeccably dressed in a three piece Brooks Brothers navy suit, white dress shirt stiff as cardboard, and red power tie. Next to him, Beatty looked like one of the homeless men on Market Street.

Logan breathed a sigh of relief. "Oh, Mr. Jacoby. Thank you for coming. They think I hurt Ran."

"Don't say a word." He looked over at Beatty and Costello. "If you don't mind, I'll have a private word with my client." They shrugged and left. "Following me into the interrogation room was supposed to be a show of intimidation," he told her.

The door closed behind them and they both sat. "Before we get started," Mr. Jacoby said, "I'll represent you until we can get you a good criminal attorney. As you know, I'm an estate attorney. I have a few names I'll give you."

"Why am I here? What's going on?"

"They didn't give me much information, except that someone hit your uncle on the head, causing serious damage. They're calling it attempted homicide. If he dies, the charge will be murder."

Logan blinked back tears. "They think I did it? I'd never hurt him. I don't understand what's happening."

"They do think you did it. That's why it's critical that you not say one word to them unless your criminal attorney is present." Mr. Jacoby placed his leather briefcase on the table, clicked open the latches and took out a yellow legal pad and Mont Blanc fountain pen. He dated the top page and wrote 'Interview with Logan O'Malley,' with the date and location.

"Why do they think I did it? I found him. Why would I call the ambulance if I was trying to hurt him?"

"They probably think you panicked when you saw all the blood. They think you two were arguing and you struck him in the heat of passion."

"That's ridiculous. I've never struck anyone in my life." She shifted in her chair. "This whole thing's crazy."

"Tell me everything that happened."

She told him about Ran's phone call saying that he'd found something interesting and she should come over.

"When did he call?"

"This morning, no yesterday morning, around eight or so I think."

"What did you do then?"

She thought. Everything was running together. She was having trouble separating and sequencing events. She kept looking up at the window, wondering what was going on in the room behind it. She realized she was cracking her knuckles, something she used to do when she was little. She'd thought she had kicked the habit, but the movements came back to her without any thought on her part.

Mr. Jacoby took her hands in his. He switched from his lawyer voice to that of a loving father. "Just take your time."

"They're watching, aren't they?"

"Yes. They want to intimidate you. They'll analyze your body language and evaluate it so they can add to the circumstantial evidence. Just take a couple of deep breaths." He let go of her hands, picked up his pen and repeated the last question.

"I got dressed and went to the corner deli for some lunch meat. I rode my bike along the bike path and took some pictures along the way. They'll have a date and time stamp on them. Mrs. Rooney can tell you when I bought the lunchmeat." She was beginning to relax. "Do the police know when Ran was attacked?"

"If they do, they're not sharing. I think they probably have some sort of time frame. Go ahead, you're doing fine." He was jotting notes the whole time she talked, making notations next to her statements. "What did you do next?"

Logan closed her eyes, picturing her movements. "I rode up to my uncle's."

"Did you see anyone on the way?"

"Some joggers, but nobody I recognized."

"Okay, good. What next?"

"I took the path that goes through the woods to the house. I had to walk my bike because it's overgrown."

He stopped her, his eyebrows furrowed. "Does anyone else know about the path?"

She thought for a minute. "I don't know. It's really hard to see. You would almost have to know it's there. But I suppose anyone could use it." She thought for a minute. "Do you think someone else went up to the house that way?"

"I don't know, but I'll have someone check it out for other signs of use."

"Jimmy."

"Jimmy?"

"Mrs. Donahue's son. She's the housekeeper at the rectory."

"Right. What about him?"

"He saw me that morning. In fact, he was hiding in the woods and jumped out at me. Scared me half to death."

Mr. Jacoby smiled. "So he was on the estate that morning."

"He lives in the little cottage on the edge of the woods. My uncle lets him live there for free. In exchange, he's supposed to take care of the property. As far as I can see, he doesn't do much of anything except smoke pot. Reeks of the stuff."

"What was his demeanor that morning?"

"I'm not sure. He usually just looks blank, stupid. I've often wondered if there were some cognitive disabilities that weren't pot induced, but I didn't know him before pot."

"Have you ever noticed any of his friends hanging around?"

"No, he's pretty much a loner. Michael might know more about him. Mrs. Donahue's been with him for years. He took her and Jimmy in after Mr. Donahue, in a drunken rage, beat her to a pulp.

Jimmy was about ten. When Jimmy was older, Michael had him do general cleanup on the estate. He was supposed to take on more of the maintenance as he got older. He doesn't do much of anything, and Ran's too goodhearted to say no."

"Which direction was he coming from when you saw him?"

Logan closed her eyes to picture the scene. "He was on my left as I came up the path, same as the house."

"You're doing great. Do you remember anything about him that morning? Was he running?"

"No, actually, he was creeping through the woods, following me. I heard a noise and called out, but no one answered. That's when he jumped out of the woods in front of me. Scared me half to death. I yelled at him."

"What did he say?"

"Nothing. Just stood there looking stupid. Then he crossed the path behind me and went into the woods on the other side. He'll be able to tell you I was there."

"I'm not sure we want to enlist his help. He might do more harm than good. But if he was coming from the house that would make him a suspect too. Do you remember anything else about your encounter?"

Logan shook her head no, then remembered. "Wait, his cell phone rang."

"Do you know who it was?"

"No, by then he was in the woods on the other side of the path, with his back to me. Do you think he could have hurt Ran?"

"I don't know if he did or not, but you can put him in the vicinity around the time Ran was attacked. Which makes him a pretty good suspect in my book. I'll get a subpoena for his phone records. What happened next?"

"I sat on the garden wall for a minute, to calm down after he scared me half to death, then went up to the house. That's when I found Ran in the attic, all bloody. I felt for a pulse and called 911. Michael came in right behind me."

"What was he doing there?"

"Ran must have called him. He was going through trunks and stuff in the attic and said he found something interesting and called me to come over. I'm sure he called Michael too."

"Okay," he said, screwing the top onto his pen and putting the pad of notes and pen into his briefcase. "Are you ready for the police to come in?"

"No, but I guess I have no choice."

"Just don't answer anything unless I say it's okay." He smiled at her and patted her hand. "You'll be fine. Whatever they think they have must be circumstantial or speculative. Otherwise, they'd have placed you under arrest." He stood, signaling to those watching that they were ready. Almost instantly the door opened, and in walked Costello and Beatty.

Beatty placed a paper bag in the center of the table, but didn't open it. He sat across from her and began the interrogation with general questions, Logan's full name, address, occupation, etc. Then they went on to her relationship with her uncle. Logan denied having any problems with him. She told them that she and Ran were very close, especially after she moved back to Philadelphia.

"Where were you before then?" asked Costello.

"My father and I moved to South Jersey when I was twelve. After that I didn't see much of my uncles. I came back to Philadelphia for college and we reconnected. We've been very close."

"How about your father, was he close to your uncles?" Beatty asked, getting up.

"When we lived in Philadelphia we were always together."

He wandered around the room, giving Logan the impression that this was just a casual conversation, but she knew better. "So your father and his brothers were estranged? Was your father upset by your relationship with his brothers?" asked Beatty.

She moved her hands off the table and sat on them so Beatty wouldn't see them tremble. "My father *died* my freshman year at college," she said with a catch in her throat.

"What about your mother. Where's she?" asked Beatty, leaning down toward her.

"I don't know," mumbled Logan.

"Speak up," shouted Beatty, making Logan jump.

Mr. Jacoby jumped up. "That's enough." He turned to Logan. "We're done here." They got up and walked toward the door.

"We're just trying to get to the bottom of what happened to your uncle. I thought you would be anxious for us to arrest his attacker," shrugged Beatty, all conciliatory.

"Well, you might want to check out Jimmy, Ran's maintenance man, and ask him why he was skulking through the woods that morning, coming from the direction of the house before Logan even got there," said Mr. Jacoby. He signaled to Logan. "We're finished here."

"Wait," said Logan. Everyone looked in her direction. "The man at the exhibition."

"What man?" asked Mr. Jacoby.

"He was arguing with Ran the night of the exhibit."

Costello took out his notebook. "Can you describe him?"

"He was in the shadows, but he was shorter than my uncle. I think he had grey hair."

"Well now," said Beatty. "Let's arrest him."

"His hand. His little finger and ring finger on his left hand were missing."

Costello jerked his head up. "You're sure?"

"Yes, I'm sure. You know who it is, don't you?"

"Did your uncle gamble?"

"I don't think so, but I don't know," she said slowly. "I'm sure he doesn't gamble," she said a few seconds later, with more confidence. "Why?"

"A minute ago you didn't know. Now you're sure he didn't gamble. Which is it?" asked Beatty.

"We'll check into it," said Costello.

"Let's go," said Mr. Jacoby.

"Don't you want to see what's in the bag?" shot Beatty as they stepped into the hall.

Mr. Jacoby and Logan stopped and turned. Logan grabbed his arm. He leaned into her and whispered, "We'd better see what he's got," and they went back into the room.

Beatty took his time opening the bag. Logan could tell he was enjoying himself and braced herself for the impact that she knew was coming. She wasn't sure what it was yet, but knew it was bad. Beatty dipped his hand into the bag and slowly withdrew it, holding a heavy object encased in a plastic bag. He placed it on the table in front of them with a flourish. Logan's hand went to her mouth and she stifled a cry.

"I thought you might recognize this," Beatty said with self satisfaction. "We got some nice sharp fingerprints."

It was difficult to see through the plastic bag, but Logan knew what it was and shivered when she saw that it was covered in blood. She knew it was the weapon used to try to kill Ran.

"My fingerprints?"

# CHAPTER 9

"D id they print you?" Mr. Jacoby asked.
"No. Yes."

"I'd like a minute with my client."

The detectives left, and he turned to Logan. "They printed you?"

"No, not now. Earlier."

"Earlier today?"

"When I got the threatening note. They printed Rose and I. We touched it and they wanted to eliminate our prints."

"When was this?"

Logan thought back over the events since the exhibit. It was two days ago. "But wait," she said, brightening, "He said they got nice sharp prints. They can't be mine. Detective Costello said that my prints aren't well defined."

"Okay. Let's bring them back in."

Mr. Jacoby looked over at Beatty. "What did you compare the prints to?" he asked, touching Logan's arm to alert her not to say a word. No one spoke. Mr. Jacoby leaned down and whispered to Logan. "He's bluffing. He doesn't have an ID on the prints yet."

"We'll be leaving now," he said, looking directly at Beatty before ushering Logan out of the room, down the hall and out the front door. The whole time, Logan felt Beatty's eyes on their backs.

Neither one spoke until they got into his car, then he turned to her. "Tell me about the weapon."

She shook her head and took a couple of deep breaths, trying to still her shaking body. "It...It was in my office. It's a bookend."

"When's the last time you saw it?"

Logan thought for a minute. She spoke slowly, trying to make sense of what she was saying. "I don't remember. It's just one of those things that's always there."

"Let's have a look." He started the car and headed for Logan's. When they got there, she took him up to her office. The bookend was sitting there, right where she thought she'd left it.

"I don't understand it."

"It's clearly not yours," he said.

"It's...it's half of a bookend set. I haven't seen the mate since I was a kid." Logan remembered playing with them when she was little. They were solid glass bookends of rearing horses, and were so heavy she could barely lift them. She smiled at the memory.

"Are they yours?"

"I remember them being together when I was little. They belonged to my grandmother. I always played with them when we visited. Somewhere along the line my father had them, but when we moved to New Jersey, I only remember ever seeing one. I assumed the other one got broken." She looked at Mr. Jacoby, willing him to make this nightmare go away. "If my bookend is here, then how did my fingerprints get on the other one? I don't understand it."

"Let's not jump to conclusions. We don't know that your prints are on the one the police have. Can you prove that you never had the set?"

"How?" her voice was panicked. "I don't think I've ever discussed it with anyone. Ran or Michael might know. They've both been here. We joked about..." She grabbed the edge of her desk.

Mr. Jacoby looked at her, eyebrows arched, head tilted, waiting for her to continue. She took a deep breath. "It's just that we joked that they were so heavy you could kill someone." Logan picked it up and turned it over in her hands.

Mr. Jacoby grabbed her arm. "The police haven't been here yet, but you can bet they will be, as soon as they can obtain a warrant. They know you recognized the bookend. It's only a matter of time before they find out it's part of a set. When they show up, you call me immediately. Don't talk to either one of them without me or another attorney present. Beatty's the one playing bad cop, but don't underestimate Costello. He doesn't say much, but he doesn't miss a thing. You should be more worried about him than Beatty. I hate to do this to you, but I need to get back to the office. Will you be okay?"

Before Logan had a chance to answer, the doorbell rang. She felt her heart rate increase and her palms get sweaty. They went down the stairs and Mr. Jacoby ushered Logan into the kitchen. The bell rang again, this time with more insistence. "You sit down. I'll get it."

She heard Mr. Jacoby and the officers murmuring, but couldn't distinguish any of the words. A few minutes later, Mr. Jacoby came into the kitchen holding a document. She already knew what it was, but the look on his face confirmed it. "They must have had it in the works when they questioned you. You don't have to be here. I'll make sure they don't do anything outside of the warrant. Is there somewhere you can go?"

Detective Beatty walked in behind him. "Mrs. O'Malley, we have a warrant to search the premises."

Mr. Jacoby walked over and stood beside her. Although he had warned her that they would probably want to search the house, it still came as a shock. She hadn't expected it to happen this quickly.

She had questions she wanted to ask, but when she tried to speak nothing came out. Mr. Jacoby led her to the breakfast nook and sat her down. He looked at Beatty. "Do what you have to do and be quick about it."

Logan watched as Beatty turned and left the room. She heard him giving orders to the officers to search everything. *All my personal things*, she thought, wrapping her arms around her body. She didn't even bother to hide the tears streaming down her face. She was vaguely aware of sounds of footsteps as the men moved from room to room, doors and drawers opening, things being moved about.

Mr. Jacoby stooped down in front of her. "Why don't we go outside," he said gently. She heard the words, but her brain wasn't comprehending their meaning. *All these strange men looking through my drawers, touching my things.* Those words played over and over in her head.

She wasn't aware of how much time passed before Beatty came into the kitchen, holding up the matching bookend encased in a plastic bag. Beatty looked from Logan to Mr. Jacoby.

"I'm bringing you in." He walked toward her, "you have the right to remain silent…"

Logan tried to speak but nothing came out.

Mr. Jacoby stepped forward. "What do you think you're doing?"

Beatty didn't bother to hide the hint of a smile. "We're investigating the assault of Kingston Ranford…To start."

"Ran? No, I didn't hurt him," she was shouting and backing away from Beatty. "You can't. Mr. Jacoby. Help me. I didn't do anything." She was too numb to think, not wanting to think. Everything was happening too fast.

"I want to confer with my client."

Beatty stepped into the hallway.

"Logan. You have to go with them."

"This is all crazy. I didn't hurt him."

"I know. They're on a fishing expedition. I'll be right behind you. Don't say a word."

Mr. Jacoby called Beatty back into the kitchen. "She's ready to go."

Costello stepped into the kitchen and spoke to Beatty, but Logan couldn't hear what they were saying. "Let's go," said Beatty.

"I'll be right behind you," said Mr. Jacoby again. He pulled Logan aside. "In the meantime, do not say a word. Understand?"

She nodded, looking up at Mr. Jacoby, tears streaking her face.

"I'm sorry," he said, taking her hand. "Remember. Not a word."

Logan was printed and escorted into a holding cell. "You can stay here. I'll be back shortly." Beatty slammed the door shut and walked away without another word.

The sound of the cell door clicking shocked her. She surveyed her surroundings and found them to be even worse than she'd heard or read. There were rodent droppings along the wall, and the smell of unwashed bodies and urine was overpowering. She tried to take shallow breaths, but it didn't help much. She was exhausted and wanted to sit, but the only available space was the bare mattress which was covered with unidentifiable stains that worked Logan's imagination. She hugged herself to stop from shaking. Pacing didn't help. Where was Mr. Jacoby? He should have been here by now, although she wasn't even sure how long she'd been here. Ten minutes or ten hours. Either one was an eternity in this godforsaken place. The sound of a door opening and footsteps brought her back.

Beatty let him into the cell. "We'd like to go to one of the interrogation rooms," said Mr. Jacoby.

Beatty sneered, but granted the request. He planned to be as accommodating to Mr. Jacoby as possible. He wasn't going to lose this case on some unfounded breach of his suspect's rights.

When they were alone, Logan turned to Mr. Jacoby. "When am I going to get out of here?" She was scratching her arms, she imagined there were bugs crawling on her skin.

"I don't know." His voice was weary and sad. "I've called a colleague who is a criminal attorney and asked her to take your case. Her name is Abigail Coleridge and she's good."

"Is she going to get me out of here? I can't go back there. Please tell me she's going to get me out."

"I can't promise you anything," he said, taking her hands. "I wish I could."

"When will she be here?"

"She's talking to the detectives now. She wants to get an idea of what kind of case they have before she meets with you." There was a knock on the door and both heads snapped in its direction. In walked a rotund woman sporting a very short afro. She hefted her bulging, battered briefcase onto the table. Logan noticed folders and papers peeking out from the broken zipper.

*Oh my God*, thought Logan, and her heart began to pound. She almost missed her attorney's extended hand and introduction. "Ms. Coleridge?" she asked, hoping the answer was no.

"Just call me Abigail. Now, let's get down to business," she was saying as she rifled through her briefcase to produce a notepad and pen. Logan's thoughts of freedom diminished by the second. "I've spoken to the detectives and got their version of the events. But I want to hear yours."

Logan recited, for the umpteenth time, the events leading up to Ran's attack, and everything that happened up until the present time. "When can I leave here?"

"They can hold you up to forty-eight hours. After that, they have to charge you or let you go."

"Forty-eight hours? I can't stay here for forty-eight hours. Please, you have to get me out of here."

"I'm working on it. Now, here's what I know about the evidence against you. They found the murder weapon at the scene with your prints all over it. Since the bookend belonged to you, it's reasonable that your prints would be on it, so that in itself doesn't necessarily mean you did it."

"I never had the pair of bookends. There's one in my office. The mate's been missing for years."

Abigail jotted down some notes. "Do you have any idea where the bookend came from or how your prints got on it?"

"None."

"Did you touch it at the scene?"

"I didn't see it...I was focused on my uncle's injuries."

More jotting. "They're not telling me anything about the injuries except that he was hit on the side of the head with the bookend, causing extensive injury. Tell me what you remember about the scene."

Logan closed her eyes and visualized everything. "Ran was on the floor."

"How was he lying?"

"On his side."

"Which side?"

She closed her eyes again. "Left. Maybe if I sketch it..."

"Anything, if it'll help give me a clear picture of the scene."

"Do you have a pencil?"

Abigail rummaged through her bag, producing a pencil and pad. She slid them over, and Logan began to sketch what she remembered of the scene.

"Stop," said Abigail so suddenly that Logan dropped the pencil.

"What? What happened?"

"You didn't do it."

"I know that," she said, exasperated. "I've been saying that all along."

"But I can prove it."

Logan looked down at the beginnings of her sketch and didn't see a thing that would cause Abigail to suddenly know she was innocent. Abigail jumped up and called the detectives in.

"She didn't do it," she announced to them.

"Oh, well, then I guess we'll have to let her go," said Beatty.

"Logan, continue sketching." The room was silent except for the scratching of the pencil.

Costello was the first to comprehend what was happening, and Abigail didn't miss it. He motioned for Beatty to follow him.

"What was that all about? What's going on?"

"I think you're about to be sprung."

"But why? What happened?"

"The detectives told me that someone came up behind him, probably while he was kneeling. He might have heard something and started to turn. That's why the wound was more to the side than back of his head."

"So, how does that exonerate me?"

"You said he was lying on his left side."

"Right."

"The wound was on his right side."

"Right. I don't get it."

"Detective Costello did. That's why they left."

"Get what?"

"You're left handed."

She began to comprehend what Abigail was saying. "I would have hit him on the left side."

Abigail smiled. "Yep. So you didn't do it. There's still the unanswered question about how your prints got on the weapon, but for now, I don't think they'll hold you."

"Detective Costello's left handed too. I noticed it when they were interrogating me. The odds of both of us being lefties."

"That's why he noticed the discrepancy."

The door opened and the detectives entered. Beatty looked none too pleased. Costello smiled. "You're free to go," he said.

"For now," added Beatty. "We'll be watching you."

"I know you're not harassing my client," snapped Abigail.

Beatty turned and left the room. Abigail and Logan followed, and continued right out the front door.

"Thank you," said Logan as they pulled out of the parking lot. "That would never have occurred to me. In fact, it didn't. I knew what side the injury was on."

"That's why I get paid the big bucks," she said, patting her hand. "Now, let's get you home and out of those clothes."

"I won't argue with that. I need a good hot shower."

Abigail pulled up to Logan's and gave her her card. "Do you want me to come in with you?"

"No, I'll be fine."

"If you're sure."

"I am. I'll be fine."

"Call me if you need me. You're still their number one suspect, but they'll have to come up with more evidence before they can bring charges."

"Do you think they will?"

"I don't know. Just stay clear of them, and you have my card if you need me." With that she waved goodbye and off she went.

*Thank God I still have Michael's key,* she thought, putting the key into the lock, but she couldn't bring herself to turn it. *Maybe I should have had Abigail come in with me. Well, I can't stand out here all night,* she thought, letting herself into the house. She wandered from room to room, assessing the damage left by the officers. It wasn't as bad as she thought. Things were in disarray, but nothing like she'd seen on television where they trashed the house. For tonight she'd ignore the cleanup and take a nice hot shower. She threw everything she was wearing into a trash bag and put it out, then made a note to call her housekeeper first thing in the morning. She was having a cup of tea when the phone jangled, jerking her out of her reverie.

"Hi Rose."

"Where've you been? Don't you check your messages. You're not answering your house phone and your cell goes right to voicemail." Logan waited patiently for a break before answering Rose's questions. She told her about the search warrant and about being arrested.

"I'll be right over." Rose pulled up a few minutes later and rushed through the front door. "Get dressed."

"I don't want to go anywhere."

"Go on, get dressed. Hurry up."

"Where are we going?"

"Nowhere in particular."

Logan wanted to argue, but there was no sense so she got dressed.

"Let's go."

"Wait, I need my jacket and purse," she said, starting toward the coat closet, then stopped short.

"What's wrong?"

"My camera bag has my wallet and keys in it. I left it at Ran's. It's hanging on the coat hook. Before…" She didn't need to finish.

They rode a few blocks in silence before Logan filled her in on all the details.

"You mean to tell me that they actually think that you packed up that bookend, which by the way weighs about ten pounds, put it in your backpack, and biked to Ran's with the intention of beating him over the head with it to kill him? And then, knowing it could be traced back to you, left it at the crime scene?"

She shook her head. "Yeah, that's exactly what they're thinking. Before that they called it a crime of passion, that we had an argument and I grabbed the bookend and hit him with it."

"Do you think it was in the attic all this time?"

"I have no idea where it was. All I know is that I haven't seen it in years. Now, it appears at a crime scene with my fingerprints all over it."

They stopped for the red light at Market Street. She spotted Jewel and her group standing on the opposite corner, and thought about the photo shoot. She needed to have them printed by Saturday, which still gave her a few days. Logan saw Jewel looking around and caught her eye as Rose moved across the intersection.

"By the way, are we going anywhere in particular or just driving around?" asked Logan

"Just driving. Do want to go somewhere?"

"I need to go to Mount Joy."

Rose slammed on the brakes. Horns blared, jerking her back to driving. "Are you out of your mind? We can't go there. It's a crime scene. If you get caught anywhere near there they'll put you back in jail and throw away the key. Besides, they'll probably have police blocking the driveway. You won't get near the place. And why do you want to go there, anyway?" Rose finally paused, giving Logan an opportunity to respond.

"Mainly to get my camera bag and bike."

"You don't need either of those things. This is a really bad idea."

"My wallet and keys are in my camera bag. I need to get them."

"The police probably have your camera bag anyway, and you don't need your bike."

"I hung the bag on the coat hook inside the front door. Maybe they didn't notice it."

"Okay," she relented. "If that's..." The car in front of Rose stopped without warning and Rose hit the brakes, hard. Logan jerked forward, grateful that the seatbelt held, but knew she'd probably have a nice bruise to attest to its secure hold. The car in front of her nosed into what looked to Logan like half of a parking space. Rose swung around the car's back end, shouting at the driver while giving him a hand signal.

"Was that necessary?"

Rose ignored her, then sighed. "We can go there, but don't be surprised if the police have it blocked off."

Logan turned to face her. "The police don't seem the least bit interested in investigating this crime. Beatty has made up his mind that I had something to do with Ran's attack and is working overtime trying to make the pieces fit. Today's reprieve was temporary. In the meantime, Costello just sits back watching. Probably analyzing me. They're going to railroad me and the only way I can clear my name is to find out who did it and why."

"The bookend doesn't help your case any."

Logan noticed that Rose turned left onto the Ben Franklin Parkway. She blew out a sigh of relief. She was heading to Mount Joy. "Thank you," she said.

"Yeah, yeah. Just don't thank me yet. We don't even know if we can get on the grounds."

"I know, but I do appreciate your help. If the driveway's blocked, we can go through the woods from the bike path."

They rode the rest of the way in silence. Rose slowed when she got to the driveway. There didn't seem to be anyone there to stop them, so she turned in.

"Just drop me off here; I can grab my bag and ride my bike back."

Rose didn't slow down.

"Rose, you can just drop me off," Logan said a bit louder.

"Forget it, I'm not leaving you here alone. Another body is liable to show up."

"That's horrible." Logan shivered. "Don't even joke about something like that."

"Sorry. But I'm still going up there with you. Besides, in case you haven't noticed, there's a bad storm coming. Look at those clouds gathering. You won't get back home on your bike before it breaks."

Logan looked up to see roiling black clouds rushing in from the west. "You're right." she said, noting Rufus's barking as they passed the cottage. "We'd better check on Rufus before we leave. I don't know why Jimmy even has a dog. He's so irresponsible." They rounded the bend. No police. One of the strips of yellow police tape had come loose and was flapping in the breeze. "I'm just going to run in and get my stuff. You wait here. I'll be right out," said Logan.

The front door was locked. She frowned, then realized that the police must have locked it. "Have to get the key," she yelled, running around to the side of the house toward the nearest outbuilding.

There used to be a neatly tended gravel path leading from the porch steps to the outbuilding, but it was buried under years of unrestrained weeds and decaying vegetation. A snake slithered across her path and into the tall grass. She pulled the vines away from the door and frame, hoping it wasn't poison ivy. It took several hard pulls to release the warped door from its frame, and when it finally gave way the opening was barely wide enough for her to squeeze through. Good thing she knew where the electrical box was, because it was pitch black inside. She heard the scurrying of what she assumed were mice and preferred not to dwell on other possibilities. The spare door key was right where she remembered. Key in hand, she let herself into the house and started up the stairs to the attic. A piece of paper on the step caught her attention and she stooped to pick it up. It was a business card. From the Preservation Society. Millicent's. But when she looked more closely at it she saw a phone number was written on the back. She was so absorbed in what she found that she didn't hear the front door open.

"What are you doing? Come on, let's get out of here."

Logan jumped up and screamed. "Rose, you scared me half to death sneaking up on me like that."

"Why are you going upstairs?"

"Not important," she said, shoving the card into her pocket.

"I hope you weren't going up to the attic." But she could tell by the look on Logan's face that that was exactly where she was going.

Logan grabbed her bag from the hook. "I'll be right back," she threw over her shoulder, taking the steps two at a time. "Watch for the police."

She had to use her flash to get any details in the dim light. The corner of the attic where Ran was found was as far from the hanging bulb as it could be. She snapped frame after frame, making sure to include every aspect of the area, high and low, without paying much attention to what she was photographing. There would be time later to scrutinize the photographs and enlarge any areas that might tell them what had happened to Ran.

"Logan," shouted Rose. "Hurry up."

"Is someone coming?"

"No, just hurry up."

"Almost through," she said, snapping another dozen shots. She looked around just to make sure she hadn't missed anything. Satisfied, she left, running down the stairs.

"Let's get out of here. This place is giving me the creeps," said Rose.

The clouds were still rolling in, but hadn't obscured the sun yet and the bright light hurt. "I'd better stop at the cottage to see what's got Rufus all riled up."

They took the path to the right which led to the caretaker's cottage, just a short distance away. The cottage was a two room white clapboard structure with a front porch. The paint was peeling and grey, and the roof sagged on one end. Logan raised her camera, taking shots of the cottage. Even in its dilapidated state, or maybe because of it, it had character.

Logan wondered again why Ran kept Jimmy on. It was obvious he didn't know a thing about being a caretaker or else he just didn't care, she wasn't sure which it was. She knew that Ran felt sorry for him. Jimmy was a pothead and clearly lacking in the brain cell department. Ran said he couldn't find work anywhere else. Besides, his mother was the housekeeper at the rectory and Michael was on Jimmy's team too. They thought he could be rehabilitated. From what Logan could see, Ran and Michael were doing all the work while Jimmy went about his business, totally oblivious to their efforts.

Logan went up the steps, carefully avoiding the rotted wood, and knocked on the door. No answer, but she could hear Rufus yelping and scratching at the door. She turned the knob and the door swung in. Rufus tore past her and ran off into the woods.

"Jimmy," she called. "You here?" She peeked inside. The stench caused her to take a step back and gulp some fresh air. The place was a mess. Stuff was strewn everywhere. She held her breath against the stench of rotted food and dirty clothing and something else that she didn't take the time to figure out. She took a deep breath and raised her camera, snapping pictures, then closed the door and joined Rose.

A noise from the woods caused them to jump.

"Jimmy," called Logan. "If that's you, get out here right now."

No answer.

"Must have been an animal," said Rose.

They heard it again, like someone moving through the brush.

"Jimmy, I'm serious. Get out here now."

Hearing only silence, they headed down the path toward the house, alert, waiting for him to jump out of the woods. But they got back to the house without incident.

"Let's take a walk," suggested Logan.

They made their way through the woods to Logan's favorite place. Logan had the camera to her eye, framing and shooting. She took close ups and landscapes, including candid shots of Rose, as they went. Rufus was barking in the background. While Jimmy loved his dog, he tended to be somewhat irresponsible regarding Rufus's needs.

They sat on the stone wall that was designed to hold back the Schuylkill River, though it was only moderately successful the few times it was seriously challenged. Logan took pictures of the lone kayaker maneuvering through the rapids, making quick sharp left and right turns to avoid the rocks.

She turned to Rose and raised her voice to be heard over the sound of the rushing water. "Rose, I'm so scared. Abigail said they still think I hurt Ran and are building a case. I have to find out who did it and why."

"I know you didn't do it, and so does everyone else who knows you."

"Character references aren't going to do me much good. I'll still be sitting in a jail cell. Oh, Rose, it was horrible. I can't go back there. We have to find out who attacked Ran."

"How's he doing?" They sat and watched the moving river for a moment.

"He's still in a coma. They'll only let me see him for a minute every few hours. At least they did. I don't know now that they think I tried to kill him. Michael's allowed in more frequently, of course, and he's been calling me with updates, but I want to be there. I need to be with him. It breaks my heart to see him lying there. No sarcastic comments, no beret, no cigar. And they don't know if he's going to get better."

They sat in silence, watching the tiny sparkles of sunlight travel downstream. "I don't know what's going on but I will find out. I tried to fit the pieces together last night, nothing makes sense. Millicent and Ran had the landmark designation in common. C.J. wants to buy the estate and Ran won't sell. I introduced Millicent and Ran, and C.J. and Sam were our best friends. That's what we know. How it all fits is speculation, and I can come up with a dozen scenarios."

"Who do *you* think attacked him?" asked Rose.

"I don't know. I'd hate to think it's someone he knew."

Rose looked at her. "But you have some suspicions."

Logan shrugged. "I don't want to think it, but I wonder if Jimmy was involved somehow. I saw him coming from the direction of the house just before I found Ran. And Ran told me last week that he found out that Jimmy was growing pot on the property. He was going to talk to him and make him plow it down. I don't know if he did, but what if that's what happened? What if Ran called him up to the house and confronted him and Jimmy attacked him?"

"What? Are you serious? A pot farm? Here? How did he find out?"

"He said he was going down to one of the old outbuildings and saw it. He was furious."

"Did you tell the police?" asked Rose.

"I completely forgot about it until just now. I'll call Costello and let him know. I assume the police have been looking for Jimmy since Ran's attack, since I told them that I saw him coming from the direction of the house just before I found Ran. You know Jimmy, sometimes he takes off for days at a time and nobody knows where he goes."

"Well, I think he's worth looking into. I wonder how hard the police are looking for him," said Rose.

"I agree, he looks good for Ran's attack, but I don't think he could have had anything to do with Millicent's accident, or mine either."

"I don't know," said Rose. "It's certainly worth a look."

"It is, but I'm not so sure about convincing Beatty. He really thinks I had something to do with Millicent's accident and the attack on Ran."

"What's he using for evidence?" asked Rose.

"The bookends, for Ran's attack. I don't know what else they could have. And I have no idea about Millicent. I was at The Gallery all evening. I don't even know what time she left."

The winds were picking up and the trees began to rustle. She listened to the birds and the water rushing by, enjoying the peace.

"Besides," she finally said, "what would killing Millicent accomplish? The only reason she even knew Ran was because of the landmark designation." Logan turned toward the sound of Rufus's barking.

"Maybe you need to start asking questions, like who was Ran arguing with the other night at the exhibition?" said Rose.

"I described the man to Beatty and Costello. Costello, at least, recognized the description, but wouldn't tell me who it was. And what about my bike accident? I just don't think Jimmy had anything to do with that. He doesn't drive, and that and Millicent's accident required a car."

"You have a point," said Rose

Logan watched the river move over and around the rocks in miniature waterfalls. The spray misted the air just above the rocks, creating rainbows. She shifted her weight. The cool dampness of the stone wall seeping through her jeans contrasted with the feel of the warm sun on her face. She watched the line of dark clouds approaching from the west releasing occasional lightning strikes, and shot a dozen frames from various angles. It wouldn't be long before the clouds blocked the sun.

# CHAPTER 10

Logan brought her attention back to her surroundings and became aware of Rufus barking in the distance. "He's really kicking up a storm," she said.

"We'd better check on him. Make sure he isn't hurt or something," said Rose.

"Yeah, you're right," Logan said, jumping down from the wall and heading in the direction of the barking. The sky was becoming overcast and the winds continued to pick up. "Looks like that storm's moving in fast," said Logan as they entered the woods. Rose followed. "We'll grab him and get back to the car." Lightning flashed, followed by the rumble of thunder in the distance, and they picked up the pace.

They went deeper into the woods, following the sound of his barks. There wasn't a path, so they picked their way through the tangled vines and debris until they caught a glimpse of him through the trees. He was jumping up and down, alternating between yelping and whining. As they got closer, his barking became more frenzied.

"Rufus," called Logan. "Come here, boy." She stooped and whistled for him, but he continued his frenzied barking. She stood and they moved toward him, tripping over the tangle of briars and detritus.

"Do you smell that?" said Rose.

"Yeah, a dead animal."

They called and whistled for Rufus a couple more times but he still didn't come. When they got to the small clearing, he rushed Logan and jumped at her legs, causing her to lose her balance and fall face down, branches tearing at her skin. She lifted her head and was staring straight into the bloated face of a human.

She screamed, breaking Rose's frozen stare. "Oh God, oh God," said Rose. Flies swarmed as Logan scrambled backwards. She swallowed several times to keep from vomiting. Rose grabbed her arm and yanked her to her feet.

"Let's get out of here," said Rose. "Come on," she said, grabbing Logan's arm but she wasn't following. "What are you doing?"

Her hand covered her face against the onslaught of flies. Logan stood there staring down at the corpse partially covered in dead leaves and branches. Rose tugged at her arm again. "Go! We have to go," she said, grabbing her shoulders and shaking her. "Come on!"

As they stood there, the flies began to resettle on the body. Logan shook her head to clear it. "Rose, I think it's Jimmy."

Rose put her hand to her mouth and looked at Logan. "Do you really think it's him?"

"It's hard to tell, but yeah, I do. Look at Rufus," she said.

"We need to call the police right away," said Rose.

"We'll have to wait until we get back to the house. My cell phone's dead." Logan reached into her bag and pulled out her camera.

"What are you doing?"

Logan turned away from the body and took several deep breaths. "Taking pictures."

"I can see that, but it's a dead body."

"Yeah, it is," Logan said. "And, just so Beatty can't try to pin this on me, I'm going to take all the pictures I can before we call them. I want an accurate record of exactly what we found."

"I guess you're right," said Rose, not sounding too convinced.

"Grab Rufus." She continued snapping while Rose tried to coax Rufus over, which was no easy task. He was in a frenzy and she finally gave up.

"Okay, let's go. We'll get him later," said Rose. "We need to call the police."

"Good thing you were with me," said Logan. "At least they can't blame this on me. But we can't leave Rufus here." They spent the next fifteen minutes trying to corral him before they were finally successful. Rose tucked him under her arm and they headed back to the house.

"This isn't going to be good," Logan said, going into the kitchen. She rooted through her bag for Costello's card and picked up the phone, but just stood there holding it before taking a deep breath. "Well, here goes," she said, dialing his number. The phone rang a few times and she was getting ready to hang up when he answered.

"Costello."

Now that she had him on the phone, she couldn't make herself talk.

"Hello? Who is this?" asked Costello.

"De… Detective, this is Logan. Logan O'Malley." Rose hovered, trying to hear Costello's end of the conversation.

"What can I do for you?"

"I think you better come out to Mount Joy."

"What are you doing out there? That's a crime scene."

"You need to come," she said again, and hung up before he could ask her any more questions. They went outside and Logan leaned over the railing and vomited. Rose stood there staring in the direction of Jimmy's body.

Within minutes they heard the siren. When Beatty and Costello arrived, Beatty immediately started to badger her about disturbing and unlawfully entering a crime scene. Logan started to say something to him, but instead turned to Costello.

"You need to follow us," she said.

"Okay, first, Mrs. O'Malley, what are you two doing here on the property?" asked Costello.

"Making sure you didn't leave any other evidence, besides the murder weapon?" asked Beatty.

Logan kept her focus on Costello. "I just came to get my camera and bike."

He looked at her, apparently waiting for more. She didn't intend to oblige. Costello stepped between her and Beatty. "You called us." His voice was low and gentle. But she remembered what Mr. Jacoby told her about him, 'Don't underestimate him.' Beatty was pacing beside the car. Logan shifted from one foot to another. Rose moved closer to Logan.

"We let Rufus out then went down by the river."

"Rufus?"

"Jimmy's dog," she said, nodding toward the porch. As if on cue, he started jumping up and down, barking. Costello looked at her, eyebrows raised and walked over to the porch.

"That's Rufus?" Logan watched as he attempted to contain his smile. "That dachshund? His name is Rufus?" He gave up trying and just laughed out loud. He had a nice laugh, Logan noticed.

"Let's get on with it," snapped Beatty. "Why'd you call us?"

Logan hesitated, then just blurted it out. "We found Jimmy. Out there," she said, pointing toward the woods and looking over at Rose. "He's dead."

"Dead? You're sure?" asked Costello.

"Show us where, right now," shouted Beatty, grabbing Logan's arm and shoving her forward.

"Let's go," said Costello.

"I'll just wait here if you don't mind," said Rose, moving toward the house.

"You wait in our car," shouted Beatty, opening the back door and slamming it shut, cutting off Rose's protests. She saw Beatty's lips moving, but couldn't hear him and smiled when he glared at her. Then he turned and followed Logan and Costello.

"Where exactly are we going?" Beatty stood with his feet apart, arms crossed.

"We're going that way," she said, pointing in a southerly direction.

Logan led the way through the woods. Beatty grumbled the whole time about the terrain, his shoes, his slacks, bugs, etc. Logan wanted to tell him to shut up, but held back. She wasn't about to give him more ammunition. Logan caught an occasional glimpse of Costello trying not to smile. Suddenly she stopped.

Beatty looked around. "Well, where is he?"

She was aware of the smell of the decaying body when the wind shifted. "Just over the rise," Logan said, pointing through the trees and down toward the river. "I'll wait here."

"You're coming with us," he said.

"Let's get a move on," Costello said, looking up at the gathering clouds.

"It's just over the rise," Logan said, pointing. "I really don't need to go."

Costello relented. "Stay here."

"And don't move," said Beatty.

She watched them disappear and waited for what seemed like hours before they came back. By now the sun was completely obliterated and she was shivering both from the sudden drop in temperature and something else. She was scared. She knew what Beatty would think, and he would let her know what he was thinking. She watched them come over the ridge and she stood up to meet them. Beatty got to her first and grabbed her arm.

"Let go of me," she said, shaking him off.

"What did you touch?"

"Nothing, for God's sakes, it's a body. We didn't touch a thing."

"The ground is all churned up. Now, what were you doing?" He was shouting at her now.

Logan looked from Beatty to Costello. Her voice was low. "I fell."

"I don't remember that part when you told us what happened. The site's a mess."

"I was trying to get Rufus, and he knocked me over," she shouted. "When I looked up I was staring at a dead body. I was trying to get up but couldn't get my balance. The leaves were wet and I kept slipping." Her voice was near hysteria.

Costello spoke, his voice low but not quite so friendly. "Why didn't you tell us that to begin with?"

"I don't know." It was a simple statement, because she didn't know. She thought of the pictures she had taken, but wasn't going to tell them, at least not before talking to Abigail.

"What else did you forget to tell us?" shouted Beatty.

"I didn't forget anything."

"So you deliberately withheld information in a murder investigation." Beatty's face was beet red and he was pacing back and forth in front of her, commandeering more and more of her personal space.

"That's not what I meant. I told you everything." She was glad she had decided not to say anything about the pictures, and told them she wasn't going to say anything more about anything until she talked to Abigail.

"Look, I'm tired of your games. We're going down to the station and you're going to answer our questions, and this time you'll be staying for the forty-eight hours."

"In that case, I'll need to call my attorney." She said it with more confidence than she felt. She was scared, but she was tired of his bullying.

Costello stepped over to them. "You're going to have to sit down with us and answer some questions."

"I know. But I'm still calling my attorney."

"No problem. Right now, though, we have to get the crime scene people up here," said Costello.

Logan turned her back on them and started walking back to the house. She thought she heard Beatty utter a word, but ignored it.

They followed behind her, Costello talking on the phone, Beatty complaining. By the time they got back to the cars, the first drops of rain began to fall. Logan went over to the unmarked car and opened the door. Rose got out and they walked to her car. The detectives pulled gear from their trunk, preparing to go back to the crime scene.

"I'm ready to get out of here," said Rose, starting the car.

Beatty's head snapped up and he all but ran toward them. "Just where do you think you're going?"

"We're leaving," said Rose.

"Turn off the car."

"You don't have any right to hold us here," shouted Rose, all the while shifting her body away from Logan, who was pinching her arm, trying to get her to shut up.

"I said turn off the car." His voice was low and his eyes bore into them. Rose turned off the car. "So," said Beatty. "What happened to him?"

"How would I know? We found him like that," said Rose.

He looked at her and smiled. He looked like a caricature, his thin lips were stretched across large teeth and his eyes were as dark as the storm clouds overhead. Logan shivered.

Costello came up behind him. "The coroner's on his way. Beatty, grab the tarps and go secure the scene while I wait for the coroner and crime scene investigators. I'll show them where the body is." Logan had thought Beatty was the senior detective, but now she wondered.

Beatty began to protest but Costello waived him off. He mumbled something under his breath, gathered up the tarps and his rain coat, and stomped away. Costello smiled at Logan, a smile that warmed his eyes.

Rose and Logan got out of the car and joined Costello. Logan watched Beatty stumble as he entered the woods, and smiled.

She turned her attention back to Costello. A clap of thunder was followed by a bolt of lightning. A gust of wind blew debris around the clearing. Logan shivered.

Costello saw that she was shaking and put his jacket over her shoulders. "You know, Beatty was right about this being a crime scene. You did notice the yellow crime scene tape when you came up."

At least she had the good grace to look sheepish. "Well, it wasn't attached."

"Just because it came loose, didn't mean you could come onto the property. I think you know better than that."

Logan shrugged and looked down at her feet. "I just wanted my bike and camera. I didn't touch anything." She left out a few things like picking up the business card with the Preservation Society logo and throwing it in her bag, and taking pictures of the crime scenes. After all, the business card probably didn't have anything to do with Ran's attack. Millicent had been out to the house a number of times. Everybody had her card. And she didn't disturb anything while she was taking pictures.

She told him again about her and Rose coming out to get her camera bag, letting Rufus out, their walk down to the river, and finding Jimmy's body in the woods.

"When you found him, what did you see?"

Logan took a deep breath and steadied herself. She started shivering again. Costello reached out like he was going to take her into his arms, but thought the better of it and instead took her arm and led her onto the porch.

"Take your time," he said.

"I'm okay." She took a deep breath and started again. "His face and a hand," she said. "It was sticking up out of the ground. That's when we called you. That's what happened."

"It's probably Jimmy, but we'll need a positive ID."

"His mother is the housekeeper at the rectory," Logan volunteered, hoping the police would have Michael or Mrs. Donahue identify him.

"We'll contact her. When's the last time you saw him?"

Logan hesitated for a minute. Maybe she should have called Abigail before calling the police, she thought. But it was too late now. She was remembering her instructions about not talking to them. But this was different. They already knew the last time she saw him. Actually, this was good. It would show she wasn't trying to hide anything.

"It was yesterday morning. Remember? He came out of the woods from the direction of the house. He scared me."

Beatty came out of the woods and walked up to them in time to hear Costello say, "I think that'll be all for now, Mrs. O'Malley. We'll be in touch."

Logan handed Costello his jacket and was moving toward the car when Beatty's voice stopped her cold.

"You aren't going anywhere until I have some answers." Logan stopped in her tracks, but didn't turn around. She could hear Beatty's footsteps crunch on the gravel as he came up behind her. Before she had time to react, he was standing in front of her, blocking her exit. "Just what do you think you're doing here? This is a crime scene. I should run the both of you in for tampering with a crime scene," he said, sweeping his arm toward Rose.

One look at Rose and she knew Beatty was going to get an earful.

"Rose," she said, touching her arm. But she didn't get any further before Rose erupted.

"We didn't tamper with anything," she shouted, sounding like a petulant child. "Logan needed her stuff. She left it here yesterday morning."

*That was just yesterday,* thought Logan. It seemed like a lifetime ago.

"First of all," said Rose, "the crime scene tape was pulled down." Logan smiled. Rose got all her information from TV crime shows. She wasn't sure how accurate it was, but Beatty remained silent. "And second," she continued, "nobody told us we couldn't be here."

He turned to Logan. "Come to make sure you didn't leave anything else incriminating?"

Rose's mouth dropped open. If this wasn't so scary and serious, Logan might laugh at the sight. Rose was speechless.

She regained her composure and turned on Beatty. Rose looked right at him, pointing at his chest. "You are the most stupid and arrogant man I've ever met. You actually think that Logan hurt her uncle?" *This isn't good,* thought Logan reaching out and grabbing Rose's arm, attempting to move her away from Beatty, but Rose shook her off. He certainly did bring out the worst in people. She continued with her tirade. "I have no idea how you made it as far as you have in the department, but let me tell you, my…"

Her voice was drowned out by a loud clap of thunder and a lightning strike somewhere so close that they felt the ground vibrate and they all jumped, even Beatty. They moved to the shelter of the porch. The heavens were close to opening up. *Not so tough now, are you, Beatty?* she thought. The wail of sirens turned their attention to the approaching crime scene team.

Beatty reluctantly moved from the shelter to meet them. When he reached the bottom step he turned, "Don't either of you move, I'll be back," he warned.

When he was out of earshot and busy with the team, Logan turned to Rose. "You're lucky he didn't slap cuffs on you."

"For what? Last I heard we still had First Amendment rights."

"Yes, we do," said Logan. "But sometimes it's prudent not to exercise those rights."

Rose rolled her eyes. "Look," said Logan. "they think I tried to kill Ran. My lawyer said to keep my mouth shut around them. I, for one, think that's good advice. This Beatty's just looking for a reason to arrest me, especially now that Abigail quashed his theory simply because I'm left handed. In fact, I think we should get out of here before he decides to arrest me."

The crime scene vehicles rolled to a stop by the unmarked car. Beatty and Costello conferred with the investigators while they were unloading their truck. It looked like they'd have to make a few trips to lug all the stuff they laid on the ground. Stuff, Logan knew, they would use to preserve the crime scene.

Just as they were all preparing to go to the crime scene, Logan went to Costello to let him know that they were leaving.

"You two aren't going anywhere. You just sit here in the back of our car and wait for us to get back," said Beatty, nodding toward the car.

They got in and he slammed the door. "Well, you did a great job of that, now, didn't you?" Logan said to Rose. "Now you're on his radar too." Rose shrugged her shoulders. "You'd better care," said Logan, "or he'll be trying to pin all of this on you, or even worse, both of us working as partners."

Rose laughed, but it was shaky, and Logan saw the worry on her face. "You can't be serious. Even he couldn't be that stupid."

"Don't bet on it."

"That's ridiculous."

"Ridiculous as it might be, I don't see him looking at anyone else."

"What about the cute one, Costello? What does he think?"

A slight smile passed over Logan's face, and Rose didn't miss it. "I honestly don't know. Sometimes he acts like he believes me, then other times…" She shrugged her shoulders. The heavens opened up.

"At least they didn't handcuff us," said Rose.

"I guess that's something," conceded Logan.

"That Beatty is a real piece of work. My brother told me all about him."

"Your brother? What does he know about him?"

"They went all through school together. St. Bernadette's, then St. Francis High."

"He's Catholic? Sure doesn't act like it. He talked to Michael like he was something he picked up on his shoe."

"Yeah, Vince said that something happened when they were in high school. It was all hush hush, and then Beatty left school.

No one knows what happened or where he went. The next time Vince saw him, he was a rookie cop. He said that Beatty turned mean. Before whatever happened he was a fun guy. Now, he hates everybody, and especially the church and anyone connected to it. Vince said that he's crazy and to watch out for him."

"I didn't need Vince to tell me that."

The rain had let up some by the time the team got back. Logan shivered and turned her head away when she saw them transporting the body, even though it was in the black body bag. "Poor Jimmy."

"Poor Jimmy? You were always complaining about him."

"I know, but he didn't deserve that," she said, nodding toward the body bag.

"How do you know? Maybe he was the one who tried to kill Ran."

"I've been thinking about that. If he was the one who did it, then why is he dead? He clearly didn't kill himself and then bury his body under those leaves and branches."

"Maybe he saw something and that's what got him killed."

"That's what I'm thinking. I wonder if he saw the attacker."

Beatty was inching his way toward them while he gave the team some final instructions. When they loaded the body and pulled away, he turned his attention back to Logan and Rose, and was about to open the car door when Costello called him aside.

Logan leaned against the window so she could hear what was going on. "We need to check the cottage and cordon it off," said Costello.

"Those two can tell us what they disturbed when they were letting out the dog." Beatty turned toward the car and opened the door. "You two, get in your car and follow us." Without another word, Beatty drove down the lane toward the cottage.

"Rose, wait. Rufus. We can't leave him here," she said, running back toward the house. He had finally settled down and was lying on the porch, head resting on his front paws, whining. She scooped him up and hurried toward the car. She held him in her lap, stroking his head to comfort him while Rose drove down the lane and pulled in behind Beatty's car. Beatty was standing in the middle of the lane, feet apart, arms crossed across his chest.

"He doesn't look happy," said Rose. "I can see his veins popping out from here."

"That's an understatement. Let's go," she said, climbing out of the car and setting Rufus in her seat. "Good boy," she said, patting his head. "We'll be right back." She could hear him whining through the closed door. "Poor little guy."

"Where were you two?" he shouted. "I told you to follow us, and look in my rearview mirror and you're nowhere to be seen."

Costello came from around the side of the house. "What's going on?" he asked, looking at Beatty.

"We had to get Rufus," shouted Rose. "We weren't going to just leave him there alone. So if you want to arrest us for that then go ahead," she screamed, offering her arms to be cuffed.

"Beatty, I think I found something on the side of the house," Costello said, nodding in the direction he'd just come from. Beatty reluctantly followed.

When they were out of sight, Logan turned on Rose. "Are you out of your mind, offering to let him handcuff you? You're lucky he didn't take you up on your offer. I've been in their holding cell and that was more than enough for me."

"I'm sorry. He makes me so mad."

"I know. Let's just answer their questions and get out of here."

Logan saw Beatty and Costello coming around toward the front. "Here they come," she whispered. "Please, don't make things worse."

Beatty walked up to them. His face had lost some of the redness and the veins were receding. "I want you to tell us what happened when you got here," said Beatty, snapping open his notebook, pen poised, ready to take down every word they said.

*Why doesn't he just tape record everything?* she thought, and shrugged.

"You mean from the beginning, or just the part about letting Rufus out?" asked Rose innocently. She gave all the appearance of being cooperative, but Logan knew better.

"Just tell us about coming to the cottage," said Costello.

"I knocked on the door, but no one answered. Rufus was inside barking up a storm. So I tried the knob and the door opened. Rufus rushed out and went toward the woods. I called to Jimmy a couple of times, but he didn't answer."

"Did you go inside?" demanded Beatty.

Logan couldn't honestly remember, but knew that wouldn't be good enough for Beatty. "I looked in and called Jimmy a few more times. The place smelled and it was a pigsty. I closed the door and left," omitting the part about taking pictures.

"Let's check it out," said Costello.

Beatty followed him up to the door, and Rose and Logan followed behind. Neither detective said anything, so they kept going. When Beatty opened the door, the smell of rotting garbage mixed with the smell of feces and urine assailed them and everyone took a step back. "She's right," whispered Costello.

They stood in the doorway for a few minutes, then ventured in. After looking around, Costello announced, "This place was tossed," and Beatty agreed.

"Come here," Beatty beckoned from the doorway. *Great,* she thought, taking a deep breath, hoping to answer his questions with a yes or no nod so she wouldn't have to breathe. She stopped just outside the door. "What time did you get here?"

She let out her breath, and turned away from the door to fill her lungs again. "I guess about an hour before we found the body."

"You took pictures. Your camera records the date and time," said Rose helpfully, then realized her mistake.

"Pictures?" Beatty's interest was immediately piqued.

"Of boaters, things like that," said Logan, watching Costello walking around inside the cottage.

"Well, let's see them."

Logan held back a groan. "My camera's in the car," she said, walking down the steps. Beatty followed. Rose popped open the trunk and Logan pulled out her camera, hoping that the sight of all the buttons would be completely beyond Beatty's comprehension or interest.

"I'll find them for you. The date and time will be stamped in the lower right hand corner." Beatty hovered over her shoulder. There was no way she could get to the scenic pictures without passing the ones of Jimmy's body.

Rose sensed her dilemma. "Beatty." He turned toward her, and Logan took the opportunity to take a quick step away from his prying eyes. "When we were looking for Jimmy, we heard a sound in the woods, here," she said, pointing to the area across from the cottage. "We thought it was Jimmy, but no one answered."

He rolled his eyes but walked over to where she was pointing. Logan shot her a thanks. Beatty didn't venture into the woods, but scanned from the perimeter. "Probably just an animal," walking back toward Logan.

"Let's see those pictures." He was beside her in two strides, moving his head in close just as she hit the forward button and replaced the last photo of the cottage with a candid shot of Rose walking through the woods. She let out her breath and showed him the date and time. He made a note in his book. She scanned forward one photograph at a time, as he jotted down the information, hoping that she had counted the number of scenic shots correctly.

If she went too far, he would see the shots of the body and he would confiscate the camera for sure.

"This is the last one."

"How long were you here before you took the first picture?"

"Maybe ten or fifteen minutes," said Logan.

Costello came out onto the porch and Beatty looked up at him. "We need the crime scene team back here. The place was definitely tossed, and I found blood spatters throughout, but no signs of forced entry." Beatty sighed, and took out his phone to make the call.

As he was finishing up, Logan asked Costello if they could leave. Before he had a chance to reply, Beatty snapped his phone shut. "Crime scene'll be here in a few minutes." He faced Logan. "We have some questions for you."

"I think it'll be okay," said Costello. "I have a full report on everything that happened. I can brief you later." Logan detected a tone that dared Beatty to argue the matter. He didn't say anything, just turned and walked away, but not before casting a look of pure disgust at them.

"You two stay away from here, and make sure we can get hold of you."

"Let's go," said Rose under her breath. "Let's get back to your house before anything else happens."

# CHAPTER 11

Not yet. I want to go to see Ran," said Logan.
"The hospital? They're not going to let you anywhere near
him. He probably has a police officer at his door. Let's just stay out
of their way and go home."

"No, you saw them back there. They've already decided that I
killed Millicent and tried to kill Ran, and now Beatty is going to try
to pin Jimmy's death on me too." She put her hand to her mouth
and gasped.

"What?" asked Rose.

"Oh my God, I just realized I was probably the last person to
see Jimmy alive, unless his mother or Michael saw him yesterday.
Oh, Rose. This is really bad. I told them I saw him yesterday
morning," she said, choking out the words. "They'll say I killed
him because he saw me attack Ran. I have to call Abigail," she said,
fishing her cell phone out. "I forgot, the battery's dead," she said,
throwing it back into her purse.

"Use mine, it's in my bag."

"Thanks," said Logan, rummaging through Rose's bag until
she found it. She selected the phone app then realized she didn't
know Abigail's number and threw the phone back into the bag.
Her business card was in her jeans pocket. The jeans she had on in
jail; the ones she had thrown out when she got home.

"What's wrong? Why didn't you call her?"

"I don't know her phone number. Her card's at home. I'll call later," she said as they pulled up to the hospital. They made it in record time. The traffic was sparse and all of the traffic lights cooperated.

"I need to see how Ran's doing and talk to Michael."

"I'll park the car and meet you at his room," said Rose.

Logan rushed down the hall toward Ran's room. She noted the police officer standing by the door and went into the small waiting room just across the hall where Michael was pacing. "How is he?"

"No change, which is a good sign." Michael looked over at the officer.

"I want to see him."

"It's not time for visiting hours yet. Let's take a walk," he said, guiding Logan past Ran's room.

"I don't want anything," she protested, and turned. "I'll just wait here."

"We'll take a walk," he said, taking her firmly by the elbow and leading her to the elevators.

"Michael, I really want to stay by Ran's room."

"We'll see him shortly, but first, tell me, how are you? Did Mr. Jacoby get there?"

"Mr. Jacoby? No. Why would he be there?" She was picturing the scene at Ran's, the body, the crime scene investigators, the coroner loading the body. "They think I killed him."

"Honey, Ran's not dead. The doctors are optimistic."

"Ran?" They stepped outside. The pavement was still wet from the downpour, but for now the rain had stopped. "Michael, they think I hurt Ran and killed Millicent, and now Jimmy. He was in the woods. He was half buried and his hand was sticking up. We had to call the police. I don't understand anything that's happening."

"Whoa, slow down." He stopped suddenly, turned and faced her, putting his hands on her shoulders. "What are you talking about?" They passed a dry, empty bench tucked under the overhang and sat. "Did you say Jimmy's dead? What happened?"

"I don't know what happened. Just that Rose and I went to the estate to get my camera bag. We had to let Rufus out, so I decided to take some pictures while we waited for him. Then he was barking a lot, so we went to see what was wrong. I thought he got tangled up. That's when we found Jimmy. He was dead." She began to shake uncontrollably. Michael held her until she calmed down.

"Then the police came, and Beatty was badgering us about why we were there, and practically accused me of doing something to Jimmy."

"Do they know what happened?"

"I don't know. I'm not sure when he died, but Rose and I found his body in the woods on the estate a couple of hours ago."

"Okay," he said. "Take a deep breath and start at the beginning and tell me everything."

She recounted everything, from the interrogation, the police searching the house, being thrown into jail, Abigail, right up to going out to the estate to get her stuff, letting Rufus out, and then finding Jimmy's body.

Michael sat there listening, interjecting questions here and there for clarification.

"Jimmy's dead. Millicent's dead. Ran's in a coma. They searched my house. They threw me in jail. Michael, what is going on? Why is this happening?"

Michael got up. "I don't know." He held his chin between his fingers while pacing. Logan watched.

"Michael, the police think I'm responsible for all this." Tears distorted her vision. Her voice cracked. "Ran was hit with one

184 | Nancy Engle

of those glass bookends. Remember them, the rearing horse bookends?" She hugged her body to keep from trembling.

He thought for a minute. "Vaguely."

"Well, they found one in the attic with blood all over it. They said it was the weapon used to attack Ran. They sprang it on me at the police station. Mr. Jacoby was there. I didn't say anything, but they knew I recognized it. Mr. Jacoby dropped me at home and I showed him the matching one."

"You still had them?"

"Yeah. I mean, no, not *them*. I only had one. The mate's been missing for years. I thought it got broken."

Michael continued pacing and massaging his chin. "Did they find the mate?"

"Of course. What am I going to do? You know I didn't do any of this. This whole thing's crazy."

He sat down next to her and patted her arm. "I know you didn't. Having the mate to the bookend doesn't help though."

"They came to my house. They searched it." Tears rolled down her cheeks. Michael took her in his arms and held her while she quietly sobbed.

"We'll figure it out. Don't worry about anything," he said, patting her on the back.

"I've been thinking about the bookend," said Logan. "Maybe it was just stored away in the attic. After all, no one's been up there in years."

"You're probably right. In which case, anyone could have been up there with him."

"I have a theory about that. I've been wondering what Jimmy was doing coming from that direction when he jumped out at me. What if he and Ran got into some kind of argument and the bookend was just there? Oh my God," she exclaimed. "I forgot."

"What?"

"Give me your phone."

"Who are you going to call?"

"The police. I forgot to tell them something."

Logan turned toward the parking lot. Rose was walking toward them and Logan waved her over.

"I don't think you should be talking to them."

"But this might be important."

"Talking to who?" asked Rose.

"The police," said Logan.

"Michael's right. It's not a good idea. And why do you want to talk to them, anyway?"

"I forgot to tell them something."

"What did you forget to tell them?" asked Michael.

"Jimmy had dark splotches all over his clothes when I saw him coming out of the woods. Right before I found Ran. I didn't think anything of it at the time. I just assumed it was dirt. But what if it was blood?"

"If it was, they'll see it when they examine his clothing. In fact, they're probably already analyzing everything," said Michael.

"You're probably right," she agreed, handing him back his phone.

"I'm going to see Ran now," said Logan, walking back inside. When they got to his room, the doctors were just coming out.

"How is he?"

"Everything looks good. His vitals are stable and the fluid is draining from his brain. He's holding his own right now. We're going to continue to keep him in the coma until the swelling goes down."

"How long will that take?" asked Logan.

"We have to wait and see."

"Can I see him?" asked Logan.

"Just for a minute."

She looked at Michael. "Go ahead. It's okay." Logan ignored the officer as she walked quietly into the room, though she felt him shift his position so that he could watch her. She stood by Ran's bed and held his hand, talked about the success of the exhibit and that she had the hundred thousand dollars the bank required. His hand twitched. She knew it was an involuntary movement, but it still gave her hope. She wondered how much he heard. The doctors told them to talk to him about happy positive things, so that's what she did.

Michael stuck his head into the room. "Sorry honey, but it's time to go."

She leaned down and kissed Ran's pale forehead. "I'll be back a bit later," she said to him as she squeezed his hand and left the room.

"Now, I want you to go straight home. I have to go talk to Mrs. Donahue."

"Mrs. Donahue," she said.

"She'll be heartbroken. Jimmy was always in and out of trouble, but he was the only family she had." He turned to Rose. "Make sure she goes straight home." He stopped and looked at her. "I have a better idea. Go to the rectory. You can stay there until this is settled."

"No, I'll feel much better in my own house." Her housekeeper would have the place neat as a pin again. "I'll be okay."

"You're not protected in your house. They can come and arrest you. If you're at the rectory, they can't just barge in. Look, I have to talk to Mrs. Donahue, hopefully before the police get there. Just stay at the rectory for now."

"I'll be okay. I have some things to do." She grabbed Rose's arm and started down the hall, hearing Michael say he would check in on her later. She waved her hand in the air to acknowledge she heard him, but kept walking.

When they got out of earshot, Rose stopped and turned to Logan. "What are you up to?"

"Let's get out of here."

The elevator doors opened and she caught a glimpse of Beatty and Costello coming out. Rose grabbed Logan's shirt, yanked her into a room and waited until they passed, then headed for the stairs.

"I'm glad you saw them. Michael's right, you shouldn't talk to them until you talk to Abigail."

They reached the car and got in.

"Now what? Where to?" asked Rose.

Logan had to shield her eyes from the sun as she turned to face Rose. "Let's review what we know so far," said Logan. "First, Millicent gets run off the road."

"Which we thought was an accident until you got that note."

"Right," said Logan. "So now we know she was deliberately run off the road. Why?" Logan made notations as they talked.

"We don't know why."

"Then somebody tries to kill Ran. Again, why?"

"How is Ran's attack connected to Millicent's death? Because I don't think it's coincidence."

"I don't either," said Logan. "But where does Jimmy fit in? The only thing we know for sure about him is that he was growing pot on the estate."

"He could have gotten in an argument with Ran over it and attacked him."

"Then what happened to Millicent, and why did someone threaten me?"

Rose shrugged, but didn't offer any explanation.

Logan continued. "But if Jimmy saw something the morning Ran was attacked, then…"

"He'd have to be eliminated," finished Rose.

"So, if he saw someone attacking Ran, then who did he see and why would they attack Ran?"

"You know, it could have something to do with drugs," said Rose. "Maybe Jimmy told someone that Ran discovered the pot and was going to destroy it. I'm sure he wasn't the brains of the operation, which means someone else was running the show. Someone who didn't want to be discovered."

"That makes sense as far as Ran and Jimmy are concerned, but doesn't explain my accident and the threat, and Millicent's accident. If we look at Ran and Millicent, the only thing they had in common was the landmark designation on Mount Joy, and I can't imagine killing someone over that," said Logan.

"It depends," said Rose. "What exactly would getting that designation mean and who would it impact, if anyone?"

"I don't think it would impact anyone. But maybe we can ask around at the Preservation Society."

"What about Ran's neighbors?" asked Rose. "You told me C.J. has been trying to get Ran to sell. She's got plans for that river front development. How would it impact Ran's neighbors if he got that landmark designation? Have they agreed to sell?"

"Whoa, slow down," said Logan, writing down Rose's questions. She looked up and Rose continued.

"What if they agreed to sell and Ran is the lone holdout? Is it an all or nothing deal? Having the property designated a historical landmark would prevent it from being sold and developed."

"C.J.? No, you're crazy. She wouldn't hurt anyone over some property."

"I wouldn't be so sure. Desperate people do desperate things and you said her company's going bankrupt. I'd say that might make her desperate. This development would put her back on easy street."

"Yeah, but I just can't imagine her doing anything like that. It's crazy."

"If not her, then what about her husband, Sam?"

"I'm not sure how involved Sam is with the financial end of things. C.J. tends to play it pretty close to the chest." Logan closed her eyes.

"What are you thinking?" asked Rose.

"I can't quite put my finger on it, but there was something the morning Ran was attacked. I've been wracking my brains to remember." She shook her head. "It'll come to me."

"Don't think about it, then you'll remember."

"What about Jimmy? How does he fit into that scenario? He doesn't have anything to do with the landmark designation."

"What if he saw or heard something? That would put him in danger. After all, this is potentially a billion dollar deal. Greed, Logan. That can push people to do things they wouldn't ordinarily do."

Logan shifted in her seat and turned to look at Rose. "Do you really think that's what this is all about?"

Rose shrugged. "Greed. It's as good a reason as anything else."

"Well," said Logan, "I guess the first thing to do is get more information about this development. Let's pay C.J. a visit."

"Do you know where she is?" asked Rose as Logan took her phone out and plugged it into Rose's car charger.

"I'll call and ask." Logan had a brief conversation then hung up. "Okay, her office manager said she's on site, down at the Italian Market. I know the project. Let's go."

They made their way through the obstacle course of traffic, delivery trucks, buses, and parked cars, which in South Philly could mean abandoned in the middle of the street or pulled part of the way onto the pavement, leaving barely enough room to get through. When they arrived they did what everyone else does and pulled the car up onto the curb, then went in search of C.J.

One of the men nodded in the direction of the corner. Logan spotted C.J.'s auburn curls first.

"There she is," she said, pointing.

C.J. had blueprints spread out on the hood of her truck and was yelling into her phone. Rose and Logan waited until she was finished then moved around to face her. Logan watched emotions rolodex on her face, ending with a smile.

"Well, Logan, Rose, this is a nice surprise. What are you two doing here? Shopping at the market?"

"No," said Logan. "We came to see you. Is there someplace we can talk?"

Logan saw what she thought was apprehension or fear, but didn't let it stop her. She was mad and getting madder by the minute.

"What about?"

"Let's go someplace more quiet," she said, and began to walk around the corner, away from the construction noise. C.J. looked like she wasn't going to follow, but then must have thought the better of it and slowly made her way to the spot Logan had picked to talk. C.J. waited for Logan to begin.

"C.J., I want to know what's going on with Mount Joy. Are you trying to get my uncle to sell?"

She shifted and chose her words carefully. "We've talked a couple of times about the benefits of selling. Why?"

"The benefits to whom? You or him."

"Well, both of us actually."

"And what did Ran have to say about your proposal?"

"You'll have to ask him."

"I can't do that now, can I, since someone tried to kill him and he's in a coma."

Suddenly C.J. caught on to where this conversation was going. "You can't seriously think I would hurt him?" It was clear to Logan that she was hurt, but C.J. was good at getting people to think what she wanted them to think.

"I'll ask you again, what was Ran's reaction to your proposal?"

"Look Logan, that's between us. But I will tell you he was willing to listen to the possibilities."

Logan was taken aback. "I don't believe you. He would never sell Mount Joy."

"It's worth a lot of money. He might. After all, he's getting older, and let's face it, he isn't able to keep up with the maintenance on the place. It's in need of major repairs."

"What about the neighbors? Are they selling too? Does the deal fall through if Ran doesn't sell? What about it, C.J.?" asked Rose.

"What happens if Ran dies?" Logan asked, to no one in particular.

C.J. spoke up. "I assume Michael or the church inherits the property."

"That's what I thought. And we all know what Michael would do. He has no use for the estate and all that money would put him in very good standing with the church, wouldn't it?" said Rose.

"Logan, I didn't hurt your uncle. All I did was bring him a proposal. That's it. Now, I have to get back to work." She stalked off, leaving Logan and Rose watching her back.

"What do you think?" asked Logan. Rose had a knack for interpreting body language.

"She was definitely nervous, but whether it was because she is guilty of something, or worried that you'll put police focus on her, I'm not sure."

"The police."

"What about them?"

"They asked me about C.J. and our relationship. It took me off guard."

"Really? When?"

"We were in Costello's office. They were asking me about Ran and the landmark designation. Beatty said he heard that we bullied Millicent into applying and that she was against it. I was leaving, and out of left field he asked about my relationship with C.J."

"Hmm. Sounds like she's on their radar. I wonder what's going on." They walked slowly back to the car. "Do you know if Michael gets the property if Ran dies?"

"I assume so. I never gave it much thought. But if that's the case, then C.J. has a really good reason to get rid of Ran."

"So does Michael."

"He would never hurt Ran. He's always after Ran to take better care of his health, making sure he sees the doctor and takes his meds."

"Something about him bugs me."

"Could it be because you're an atheist?" Logan laughed as she nudged Rose.

Rose laughed too. "That might have a little something to do with it."

Logan rolled her eyes and shook her head. They got into the car.

"Okay, where to now?" Rose asked.

Logan thought for a minute. "We didn't get very far with her, did we?"

"I'm not so sure. She's definitely nervous about something. We just have to figure out what it is."

Logan nudged Rose. "Look, she's calling somebody."

"Could be business, but I wish we had one of those gizmos that amplifies. Maybe we could hear what she was saying."

"It would also amplify the city and construction noise."

"Right."

"She's looking around like somebody might catch her. No, something's up. We need to get more information on her and that land deal."

"Let's head over to the Preservation Society and find out exactly what the landmark designation would do for Ran, but more importantly for his neighbors. Then I guess we should check on this development project and find out exactly what it entails, and again what it does for the neighbors. I noticed C.J. didn't answer the question if it's an all or nothing deal. If it is, that would give not only C.J. but any of the neighbors a reason to get rid of Ran."

"The police don't seem to be pursuing any of these ideas," said Logan.

They threaded their way through the city and were lucky to find a parking space directly in front of the Preservation Society.

"Well, here goes. I just hope our friend Jane isn't here today," said Rose.

"I think we can count on her being here," said Logan. "Remember, when I asked about meeting with the person who will be taking over Millicent's position, she told me that she wouldn't have any time in the foreseeable future to meet. She made it sound like she was that person. And refusing to meet with me makes it look like she doesn't intend to work with us on the landmark designation."

"I find that rather curious," said Rose. "After all, why should she care one way or the other?"

"Well, that's a good question. Why don't we ask her? And I also plan to talk to Millicent's supervisor to see what she can tell us about the project, and hopefully what Millicent found that she was so excited about."

Just as they were getting out of the car, Logan's cell phone rang. She looked at the display. "It's Costello." She debated whether or not to answer it, but curiosity got the better of her. "Hello?" Rose just rolled her eyes. Logan listened for a moment. "What, now?"

"What? What?" Rose said. She was tapping Logan on the arm.

Logan put her finger to her lips. "All right, I'll be right down." She closed her phone and looked at Rose. "I have to go down to see Beatty and Costello.

"Now?"

"Yeah, right now."

"I don't think you should go without a lawyer."

"You have a point. I'll call Abigail and have her meet me there," she said, pulling up the contact information on her phone. Rose waited while Logan talked to her assistant.

"Darn right I have a point," said Rose.

"Let's go," said Logan.

"Is she going to meet us there?"

"She's in court and won't be free for a couple of hours."

"So call Costello and tell him you can't meet him until this afternoon."

"You know, if I won't go without a lawyer they might think I'm trying to hide something."

"Better that than have them trying to pin Jimmy's death on you too."

"It won't hurt to just listen. After all, I don't have to say anything. And you can be right there."

"You're determined, aren't you?"

"Yes, I am. I'm tired of walking around on eggshells. I didn't do anything."

"There are lots of inmates singing that same song." She saw the look of determination on Logan's face and sighed. "Come on, let's get this over with," Rose said, driving to police headquarters. They parked in the lot and Rose turned to Logan. "You're sure you don't want to rethink this?"

"I'm sure. I just want to get it over with. Let's go."

They walked into the station and went through security. Fortunately, this time Rose was wearing shoes without any metal ornamentation. The officer at the desk made a call while both Logan and Rose paced. After waiting a few minutes, Costello came down the hall and told Logan to come back to his office. Rose started to follow but Costello told her to wait. "No," said Logan. "She comes with me or I don't come."

She saw him roll his eyes. "Okay, come on."

They walked back to his office. Of course, Beatty was waiting for them. He eyed Rose, but didn't say anything.

"Why are we here?" asked Rose.

Costello cleared his throat. "We came across something."

"What? More circumstantial evidence to pin everything on Logan?"

Beatty shifted toward Costello and started to say something, but Costello caught his eye and he remained silent.

"Look, despite what you think, we're just trying to find out who tried to kill your uncle," he said, looking at Logan. "And who killed Millicent and Jimmy."

"I keep telling you, I had nothing to do with any of this. Have you looked at the landmark designation and the development project? Who benefits? What about the neighbors? Is it an all or nothing project? It seems that none of these questions are being asked."

"Despite what you may think about our handling of the investigation," said Beatty, "we do know what we're doing. You aren't privy to who or what we're investigating."

"Look," said Costello, shooting Beatty a look, "we just have a few questions. Why don't you sit down," he said, indicating the chair in front of the desk.

"We'll stand, thank you," said Rose.

Costello sat on the edge of the desk, facing them. "Did you know about the pot?"

"You mean that Jimmy was a pothead? Yeah, who didn't?" said Logan.

"Do you know where he was getting it from?"

She hesitated just long enough to catch the attention of both of the detectives. "I never thought about it." They knew she wasn't being honest, but let it go for now.

Beatty moved and stood in front of them. Costello spoke before Beatty had a chance to. "So, you were never curious about where he was getting his pot?"

"No, why should I be?" asked Logan.

"Seems to me you should be the ones who are curious about where he was getting it," said Rose.

Both detectives ignored the barb. Costello spoke again, watching both Logan and Rose. "We took a walk around the property today." Logan and Rose waited. When they didn't respond, Costello spoke again. "We found out where he was getting it from."

"Well, now maybe you can shut down that source," said Rose, not even trying to keep the contempt from her voice.

Costello continued. "It seems he had himself quite a business going. Had a whole plot of weed growing right there in the woods."

Logan could feel Beatty's eyes drilling into her. "Really?"

"Yes, really. Right there in the woods," said Beatty. "Funny you never saw it. What with the Preservation Society poking around and all."

"First of all, there's a lot of property. Second, the Preservation Society, at this point, is focused on the house. They have a plat of the property, but haven't walked it. At least, as far as I know."

"So, it looks like you need to look somewhere else for your suspect," said Rose. "Just maybe drugs are involved in what happened to Ran and Jimmy."

Beatty sneered at her. "Aren't you two forgetting someone?" Logan looked confused, then it hit her.

"Millicent."

"Yes, Millicent," said Beatty. "Unless she was dealing drugs or using drugs I doubt she had any knowledge of what was going on out there."

"She might have been vulnerable if the landmark designation threatened Jimmy's business, which it would. Drug dealers don't like to lose their supplier," said Logan.

"Maybe she stumbled on the harvest or overheard something," suggested Rose.

"Not likely," said Beatty.

"You don't know that," shouted Rose. "Come on, we're getting out of here," she said to Logan, taking her arm.

They turned to leave when Logan noticed a photograph on Costello's desk. It was a close up of the man Logan had seen Jewel hanging out with. The one with the cane with the skull handle. He was holding the same cane in the photograph. She could just make out Jewel in the background. Costello followed her gaze and quickly blocked her view.

"Why do you have a picture of him?" she asked, pointing to the picture.

"That's none of your business," snapped Beatty, throwing Costello a nasty look.

Costello ignored him. "Do you know him?"

"Of course she does," said Beatty, his eyes boring into her. "Maybe we're a lot closer to finding the major players."

"Logan, we need to go," said Rose, pulling her toward the door.

Costello let his question go unanswered, and instead asked another one. "Aren't you curious about what else we found out?"

Logan and Rose stopped and turned toward Costello. "What else?" asked Rose.

"Well," he said, looking at Logan. "We talked to your uncle's attorney today."

"He can't tell you anything," Logan said to him.

"He's her attorney," said Rose.

"We didn't discuss Logan, but he did tell me something very interesting."

Neither spoke. Beatty picked up where Costello left off. "It seems your uncle met with his attorney two weeks ago."

"I know. He told me."

"Did he tell you what he was meeting him for?"

"I think it was to talk about the landmark designation. He wanted to know the legal ramifications."

"It seems he talked about more than that."

"Well, I wouldn't know. He didn't share that with me."

"Are you sure?"

"Look," said Rose. "Stop playing games. If you have something to say, then say it, otherwise we're out of here."

Costello spoke. "It seems he changed his will."

Logan just stared at him wide eyed, her mouth worked, but nothing came out.

# CHAPTER 12

It was Beatty who spoke first. "Aren't you curious about what the new will says?"

"It doesn't matter," said Logan. "What my uncle planned to do with his estate is his business. I was only helping him with the landmark designation. The architecture and the house's past are of significant interest to the Society. I'd hate to see it torn down, but if that's what Ran decided to do, then that's his choice."

"It seems he made you the beneficiary," said Beatty. He stood inches from her and leaned in to close the gap. She tried to step back but there was no place to go.

"What? What are you taking about?" asked Logan.

"You know," sneered Beatty. "Beneficiary? You get it all when he dies?"

Logan just stood there, mouth agape. It was Rose who rallied first. "Let's get out of here," she said, literally dragging Logan down the hall and out the door. Logan glanced back and saw Beatty standing in the hallway, arms folded, glaring at them.

Rose started the car and barely kept it under control as she shot out of the parking lot. They were several blocks away before Logan found her voice. "I don't understand. Why would Ran do something like that? What about Michael? There's got to be more to it than that. He wouldn't write Michael out of the will."

Rose hadn't said a word during Logan's stream of consciousness. "They probably talked about it. But, I hate to say this, it gives the police motive. If they can prove you knew about the new will, then in their minds they have motive."

"This just keeps getting worse. It's almost like someone's trying to set me up."

"Almost? I'd say they're doing a pretty good job of it."

"But who would do that to me? None of this makes any sense. I'm totally against the development."

"It makes perfect sense. If you're convicted of murder and attempted murder, then you can't inherit the property. I expect it'll go to Michael and we know he has no use for the property. Remember, C.J.'s been working on him, trying to get him to convince Ran to sell."

"I wonder where C.J. was the morning Ran was attacked?" mused Logan.

"Good question. Maybe we need to ask her. You need to call Abigail right now and let her know what happened."

"You're right," said Logan, fumbling for her phone. She called her office and made an appointment to see her at eight the following morning. "I'd be suspicious of me too," she said as she hung up.

"Stop that talk, right now. Let's go to the Preservation Society," said Rose, turning right. "Maybe someone there knows what Millicent found. She might have something in her files or on her computer."

"Did you notice that picture on Costello's desk?"

"Yeah, so?"

"I know that guy and the girl who was in the background. And both Beatty and Costello know I recognized him."

"Who are they, and why are the police interested?"

"I don't know why they're interested, but they hang out on Market Street. The guy seems to be the leader of the group. It's a bunch on teen misfits. The girl's name is Jewel." Logan filled Rose in on how she met Jewel and how impressed she was with Jewel's creativity with the camera.

Rose hadn't spoken or asked any questions. Logan turned toward her. "What're you thinking?"

"I'm not sure, but what if they are Jimmy's drug dealers."

"I don't think Jimmy could organize his morning routine, let alone a drug empire," said Logan.

"I don't think he did. I think he was the flunky. Someone else, someone a lot smarter than Jimmy, is in charge."

"Like who? Do you have anyone specific in mind?"

"I don't, but I'll bet the police do," said Rose.

It only took a second for Logan to see where Rose was going. "Me?" she squeaked. "Me?"

"You."

"How could they possibly think it was me?"

"Logan, think about it. You're the common denominator."

"Then why would I have Millicent trampling all over the property if I had this drug empire going on?"

Rose was silent for a moment. "How did Ran and Millicent meet?"

"She had approached him a couple of times about having the property designated."

"And he said no the first few times. What made him change his mind?"

"We talked about it. He was leaning in that direction, but wanted my input. I told him it wouldn't hurt to hear what she had in mind and then talk to his attorney."

"You went along with it because it would look suspicious if you tried to talk him out of it."

"I did not. Whose side are you on?"

"Just playing devil's advocate. That's how the police will look at it. You went along with it, biding your time until you could get Ran to change his will. Now, it's time to eliminate anyone who might interfere with your growing drug empire."

"You're out of your mind. No one could possibly believe that. I've never been in trouble; not even a parking ticket."

"That's why the police haven't been able to connect you with running a major drug empire. You're under the radar. And until this week they didn't even know where the drugs were coming from."

"But…"

"No buts."

"Wait. Abigail proved I couldn't have attacked Ran because I'm left handed."

"*Dominant* left hand. How long do you think it'll be before they realize you're ambidextrous? They're watching every move you make."

"This can't be happening. Rose, what am I going to do?"

"Make sure you keep that appointment with Abigail tomorrow."

The Preservation Society was just up the block. Rose slammed on the brakes. Logan's purse flew off her lap and dumped on the floor.

"Great," she said, leaning over to scoop up her stuff.

"Sorry, I spotted a car pulling out. Gotta grab a spot when you can get it."

"Right." The business card she found at Ran's was lying on the floor, and she took a closer look. It was from the Preservation Society and had Millicent's name on it. There was a phone number on the back. Logan picked up her cell phone and punched in the number. After a few rings she heard the generic voicemail message.

"Who were you calling?" asked Rose.

"I found Millicent's business card on the steps when we went back to get my camera. There's a phone number handwritten on the back, but it's not her cell number. When I called it I got the generic voicemail message," said Logan, picking up the contents of her dumped purse.

Rose parked and they walked the half block to the building.

"Well, brace yourself. If Jane's here, she'll go on the attack as soon as she sees it's me," said Logan. "We need to get past her to Millicent's supervisor and see if we can find out what Millicent wanted to show us."

They climbed the four steps to the ornately carved oak door, pushed it open and entered the vestibule. The leaded French doors leading to the interior were open, welcoming visitors. The hushed tone created by the thick carpet inside the Society was in stark contrast to the marble vestibule. They approached a middle aged woman who was manning the information desk. She looked up and smiled at them. "So far so good," whispered Rose.

"May I help you?" she asked in a soft voice. The name plate on her desk said her name was Velma Thompson.

"Velma, I'm Logan O'Malley, and this is my friend Rose Parker. If it's possible, we'd like to speak to the person who was Millicent's supervisor."

"That would be Gina."

"Could we see her?"

"I'll call up to her office and check," she said, picking up the phone.

"What are you doing here?" a voice screeched. The receptionist froze with the receiver halfway to her ear and her finger poised over the keypad.

"Great, we almost made it," whispered Logan. "That's none of your business," said Logan.

"You can put that phone down," Jane ordered the receptionist. "I'll take care of this."

"Actually, we're not here to see you. We have an appointment," said Rose, stretching the truth a bit.

"Right, who with?"

"That's none of your business. Now, if you'll excuse us, we're late," said Rose, looking at her watch.

"Could you ring up our appointment?" asked Rose. looking at the receptionist. "Let her know we're down here. Or better yet, if you'll just point us toward her office…"

"I'll take them," said Jane. "Who are they here to see?"

The receptionist looked from Logan to Rose. Logan nodded her head imperceptibly and fortunately the receptionist caught it.

"How about I take you up," she said, giving Jane a look that Logan interpreted as dislike.

"That would be great. Can you leave the desk?"

"Of course. Just follow me." She walked with a straight back, her chin up, and didn't bother to look back.

They followed her through the stacks full of old leather bound books lined up on the oak shelves. The sound of their footsteps died in thick carpet. They wound their way up the hand carved spiral staircase to the loft, where the offices were located. Logan dared to glance down at the reception desk. Jane was busy talking on the phone. They stopped in front of Gina's office door and knocked.

"Come in," came the voice from beyond.

Logan turned to the receptionist. "Thank you, Velma, for your help. I hope you won't get into trouble."

"Not to worry. I've handled more difficult situations than your friend down there." She smiled and waved as she turned and went down the stairs.

Rose and Logan went into Gina's office. She rose from behind the antique desk and came forward to shake their hands, smoothing her red silk skirt. Logan noticed the matching jacket hanging on a padded hanger on the coat rack. Her black hair and exotic features were a compliment to her suit. They shook hands and made introductions.

"Millicent kept me up to date on the progress with your uncle's place. I hope we can continue to work with him when he recovers."

Logan stood there with her mouth open.

"You look confused."

"I guess I am. I was led to believe that this was Millicent's project and that the Society didn't necessarily back her or agree that the property was worth pursuing."

"Sit, please. Can I get you something to drink?"

"No, we're fine," said Rose.

"Now, where did you get that idea?"

Logan shifted in her seat. "Well, perhaps we misunderstood."

"Misunderstood, my eye," said Rose. "Jane specifically told us the Society wasn't interested in pursuing the landmark designation on the property."

"When was this?" asked Gina, picking up the phone.

"A couple of days ago," said Logan. "But, look, there's no need to make a big issue."

"Oh, I'm going to make an issue of it all right. The Society is very interested in his property. The history of the property, as well as the house's architectural attributes, are of vital importance."

Logan was dumbfounded. "We didn't know it was of so much importance."

"Yes, it is. And even more so now."

"Why?" asked Rose.

"Millicent just uncovered some important information." Gina looked down at the notepad on her desk. When she looked up,

Logan saw that her eyes were moist. Her voice trembled as she spoke. "Millicent was a valuable asset to our organization. She'll be missed."

"We'll miss her too. I really enjoyed working with her."

"Do the police know anything more about what happened?"

"No, only that they don't think it was an accident."

Gina raised her eyebrows. "I thought it was weather related?"

Rose spoke up. "That's what the police thought at first, until Logan got a threatening note." Logan wasn't sure Rose should have shared that information, but it was too late now. "The note said, 'A CAR ACCIDENT CAN HAPPEN ANYTIME, ANYPLACE.'"

"The police think she was deliberately run off the road," said Logan. "A witness saw a dark car run her off the road, but they weren't sure if it was accidental or deliberate. When I got the note…"

Rose spoke up. "The police think that Logan had something to do with it, especially after someone tried to kill her uncle. They think that Logan wants the property so she can sell it."

"Gina, do you know what Millicent found?" asked Logan, in an attempt to get the conversation back to the research and away from the investigation.

Gina held up her finger, picked up the phone and punched in a couple of numbers. "Jane, would you come up to my office, please." Her voice was syrupy sweet, smooth. Logan was glad she wasn't going to be on the other end of that conversation. "Yes, right now," she said, and hung up. She turned to Logan and Rose. "We'll get to the bottom of this right now."

"Look, I don't want to make any trouble for her."

"You're not. She made her own trouble." Gina made some tea and was serving it when there was a timid knock on the door. "Come in."

Jane entered cautiously, making an effort not to look over at Logan and Rose. "Jane, sit down." *She doesn't look quite so arrogant now,* thought Logan. She should have felt satisfied, but somehow she felt sorry for her. "Jane, maybe you can help us," Gina said, using that syrupy voice again.

"Sure, if I can," she said cautiously. "What is it?"

"You know Rose and Logan?"

"Yes."

"They're here about the work Millicent was doing on Logan's uncle's property."

"Uh huh."

"Bring me all of her files, and I want her password for her computer."

"I'll get the files to you by the end of the week."

Gina smiled at her. "No, you'll get them to me now. We'll wait."

Jane got up and moved toward the door. When her back was turned to Gina and she was facing Rose and Logan she gave them a look that was pure venom. *So much for feeling sorry for her,* thought Logan.

"Jane," said Gina, "write down the password before you go." Gina handed her a pad and pen.

Grudgingly, she wrote it down. As soon as she left the room, Gina logged on and changed Millicent's password.

"I don't know exactly what Millicent found, but I know she was excited. Whatever it was should be in the files. She was a meticulous record keeper. If you don't mind waiting here, I'll go and help Jane." She left the room. Logan and Rose looked at each other.

"Well, Jane seems to be *persona non grata* around here," said Rose.

"It would appear so," agreed Logan. "What do you suppose is going on?"

"I would say that our friend is about to be escorted to the curb," snickered Rose.

Gina returned about thirty-five minutes later with her arms loaded down, followed by Velma, who was equally loaded down.

"That should be everything," said Velma.

"Thank you," said Gina with a smile.

"No problem. Anytime."

Logan and Rose looked at the piles. "Is all of that about my uncle's property?"

"It is. It's amazing how much paperwork is involved in documenting the property and filling out forms."

"I had no idea. Millicent never said how much work it would be."

"No, she wouldn't. She was a professional. And she loved doing the research. For her it wasn't work." Logan saw the sadness in her eyes. "She'll be missed."

"Didn't Jane take her place?" asked Rose.

"Not to my knowledge. Although, she might think she did." Gina looked at the stacks of research. "Let's take this into the conference room so we can spread it out and sort through everything to see what we have."

They carried the stacks of files down to the conference room and set everything on the floor in the corner.

"How should we go about this?" said Logan.

"The folders are all labeled. Let's just see what we have," said Gina, picking up the top one. She looked puzzled.

"What?" asked Logan.

Gina didn't answer her, but went back to the stacks and picked up another folder and shuffled through the papers. She checked a few more files before saying anything. "This can't be right," she said.

"Why, what's wrong?" asked Logan.

"Most of the folders are labeled, but the papers in the folders aren't related to what's on the labels. For that matter, the papers don't seem to be related to each other. It's like someone just threw everything up in the air then scooped up a few at a time and shoved them into folders. This isn't like Millicent…" She never finished the thought. Logan noticed that Gina's face was the same tomato red as her skirt, but she didn't say anything. Rose and Logan watched her grab some folders and rush out the door, hair flying.

"Jane," they said in unison. "I don't even think I want to watch," said Logan.

"Me neither. This is going to be ugly." They waited, but didn't hear any shouting. The place was quiet as a tomb.

"Maybe she already left. What would ever possess her to sabotage the files?"

"She's crazy?" said Rose.

"This is beyond crazy. I know she hates me, but this isn't about me, it's about Ran."

"And he's related to you. If she hurts him, she hurts you."

"Yeah, but this is really over the edge. Scary."

Gina came back into the room. She appeared to be somewhat composed, but Logan could see the anger just below the surface. Her body was rigid and jaw muscles tight. Logan spoke. "Let's take each folder and put the contents into categories, then we can sort them according to date."

"That's all we can do now," conceded Gina. "Will you two excuse me, I have to make a couple of calls."

After she left the room, Rose whispered. "I guess it's the old boot for our dear Jane."

"It looks like it. But that's only going to strengthen her resolve to get me. Why would she do such a thing? I don't get it. Does she hate me that much that she would keep Ran from getting the landmark designation?" Logan shook her head. "Well, we better dig in. This could take weeks to sort out."

They spent the next few hours sorting the papers into categories without really taking the time to read them. Gina came back periodically to see how they were doing. "I'm going to check Millicent's file cabinets and drawers to make sure we didn't miss anything. Can I get you anything?"

"We're good," said Rose.

Logan stretched. "I think I'll call the hospital," she said, reaching into her bag for her cell phone. "Oh, no. I missed some calls from Michael. I hope Ran's okay," she was saying as she speed dialed. "Michael, I'm sorry I missed your calls. My phone was turned off. Is Ran okay?"

"He's fine. No change," she repeated for Rose's benefit. "That's good news. No, we're at the Preservation Society. I know, but I wanted to get some information." She listened for a minute. "I'll fill you in when I see you." There was another pause while Logan listened. "We will. Talk to you later."

"What was he saying?"

"He's worried about me. I was supposed to go home and rest." Rose rolled her eyes. "I have to admit that sounds like a good idea. I'm running on adrenalin right about now."

Gina came back into the room. Her face was flushed, and she was excited about something. She was waving a handful of papers. "I found these stuffed in the back of Millicent's desk drawer."

"Tell us," said Rose.

Gina laid out the papers. "It seems that there is some indication that your uncle's estate was used as a stop on the Underground Railroad."

"Are you sure? I never heard that."

"I'll have to dig a little deeper, but it looks like Millicent found some information that points in that direction. These are copies of some documents the Armstrong family descendants apparently donated to the Society. It sure looks like there might be something to it.

"That must be what she wanted to tell us." Gina looked at Logan questioningly. Logan explained, "We saw Millicent the night she had her accident."

"I didn't realize that."

"She came to the photo exhibit at Rose's art gallery. We displayed my husband's work," said Logan, looking over at Rose.

"Your husband's an artist?"

"He's a photographer. Was."

Gina looked up.

"He died two years ago," said Rose.

Before Gina could ask any questions, Logan continued. "Millicent told us that she found the original blueprints and that they showed something interesting, but she wouldn't tell us what it was. She said that she would have to show us and that she would meet us at Mount Joy in the morning," said Logan

"But she never said what it was?"

"She said she had it in the car, but didn't want to bring it out with everything going on with the exhibit and all."

"She probably made copies to bring to you." Gina looked thoughtful.

"Did they find anything in her car that belonged to the Society?" asked Logan.

"No," said Gina. "The police said mostly everything was destroyed."

Logan again thought about the papers in her office, then furrowed her brow. Rose looked at her and Logan gave her a 'not now' look.

"Did you come across anything like blueprints in the papers you sorted?" asked Gina, sweeping her arm toward the table.

212 | Nancy Engle

"Wouldn't we be able to spot a blueprint? It would be bulky," said Rose.

"Not necessarily," said Gina. "We started digitizing a lot of stuff. It could be several sheets of 8x10 paper."

They spent the next two hours looking through the files without success.

"I don't think it's here," said Logan.

"Let's not give up yet," said Gina. "Now that we know what we're looking for, I can check some outside sources. But it's too late to do anything tonight. Come back in the morning and hopefully I'll have something for you."

Reluctantly, they left. Jane was nowhere in sight when they passed through the building and out the front door.

"She's probably gone for the day, or with any luck, permanently," said Rose, reading Logan's thoughts. She looked at her watch. "No wonder I'm hungry. It's eight thirty. You can really lose track of time in there."

"Let's get a bite to eat before heading home," suggested Logan. "Antonio's is just around the corner. We can leave the car here and walk."

"I can smell the garlic," said Rose, taking in a deep breath.

During dinner they discussed all that had happened and the discoveries they'd made. "Do you think Gina will be able to find the blueprints?"

"I hope so. She said they digitized some of the material. I know Millicent was really excited about those blueprints and I have to admit, I am too," said Logan.

Logan paid the check and they walked back to the car. Neither spoke on the way back to Logan's.

"You're awfully quiet," said Rose.

"I was thinking about something. Remember the papers I found at the scene? I had them in my office. When I went up there the other day something felt wrong, but I couldn't put my finger on it. I thought I was being paranoid. When we were talking about the blueprints at the restaurant I realized what was bothering me. I didn't see the papers on the work table where I laid them."

"You mean they're gone?"

"I'm not sure. It's been so crazy the last few days that I could have misplaced them."

"You're the most organized person I know. It's not likely you misplaced them."

"I probably just missed them. After all, I wasn't looking for them. I was looking at the work table and just had a sense that something was different."

They got out of the car. "Let's go see," said Rose.

Logan followed her into the house, reset the alarm, and they headed upstairs to the office. Logan looked around first, then walked over to the table. She shuffled through the papers.

"They're not here. I'm sure I left them right here." She circled the room looking at everything. She shook her head. "I'm just not sure."

"Maybe the police took them."

"I don't think so. Beatty wouldn't have missed an opportunity to wave them in my face and accuse me of tampering with a crime scene. No, I don't think they were here when they searched. Maybe I put them somewhere and just don't remember."

"I know you have copies. Let's look at them."

Logan booted her laptop and went to the file. "It's gone." The realization hit her hard. Someone had been in her home. She did a hasty search of the other files on her computer. Everything else was there. The only things missing were the photos of the papers from Millicent's car.

"Maybe you put the file in another directory," suggested Rose without much conviction.

"I did a search for the file name. It's gone. And the trash has been emptied."

"Someone didn't want you to have those papers."

"I'm exhausted," said Logan. "Wait, I just thought of something. When I uploaded the file from my camera it did it through dropbox. The file should still be there," she was saying as she navigated to dropbox. "And, here it is," she said, sending it to print. "I'm going to e-mail a copy to you, Rose."

Rose pulled the copies off the printer. "There's a lot of information missing."

"I know, but we can still read some of it. I looked at them briefly after I printed them, but nothing jumped out at me," said Logan.

"We'll take them tomorrow when we meet with Gina. We might be able to find the originals."

"Great idea," said Logan. "I think I'm going to call it a night. I can barely see straight."

"Me too. I'm going to head home. Unless you want me to stay."

"No, I'm perfectly fine. I'll set the alarm, and then I'm going to take a nice hot bath and go to bed."

"If you're sure."

"I am. I'll be fine. See you in the morning."

"I'll pick you up at nine sharp."

"I'll be ready." They hugged, and she watched Rose drive away. She gave a quick scan of the street and didn't notice anything out of the ordinary. She realized she was looking for the car that spooked her the other night, or was that last night? She didn't remember any more. Everything was running together. The result of the events of the last few days: exhaustion and paranoia. She closed and locked the door.

Even though the alarm was on, she still checked all the downstairs rooms before heading up. She decided to forego the bath, and instead crawled between the crisp cotton sheets. After much tossing and turning, she finally fell into a fitful sleep.

# CHAPTER 13

Logan started awake. A cold wind was blowing her curtains into the room. Crashes of thunder were followed closely by flashes of lightning. She lay there debating whether or not to leave her warm bed to close the window. A gust of wind blew the curtains straight out, and she felt the light spray of rain on her face. No choice, she had to get out of her nice warm bed and close the window, but she continued to lay there. Suddenly, the hair on the back of her neck stood up. Her heart began beating too fast. Her skin was clammy. *You're just overreacting,* she told herself.

A couple of slow deep breaths and her body began to relax and the wave of fear subsided. Another gust of wind got her attention and she had no choice but to close the window, scanning the street as she did. The trees were blowing, and debris skittered along like tumbleweed. Another clap of thunder with an immediate bolt of lightning caused her to jump. In the quiet that followed, she was sure she heard something and looked out onto the street again. She knew she should check the house to make sure everything was secure, and gathered her courage. She moved toward the door, listening, and heard the noise again. This time she was certain it was in the house and looked for something to use as a weapon, but the best she could come up with was a shoe with a stiletto heel.

She took a couple of deep breaths and opened the door a crack. She didn't hear anything. She opened the door a little further and looked to her left, down the dark hall. She'd been meaning to put a night light at the end, but never got around to it. Tomorrow, she promised herself. She looked to her right, down the stairs into the foyer, and when she didn't see anything unusual stepped lightly into the hall. She was standing at the top of the steps debating whether or not to go down and check things out, when she sensed movement behind her and turned, but she wasn't quick enough. A black clad hand and arm covered her mouth and nose. She struggled but couldn't break away, then the sickly sweet smell invaded her nostrils. Her surroundings began to fade until everything went black.

Logan slowly returned to consciousness. She tried to move and the searing pain broke through the rest of the haze. It took a few seconds for her to become aware of her surroundings. She was lying on her side, in fetal position. She shivered from the cold. Her shirt was plastered to her body and she could feel the slippery mud of the floor. It was pitch black. Not a speck of light seeped in from anywhere. She tried to move her arms and realized that they were bound behind her back. She tried to move her legs, but they too were bound. She was unable to see anything, including her own body. Every time she tried to move, the bindings bit into her wrists and ankles, making even the smallest movement excruciating. Jagged rocks dug into her side. Her prison smelled of earth, sweat, and rot. Her recurring nightmare was now her reality. She cried. Heart wrenching sobs, not caring that the movement intensified the pain.

She tried to remember how she came to this prison. Her head ached and from somewhere came the coppery smell of blood, but she had no memory of anything after waking in the middle of the night.

She closed her eyes and tried to put the pieces together, but it was no use. She shifted her position and screamed as the pain shot up her arms and legs. A sound. Fear caused the hair on the back of her neck to stand up. In that instant she knew she was being watched. She shrank backward, causing the binding to slice into her wrist. She felt a warm trickle of blood run down her hands. She needed to sit up but gave up after several tries and just lay there, eventually fading into darkness.

When she woke, she shifted and held her breath against the pain. She tried scooting backward toward something, anything. She had to find a way out. Then she heard a scraping sound. Something was moving. The beating of her heart pounded in her ears, drowning out the direction. She was soaked with sweat, freezing, shivering. The noise got closer. A scurrying sound. Rats, she realized, horrified, and moved to scare them away, almost passing out from the pain. She started scooting backward again. She had to find a way out. If she could find a wall, she could move along it. Eventually it would lead her to a door. Something brushed against her leg and she tried to scream, but all that came out was a small raspy sound.

She brought her knees up toward her chest, scraping her leg over a sharp rock imbedded in the floor. She used the rock as leverage and pushed against it with her feet. Her body moved a few inches. She stopped to breathe before pushing again, and did this several times, each time moving another few inches. Something ran over her legs. She tried to scream, but nothing came out. Her throat was raw and sore.

She took a deep breath and pushed again. She was sure all the skin on her left side was stripped off, but she kept moving. Her head hit something solid. She closed her eyes, exhausted, and drifted again into nothingness. She woke again. She had no sense of time.

She remembered finding a wall, and twisted her body so that she was parallel. Using the wall as leverage, she finally managed to sit up and began moving to her right a few inches at a time. She was freezing, thirsty, exhausted, and in pain. Each time she stopped to rest, she sensed rather than felt a presence.

"Who's there?" she asked, her voice raspy. "Please, is anyone there? Help me. Please," she said to the empty black space. "Is someone here? Please, help me." Tears of pain and frustration streamed down her face. There was no response, but she knew she was being watched. She kept moving and bumped into something solid but soft. She felt the object as best she could. Someone was lying on the floor. Somehow, knowing she wasn't alone made her feel better.

She nudged the prone figure to get their attention, not wanting to alert their unseen captors. She heard that scratching sound again and cold sweat ran down her back. She had to get them out of here. *God, please help us.*

She kept perfectly still and listened to see if she could hear the person breathing, then froze, sensing someone to her left. She thought the person was standing. Their captor. Sheer terror ran through her like ice. Before she could do anything, someone jerked her up by her hair. She lost consciousness. When she opened her eyes, nothing had changed. It was still dark but she knew someone was standing over her, watching her.

"Wake up," she was saying, nudging the prone body. "We have to get out of here," but whoever was lying next to her wasn't responding.

"Shut up," came a disembodied voice from somewhere on her right. She tried to place the voice. There was something familiar but she couldn't…Everything was distorted. Her captor kicked her. Tears welled up. She took a deep breath and tried to steady her voice.

"Who…who are you? What do you want?"

"You stole everything from me," her captor said in a voice devoid of any feeling or emotion.

She tried to see her captor's face, but it was too dark. She couldn't even tell if it was male or female. She drifted in and out of consciousness. She couldn't focus. "Jane?"

*Focus*, she told herself. You have to stay awake. She took a couple of deep breaths, ignoring the pain, and tried to clear her head. "… talking about?" she asked, using all of her strength.

"Shut up. The estate was supposed to be mine. How did you get Ran to leave it to you, you manipulative bitch?"

"No idea…C.J.?" She wasn't making any sense. She struggled to get her thoughts in order. "I don't know what you're talking about." She didn't recognize her own voice.

"Liar."

"Never yours. Ran would never sell." Her voice was weak and cracking. "Wake up," she said, nudging the body again.

"You're not going to get your greedy hands on what's mine."

She shifted, but the straps bit into her skin and she yelled out in pain. "My friends will miss me." Her voice sounded weak and unconvincing, even to her.

Her captor let out the most primal laugh she had ever heard. "I've taken care of that," the voice said, and laughed. "They'll all be getting a nice letter from you talking about your grief over losing Luke, how you didn't know if you could go on, and that you were going back to Tennessee, to the place where he died." That laugh again, a sound that was pure evil. She began to tremble.

*Would they believe the letter?* she thought. It was in that instant that she knew the truth. Her terror permeated the very marrow of her bones. She began to shake violently and her stomach heaved. The bile burned her throat.

"Michael?" She squinted, trying to focus on the figure that stood a few feet away. Without any light filtering in, she couldn't tell who was there and she was still groggy from whatever her attacker had pressed onto her face. Her attacker. Michael? *It can't be*, she told herself. Her stomach lurched and she took some deep breaths. Her head was beginning to clear a bit. Then it hit her. What she was trying to remember. The morning she found Ran she had smelled Michael's aftershave, before he got there. This time she couldn't keep from vomiting.

"Michael? I don't understand."

"The estate." He said it as calmly as if he'd been ordering a coffee.

"This is all about money? Ran would have given you anything you needed."

His laugh was bitter. "Yeah? Your precious uncle cut me off."

"I don't understand."

"He cut me off. He refused to give me any more money. Said he was tired of supporting me." He didn't try to disguise his hatred.

"Supporting you? You're a priest. The church supports you. How much more could you need?" Her voice began to rise. She had to calm down and think. "My friends will miss me," she said, in a lame attempt to get him to realize he couldn't get away with this.

"Yeah, well, I've been in touch with your friends. I told them how you've been putting on a brave front. I let them know how much you miss Luke and how you're struggling just to get through each day."

"They'll never believe it," but her voice held some uncertainty and he pounced on it.

"You're not so sure, are you?"

"They won't believe it," she said with more conviction than she felt.

"Ah, but they already do. I must say I've been pretty convincing, feeding them bits at a time. They asked me to look after you and I happily accepted. After all, who could be a better protector and guide than a priest?"

Bile burned in her throat and it took all her strength to keep it down. She knew in her heart that he could be very convincing. She thought of Ran and her friends. She thought of herself and knew she didn't want to die. She wasn't going to die in this prison. A new strength filled her body.

"Where are we?"

"Someplace where no one will ever find you."

*Keep him talking while I think of a plan*, she thought. First, she had to know where she was. "Why not just tell me if you're so sure no one will ever find me. You plan to kill me, so what difference does it make?"

She felt him smile. "Sure, why not? You're right, I am going to kill you, but not before you sign a new will making me beneficiary," he said. His normally warm voice was now glacial and sent a shiver through her body.

"You're forgetting one thing," she said.

"I seriously doubt that," he laughed. "This was a very well thought out plan. That is, until you meddled. I've had to improvise a bit, but it's still a pretty solid plan. And if you're thinking the police will find me, think again. Those two detectives couldn't find me if their lives depended on it. Or rather, your life." He laughed at his own joke. "They're too stupid to see what's right in front of them."

"Ran is still alive."

He laughed. "But not for long. You see, they don't pay much attention to a priest visiting the sick, especially if they're related."

Logan knew he was right. She started shifting closer to where his voice was coming from, ignoring the pain in her arms and legs.

She bumped the body next to her and wondered who it was and why they were there. She concentrated every ounce of her power on getting information she could use to get herself out of this prison he had created. She had to keep him talking. "Your plan wasn't too well thought out. You didn't know Ran changed his will."

"A minor detail. You're right, though, I didn't realize it was already done, but I knew he was going to look at making other arrangements. That's why he had to go," he sniggered.

"But he'd already changed his will."

"No problem, kill him, kill you. Not a big deal. You're going to sign a new will making me sole heir."

The pure cold calculating evil she heard in his voice and his words froze the blood in her veins. "You're going to kill me anyway, so why would I sign it?"

He noted the defiance in her voice. "Oh, you'll sign. By the time I'm through with you, you'll be more than happy to sign."

She made what she knew was a feeble attempt at reasoning with him. "You're a priest."

"Please, my dear Logan. I'm a priest for convenience purposes. I can do whatever I want. Just as you've said several times, 'I'm a priest.'" He laughed that horrible bone chilling laugh.

"Please, can you turn on a light?"

He didn't answer and she thought he was going to ignore her. Then he spoke. "Maybe I should let you see your final resting place." He snapped on the lantern.

The sudden light hurt her eyes and made them water. She closed them and took a few minutes to adjust. When she opened them, Michael was stooping in front of her. She tried to move backward, away from him. This wasn't Michael. His face was distorted. His hair and clothing were in disarray. His eyes appeared unfocused. *He truly is insane,* she thought. *How could I have missed it?* Logan blinked back tears and tried to steady her voice before continuing, as the full impact of his words hit her. He planned to kill Ran and her. Then a horrible thought hit her.

"Millicent. It was you."

"Ah, yes. I was surprised the crash not only killed her, but set the car on fire. The plan was to run her off the road and get the papers, although I did realize that I'd probably have to kill her. But it worked out okay. That is, until you started snooping around the crash site. And then you found those papers and just had to preserve them. I had to steal them from your office."

"My office? It was you who stole them?" He'd been in her home when she wasn't there. The thought that he had violated her home made her angry. But she had to keep a clear head.

"Well, I couldn't have them just lying around now, could I? Any little piece of information about that damned estate might get the police looking in another direction. All Ran had to do was sell it and let C.J. develop it and we'd all be sitting pretty. He caused this whole chain of events."

"Ran? Ran didn't cause this, you did. You selfish, greedy bastard." The name calling sounded childish and stupid, even to her, but she was so full of rage she couldn't think straight. *Breathe,* she told herself. *Calm down. Deep breath in, breath out.* She did that a few times until she felt somewhat under control.

Logan thought back to the night of the exhibit. "What were you and Ran arguing about at the exhibition?"

"The usual. I needed money to pay for my gambling debts and he was refusing."

"Gambling? What are you talking about?"

"I like to place a few bets on the football games and Ran was denying me that pleasure."

Logan was having difficulty making sense of what he was saying. "You said gambling debts. That's not just a few bets on some football games."

"I like to get away from the parish and all those sniveling, needy people and play some poker in Atlantic City. There's nothing like bluffing the other players into betting big when you know you have the winning hand. Then just sit back and watch them watching your every expression—trying to decide if you're really holding the winning hand or bluffing." His eyes glazed over just talking about it.

"You must not be too good, if Ran has to pay your gambling debts," she said sarcastically.

The punch to the side of her head came without warning, and sent her head crashing into the jagged stone wall. Her body slumped over. When she regained consciousness she cracked open her eyes just a bit; the lantern was out, but she sensed him sitting there waiting. She felt liquid running down the side of her head and knew from the sharp pain in her left ear that her eardrum was punctured. She didn't move; she wanted him to think she was still unconscious, but her stomach was churning from the massive headache. She swallowed several times, and took slow deep breaths, but in the end gave in and vomited. It was mostly dry heaves, but afterwards she felt a little better.

She remained silent. She wasn't going to deliberately antagonize him again. She needed to keep him talking while she figured out how to escape. In the end, Michael broke the silence.

"I see you're finally awake." His voice was soft, caressing. It was a simple statement, said as though she'd just laid down for an afternoon nap.

She tried to remember what they were talking about before... The exhibit—Michael and Ran, they were arguing. She remembered the man in the alley. "Who was the man Ran was arguing with?"

"My bookie."

She waited, but he didn't offer anything else. "Did he threaten Ran?"

He laughed. "No, my dear. He could care less about Ran. He threatened me. You see, for all his righteous indignation about my hobby, he couldn't...wouldn't, sit back and watch them hurt me, knowing that all he had to do was give them the money."

Logan asked herself for the millionth time how could she have missed all this.

"You killed Jimmy." It was a statement. "Why?"

"He saw me attack Ran. He was getting harder to control, so I knew that he had to go."

"Control, what do you mean?"

"You don't think he came up with the idea to grow pot on the estate on his own, do you? His brain was too fried. That was my brainchild. He just did what I told him to do. Planted, harvested, delivered the goods to the dealers when they pulled up on shore. In return, he was allowed to smoke whatever he wanted. Whatever he was taking for personal use didn't put a dent into the profits. But then Ran found the patch and was going to talk to him about it, and Jimmy got scared. He was going to tell Ran everything. First, he consulted me. I asked him to wait until I could talk to his mother and he agreed." He laughed, and the hair stood up on the back of Logan's neck again.

"You said he saw you attack Ran. What was he doing in the attic?"

"I asked him the same question. He was there to see Ran. To tell him everything. He walked in just as I hit him."

"I saw him coming from Ran's. Then he got a phone call."

"That was me. I told him to keep his mouth shut and I'd talk to him later. I promised him a lot of money. Figured that'd keep him quiet until I could do it permanently."

"You killed him at the cottage."

"That place was a pigsty. I don't know how anyone could live like that."

Logan thought for a minute. "But why toss it?"

"To get the ledger."

"Ledger?"

"Yeah, when I was beating him he told me he had my ledger. It contained all of the information about the business—names, dates, amounts, payments. It would lead directly to me. I assumed it was hidden in the cottage. Except it wasn't there. And Jimmy was dead."

There weren't any words to convey her rage and, she realized, it didn't matter. He didn't seem to care. "I'll find it though. He wasn't that clever. I just need a little time to think like he did and I'll know where to find it."

# CHAPTER 14

It turned her stomach to hear him describe this horror in such matter of fact terms, but she had to keep him talking. If, no, *when* she was free she needed to be able to tell the police everything. So she plunged ahead. "Was using the bookend to attack Ran coincidental?"

"Of course not. I told you everything was well planned out. I knew the bookend was in the attic, but then thought what if I switched it with the one in your house. Your fingerprints would be all over it. It was perfect."

She could hear in his voice how clever he thought the plan was. And maybe he was right, they had arrested her. As if reading her thoughts, he said, "The police thought they had an airtight case. They had the weapon with your prints all over it and the motive, the will."

"You forgot one thing. Ran was hit on the right side of his head from behind. As soon as they realized I was left handed, their case had a huge crack in it."

"Mr. Jacoby didn't know that. I didn't expect him to call Abigail. I didn't think he was smart enough to get you a top notch lawyer."

"Lucky for me he was. How do you know what the police thought?"

"When they questioned me, I, of course, was reluctant to say anything negative about you. Sadly, I had to reveal a few facts about your past."

"My past? What past?"

"How, unprovoked, you attacked poor Jane while you were in college."

"What? Jane fabricated those charges. The police didn't find any evidence to support what she was saying, so they closed the case. I never attacked anyone."

"Well, that's not how they saw it. You see, Jane was poor, you weren't. She was from the, how shall I say it, the wrong side of the tracks. That's just the way the justice system works. And Jane believed you bought your way out of the charges."

"Jane was crazy. She hated me and was always making unsubstantiated accusations. Nobody listened to her."

"Well, let's just say, the incident peaked their interest."

"This is crazy. Surely, all they had to do was look at the case to know Jane filed a false report."

"Then, of course, I had to tell them about your unfortunate hospitalization. They sympathized, but Beatty became convinced that you were unstable."

"I was hospitalized after Luke died. And his body was never recovered. I was devastated." Then she stopped as a horrible thought occurred to her. "You talked me into going into the hospital."

"Yeah, I did, didn't I? Insurance. You never know when something like that can come in handy."

Silent tears slid down her cheeks. She didn't even try to stop them. "Rose was so right about you. She never liked you. Said you gave her the creeps. I guess she was more observant than I was."

"Ah, yes, Rose. She is very clever. A lot like her mother, you know."

"Her mother?"

"I knew her. Catherine Parker. A real beauty. We were from the same neighborhood. Went to the same school. You wouldn't know that, of course. "

"You never said you knew her."

"Of course, Rose doesn't know we were acquainted, it was better kept a secret."

Logan was trying to put his words into some sort of logical picture, but the pieces were still scattered. She ignored the pounding in her head and pressed on. She needed more information. "Why would you keep it a secret?" she asked, not sure she wanted to know the answer.

"Well," he said thoughtfully, "I guess it really doesn't matter at this point. After all, you won't be telling my secrets." He laughed. She continued working her way down the wall toward him. "You see, we dated in high school."

Logan stopped. That wasn't the response she expected. He dated Rose's mother? "So you dated. What's the big secret about that?" She attempted to sound nonchalant.

"Well, you see, she turned on me. We were having sex behind the old outhouse and she ran off. She told my mother that I raped her." He stopped talking for a moment. "My mother believed her, of course. She never really liked me, you know. My mother, that is. Ran was always her favorite."

Logan was stunned. Michael raped Rose's mother? Her best friend's mother? She wondered if Rose knew about it and that was why she disliked Michael so much.

"You know, it was my mother who forced me into the priesthood. At the time, I don't think she realized how much of a benefit it would be to me. I'll tell you a secret if you promise not to tell anyone." He laughed at the thought because he knew she wasn't going to be able to tell anyone, ever. "Rose is my daughter."

Logan gasped. "Shocked you, didn't I?" he said, laughing. *Rose?*
*His daughter?* His maniacal laugh brought her back to reality. "You
should see your face."

Logan didn't need to see her face. She knew the horror of
what he was telling her, and the revulsion would be clearly evident.
It was always easy for others to read her thoughts, feelings, and
emotions. Her face always betrayed her. Her head hurt and her
mind was reeling. Maybe she misheard him. "What?"

"I believe you heard what I said. I guess that six degrees of
separation thing is true. My mother talked Catherine into keeping
quiet. Gave her money and told her I was going into the seminary.
She thought it would straighten me out. Change me. It didn't take
long for me to realize that it was the perfect place for me." She
could hear him walking back and forth as he talked. The noise he
made pacing covered any noise she made trying to get closer to
him.

Michael was talking again. "I want you to think about your
surroundings."

She did. The light from the lantern had illuminated the
immediate area, but was quickly swallowed up by the blackness
on either side of her. The lantern was off now, and the blackness
enveloped everything.

"I can still hear the fear in your voice," he said. "It won't be
long now though, until resignation starts to take over. Then I can
turn on the light again. You see, fear can motivate a person to fight,
to try to escape their situation, and the light would guide you. I
can't have that, now can I?"

She remained silent. She was trying to follow him, process
what he was saying, but her head was throbbing and the slightest
movement caused excruciating pain to her arms and legs. "Well,
now, where were we? Oh yes, Rose. My daughter. Your cousin."

*My cousin*, thought Logan. *She's my cousin.* All the love she felt for Rose suddenly flowed through her, giving her a new resolve. She always knew that they had a special bond. They could read each other so well. Then she remembered Michael's words about fear and resignation, and was determined not to show either. She was still afraid, and knew she was nowhere near resignation.

Her voice took on renewed strength just thinking about Rose. "You won't get away with it."

"Oh, but I already have, many times."

Many times? She knew if she opened her mouth she'd be sick. He waited patiently for her reaction. His revelation was too horrific to comprehend.

Michael broke the silence. "This isn't the first time I've killed," he bragged.

She had to ask the next question, but did she really want to know the answer? No. No, she didn't. She had been so wrong about him. She had trusted him. Her faith was completely shattered. *How could God let this happen?*

"Who...?" Her voice stumbled.

He laughed. "Who have I killed?" She heard the joy in his voice and cringed away from him.

"Well," he continued, like a small child proud of his accomplishments "when I was a kid I found it fascinating to see how animals reacted when they were trapped. Did you know you can actually see the fear in their eyes? I came to be able to see the exact moment when they knew they were going to die, when fear turned to resignation. Then, I just had to see if humans reacted the same way. Animals react purely on instinct, but humans have the ability to reason out their situation."

"What are you talking about?"

"Ah, curiosity. Interesting." She could hear him pacing back and forth, and could picture him stroking his chin, that gesture that always caused her to smile. Now, though, she felt nothing but hatred and revulsion for him and what he was. "Could it be that your dark side is wondering what it feels like to kill?" He laughed and Logan moved a little closer.

"Well, maybe I can satisfy that curiosity. Let's see. The first person I killed. Ah, yes. Less than satisfactory. The fear was there but not the resignation. It was too quick. But then, it was an impulsive action, not planned out like with the animals. Those I took the time to observe, but it was an interesting learning experience."

The urge to vomit was so strong that she had to keep swallowing and taking slow breaths to keep the bile down. She remained quiet, wanting to hear who his victims were, needing to know who they were, but afraid to hear more. She heard his breathing quicken. He was getting off reliving the experience, she thought with horror.

He started talking again. Suddenly, she didn't want to know anymore. Bile burned in the back of her throat. Her eyes stung from unshed tears. She couldn't keep her body from trembling. He seemed to sense her distress. "Let's see, where was I? Oh yes, my first human victim. My brother, Peter." He heard her sharp intake of breath. "Actually, he never left the property. They spent weeks looking all over the neighborhood, dragging the river, but he was right here the whole time."

"What are you talking about? Who's Peter?"

"Why, our brother. Your father's brother. You didn't know about him?"

She refused to answer him. How could her father never have told her?

"Well, I guess now is as good a time as any to fill you in on the family history."

She wanted to tell him to shut up. She didn't want to hear any more.

"Let's see. Peter was the second child. Your father was the oldest, then Peter, me, and Ran. Peter was born in 1952. He was eight when he disappeared. I was seven and your father was thirteen. Ran was about four. Peter was damaged. He was weak and puny."

Logan thrust her body to the right. She had to get away from him.

"Stop," she shouted. "I don't want to hear any more. You're a monster." She knew it was a feeble attempt to hurt someone who had no feelings, but she couldn't help it.

"But you've been wanting to know about the family history. I'm just filling in the blanks."

"Shut up. Shut up." She wanted to cover her ears so she didn't hear any more.

He ignored her and kept talking. "We weren't allowed to mention his name. It was my mother's unspoken message." Logan remained silent. "They started looking for Peter when it was time for lunch. I told my mother I'd seen him playing out back in the dirt. She sent me to get him, but of course I knew he wouldn't be there."

Logan struggled to keep her body still. She had to focus on getting out of here, getting away from him. She had never realized how completely evil he was. Then she realized what he'd just said. 'He was right here the whole time.' Was she at Mount Joy? She tried to remember what she knew about the basement. She moved down the wall a few more inches and her wrists struck a rock as sharp as a knife. Her hopes soared. The adrenalin pumped. At last, something that might just cut through the plastic ties. She positioned herself but could only move her arms about an inch or so over the rock. She had to be careful not to make a sound, not to alert him. He was talking again.

"I don't think he knew what was going to happen to him. It was actually too easy. No struggle."

"Why? Why would you do that to your own brother?" she asked, moving her wrists back and forth over the rock.

"He wouldn't let me play with his truck." It was a simple statement. A horribly simple statement.

"You would kill another human being over a toy?" She stopped. Truck? There was a toy truck sitting on his desk. *No*, she thought, *impossible*. Even he wouldn't be that evil, but in her mind she knew he was. "The truck on your desk," she half-whispered.

"The very same one." And she knew he was smiling. She had to get out of here, and continued working her arms while talking to keep him distracted. Then she remembered something.

"He was older than you."

"He was inferior. Not normal. My mother spent too much time taking care of him, protecting him. The funny thing is, I believe she always suspected that I was responsible for his disappearance. She always hated me, but even more after that. My father, though, tried to protect me from her. Until one day he just wasn't there anymore. My mother said he went back to Ireland, but he never said he was leaving."

*My grandfather. I don't remember anyone ever talking about him,* she realized. *The focus was always on my grandmother. She was the dominant one.* Logan took a deep breath. She had to find out where Michael was holding her.

"Is Peter here, in this place we're in now?" She hoped he would tell her where they were.

He laughed. "No, of course not. I didn't know about this place until I was a teenager. I found it quite by accident."

"This place?"

"You think you're clever. But you're not near as clever as me. This place is a secret. I might tell you just before you die, or I might not. I haven't decided."

"Where…where is Peter?"

"Just where he should be. Buried under all the debris in the outhouse." His laugh bounced off the walls.

Logan shivered. She was afraid to ask the question, but had to know who else he had killed. "Who?"

"Caroline. Your mother."

Logan couldn't breathe. *That can't be right.*

"I can see that you're trying to convince yourself I'm not talking about your mother, but deep down, you know I am."

Logan began to shake uncontrollably. She let out a primal yell that would have wakened anyone for blocks. She didn't care that her head felt like it had exploded into a million pieces.

"Go ahead, yell as loud as you want. If I thought anyone might hear you, you would have been gagged."

This time she didn't try to swallow the bile. She leaned over and dry heaved until her body collapsed. She let the heart wrenching cries take over. Then came a sharp kick to her ribs.

"Shut up. She wasn't worth the tears."

She took a sharp intake of air, and pain seared through her body. She had to take slow shallow breaths to keep from passing out from the pain. He was talking again, but she didn't care. She didn't want to hear any more. She wasn't going to get out of here alive. He would make sure. She was resigned to her fate. Then those two words echoed back—fear and resignation. She didn't want to die. She wasn't going to die. Not yet. Not here is this place.

"You and your mother were at the estate that day. She wanted to talk to me about your father." At the mention of her father, she became alert, but remained silent. "She knew they couldn't divorce, but she didn't think she could go on living with him."

Divorce? Her parents? "You're lying. They loved each other."

Michael ignored her. "We were walking down by the river. She was pouring her heart out to me. I tried to console her. I tried to show her what a strong man could do for her, but when I kissed her she slapped me and started to run back toward the house. Just like every other woman. Pretends she's helpless and flirts, and when some man responds…Well, I couldn't let her get away with that."

He continued talking. "I grabbed her and she tried to get away. I was going to show her what it was like to have a real man. I reminded her that you were wandering around the property and that if she screamed you might find her, then you would know the kind of woman your mother really was. Adulteress. And with her husband's own brother. Seducing a priest. Well, that stopped her. She was willing to give herself to me then, but in the end, she knew she was going to have to die. She was resigned to that. All she asked—no begged—was that I not hurt you."

"You're a monster. You'll never get away with this." She shivered, thinking of all the times he had consoled her, put his arm around her, hugged her. She cried out, the anguish ripping her body and soul apart.

"Who's going to tell? You? They'll never find your body. But if you cooperate and sign the will, I'll make your final resting place right next to your mother."

*My mother. She must be somewhere on the estate.* "Where is she?" Logan wanted to keep him distracted while she continued to try to free her hands. He was not going to win. She would live and make sure he paid.

"She's close by. Maybe you're sitting on her. Or perhaps she's over there," he said, pointing into the darkness.

"They'll find the bodies. Even if you sell the property to developers, they'll do an archaeological excavation. They'll sift through the debris in the outhouse and find Peter."

"I have to admit, Millicent and the Preservation Society were a problem. I knew she would have to go, that if they started doing any excavation they'd find the bodies, and I couldn't have that. Now, I'll sell the land and be long gone before anyone can get the paperwork together to even begin excavating. Even if they figure out it was me, they'll never find me." He laughed.

She would get away from him. She would get free. With new resolve, she put every ounce of her energy toward freeing herself. No time for rage now. She needed to keep a clear head. She strained her finger to feel her progress, and found that the tie was close to breaking. Adrenaline flowed and she renewed her attack.

Her mind was trying to grasp all that he told her. Boasted about. That was what was so horrifying to her. He was actually boasting about his kills. *He raped and murdered my mother.* All this time Logan and her father believed that her mother just left them. Her eyes stung with tears. She shook her head. *No, focus on getting loose.* She raked the binding over the jagged rock a few more times and felt the binding snap. Her hands were free, but she kept them behind her back, massaging them to get back some of the circulation. She moved her shoulders lightly, and felt her arms tingle as the blood began to flow.

# CHAPTER 15

"Where are we?" she asked. Her hands were free, and soon her feet would be. She had to know where she was and how to get out.

"Maybe I'll tell you that when I get back."

With that, she heard him walk off. He didn't use a light of any kind, so she wasn't able to see how large the room was. Once she was sure that he was gone, she shifted around and began to work on getting her ankles free.

The position was awkward and the pain from her injuries almost caused her to pass out. She lay on her side with her back to the wall and moved her legs back and forth, but the ragged rock was tearing up her flesh. She shifted her body back around to rethink her options. Her hands groped around the floor, searching for something she could use to get free. She touched the prone body. She was going to die alone in this hole. Tears sprang to her eyes. *Just like Luke,* she thought.

"Ah, I sense you are now resigned to your fate," said Michael.

Logan jerked up and cried out from pain. She hadn't heard him come back.

"Did you really think I wasn't aware that you were freeing your hands?"

Fear consumed her body, but she remained silent. He yanked her up and she screamed. Her arm separated from her shoulder, shooting red hot pain throughout her body and making her nauseous. He shoved her up against the wall and pressed his hand against her throat. White spots danced before her eyes. Everything began to go grey. She fought to stay conscious. She couldn't breathe. Her lungs were burning. Just as she was about to pass out, he let her go and she fell to the floor, her back scraping all the way down. She felt blood oozing from her wounds.

"Now that your hands are free, you can sign your new will."

"I told you I won't sign. Why should I? You're going to kill me anyway."

"You'll sign."

"Nothing you do to me can make me sign it. You confessed everything. I know you won't let me live. There's no reason for me to sign it." Her voice was weak from pain and lack of water.

"There's something I can think of that will change your mind."

"What can be worse than being murdered?"

"Rose."

That one simple word. She would sign. She had to save Rose.

"It looks like we've come to an understanding."

She lay crumpled in a heap, drifting in and out of consciousness. Every breath sent searing hot pain through her body, threatening to sink her into total unconsciousness. She thought of Rose, and her tenacity. Rose wouldn't just lay there resigned to her fate, and she wouldn't either. She wasn't going to die. Not here. Not now.

She fought her way back to consciousness. Her resolve returned. She listened but heard only dead silence. "Michael?" she whispered. No response. "Michael, please?" Her cheeks were wet from silent tears. She choked down the sobs that were rising to her throat, determined not to let him see her cry.

A movement. What was it he said to her? Think. Something about being resigned. She had to keep him thinking that. It would give her the element of surprise. "Michael? Please answer me."

He began to laugh, but it wasn't his normal laugh. The sound coming from him was demented. That was the only word that came to mind. She knew where he was, and he was close. Then he took a step toward her.

She gathered all her strength and drew her legs up to her chest, clenching her jaw tight against the pain. She couldn't see him but rather sensed where he was, and kicked out, hoping her aim was true. The cry that emerged from him told her she'd hit her target. She heard him fall to his knees. She had to hit him again. Lying on her back, she raised her legs and brought them down hard on what she hoped was the back of his neck. She rolled up to her knees and grabbed a handful of his hair with one hand while trying to gouge his eyes with the other. The rage she felt for the death of all those innocent people surged through her. Her fingers found an eye socket and she pressed with all her strength. He screamed.

Something streaked past her and distracted her for a split second. Just enough time for him to regain control. He flipped her over on her back. Her head hit the floor hard. He drew back his fist. A shot rang out and he dropped on top of her.

When she finally came to, she tried to open her eyes, but the light hurt. There were voices. She forced her eyes to open a little at a time, and saw that she was in the library at Mount Joy, and there were people all around her. Her eyes stung and watered in the blinding light. Someone, a man, was patting her cheek and saying her name. She squinted and focused. Costello. She smiled and the tears broke loose.

"You're okay." She felt his fingers brush the tears away, which only caused her to shed more. "You're safe now."

She tried to talk, but her throat was dry and sore. "Wh…"

He pushed the hair back from her face. "Shh. Don't try to talk. You're safe now. The paramedics are going to take you to the hospital." He squeezed her hand and she didn't even try to blink back the tears. "You're in good hands now."

She heard Rose's voice. "You're okay, now," Rose said, patting her hand. "I'll follow you to the hospital."

Logan closed her eyes and smiled. Rose was always there for her, since first grade. She felt herself being lifted and strapped onto the gurney. Her ankles were free. She opened her eyes and looked up into Costello's face.

"How?"

"There'll be plenty of time for explanations. I'll see you after you get to the hospital," he said, patting her hand. "I'll be along in a bit." With that, he waved the paramedics to take her to the hospital.

"I have to tell…", and then she slipped away.

The next time she woke, she was tucked into a hospital bed, tethered to all kinds of equipment, and two faces looking down at her. Rose and Costello.

She tried to talk, but her throat hurt. In fact, her whole body hurt. Rose picked up the glass of water and put the straw to her lips, and Logan took a sip.

"Michael."

"Yes, we know he kidnapped you, but don't think about that now."

"No. Have to tell…"

Costello jerked his head up, instantly on police alert. "What?" he asked, holding her hand.

"My mo…mother." Tears welled up. Costello smoothed her hair. "He killed my mother and my Uncle Peter," she said, sobbing.

"Costello, he's so evil. I never knew. He said that he dumped Peter's body in the old outhouse. I think he buried my mother where you found me."

"I'll get some men out there and check the outhouse. The forensic team is going through the tunnel now. They've reported some anomalies. We're waiting for a team from Temple's Anthropology Department to help with the excavation."

"Please find my mother."

"You lay back down." He took out his cell phone and stepped into the hallway.

Rose held her hand. "I'm so sorry."

"All these years he said she just walked away from me."

"I know. Try to get some sleep."

Costello walked back into the room and gently took her other hand. "A team's going out this afternoon."

"Thank you." Tears welled up, and both Rose and Costello reached up to wipe them away. Logan took a deep breath. "I'll be okay."

"I know you will," said Rose.

"Why don't you try to get some sleep? We'll both be right here," said Costello.

Logan was already drifting. The next time she woke, Rose was still by her side, holding her hand. Logan looked around.

"He just stepped out in the hall," she responded to Logan's unasked question.

"How did you find me?" Logan asked.

"I called you yesterday morning, but you didn't answer so I went over to the house. We had plans to go back to the Preservation Society, remember?" Logan tried to nod but her head hurt. "When you didn't answer the door, I got out my key, but Mrs. Rosen popped out before I could go in." Logan moaned and Rose laughed. "It was a good thing." Logan looked at her with lifted brows. "I know, hard to believe. But, believe it or not, she was helpful."

Logan tried to laugh, but it hurt too much.

"She was the one who put us on to Michael."

Logan took another sip of water. "Huh?"

"She's right," said Costello, walking back into the room. "She told us that a man was coming and going every time you were gone."

"How did you know it was Michael?" she whispered.

"She told me that you left with that man around two in the morning, and that you were dressed in night clothes and drunk."

"As soon as she said that," said Rose, "I knew something was very wrong."

"That's when she called me," said Costello. "We already suspected that someone was trying to frame you, but we didn't know who or why."

"We? Beatty?"

Costello smiled. "Even Beatty. I know he gave you a rough time, and he really thought you were involved, but in the end he realized that things just weren't adding up."

"Costello and Beatty came right over. I had to pave the way before they went to see Mrs. Rosen. She told them everything that she had witnessed, including you leaving in the middle of the night. We showed her some pictures and she picked out one of the faces. A lot of things began to fall into place."

"Michael," whispered Logan. Her voice was raspy.

"Yeah, Michael," said Rose. "I always knew there was something off about him."

"You did."

Costello picked up the story. "After Mrs. Rosen picked out Michael's photo, we went over to have a talk with him."

"Mrs. Donahue didn't want to let us in," said Rose, "so while Costello was trying to get her cooperation, I just walked right in. Costello has to play by the rules, but I don't."

Costello laughed. "She was pushy, but she got us in the front door. As soon as Mrs. Donahue ran after Rose, I followed. Rose burst into Michael's office without even knocking, but of course it was empty."

"Mrs. Donahue was grabbing at us, trying to get us out," said Rose.

"I was beginning to feel sorry for her," said Costello. "She actually looked terrified." Logan looked from one to the other. "While I was trying to find out where Michael was, Rose saw the cat run behind Michael's desk and disappear."

"It was like he just ran right through the wall," said Rose, "so I went over to where he disappeared."

"I was facing Mrs. Donahue and her face went ashen when she saw where Rose was going."

Rose picked up the story. "I noticed that the bookcase was pulled out from the wall about six inches on one side, and I called Costello over. He came over and pulled it back farther. It was pitch black in there. And musty. I thought it was some kind of room and took a flashlight and went in and walked a short distance. That's when I realized it was a tunnel and came back into Michael's office.

"Mrs. Donahue tried to sneak out when we found the opening, but Beatty grabbed her arm and pushed her down into a chair. He told her that she'd better start talking or she was going to prison as an accessory to kidnapping, and if you died he'd make sure she was charged with murder along with Michael. That's the first time in this whole investigation that I actually wanted to hug him," laughed Rose. Logan was trying hard not to laugh because it hurt too much.

"We might never have known about the tunnel if the cat hadn't slipped through," said Costello. "Anyway, the housekeeper spilled her guts. I guess the prospect of jail time was enough incentive."

"She knew?" whispered Logan. "She knew?"

"Yeah," said Costello. "She knew. Apparently, Michael threatened her with jail time for Jimmy if she didn't cooperate with him. He might not have abused her physically, like her husband, but he abused her all the same."

"That poor woman," said Logan.

"She told us that the tunnel runs from the rectory into the library in the house."

Logan did some quick calculations. "Five blocks?" she whispered.

"Yep," said Rose. "He could move back and forth without ever being seen. That must have been what Millicent found, the tunnel. Michael knew if she ever showed you the blueprints, his secret would be out. He could have acted as surprised as everyone else, but Mrs. Donahue told us that he had suspicions that the tunnel had been used as part of the Underground Railroad. He knew once that came to light, his chances of selling the property would fall apart. Even if he was able to sell, it could be tied up in the courts for years. Every organization you could think of would have a say in any proceeding, including the church.

"Mrs. Donahue said that you were somewhere in the middle of the tunnel. He didn't want to take a chance that someone would discover his secret and find you."

"Dark."

"Right," said Costello. "She told us that he used night vision goggles so he could move around without using any light. When you attacked him, you knocked them off."

"I couldn't see him."

"We called the station to get some officers and an ambulance out here and told them to bring some goggles with them."

"They took forever to get here," said Rose.

"Actually, it was less than half an hour, but it did seem like forever. We didn't want to go in with flashlights and alert him, so we just had to wait for the right equipment."

"When they got there," said Rose, "the police and Beatty took Mrs. Donahue to the house and she showed them how to get into the tunnel from that end. Then she was arrested and taken to the station. Beatty called when they were ready to go in. Costello, me, and some of the police officers went in from the rectory end.

"We had to take it slow and be careful not to make any noise. The floor was slippery from the water that had seeped into the tunnel from the recent rains.

"Costello here," said Rose, nodding in his direction, "stepped on a loose stone, fell against the wall and yelled out. Fortunately, Michael didn't hear us. We came around a bend just as Michael flipped you on your back. He was going to hit you. That's when Costello shot him."

"Where…" She took a deep breath.

"He's in surgery having the bullet removed from his thigh. It's not life threatening," said Costello.

"You should have killed him."

"Don't think I wasn't tempted."

"Did…" She took another sip of water . "There was someone else."

"Jane," said Costello. "She didn't make it."

"Jane?" Logan didn't know what answer she was expecting, but it definitely wasn't that one. "Why would he hurt her?"

"According to Mrs. Donahue," said Costello, "Jane was helping Michael."

She took another sip of water. Her mind was clearing, although her body was hurting. She was sure they weren't giving her pain meds. Rose must have told them about her drug allergies. She had to be able to think clearly, to be able to tell Costello everything. "I don't understand. Helping him how? Why?"

"Mrs. Donahue filled in some of the gaps. For a plea bargain, of course. I hated to do it, but she did help put all of the pieces together."

"I can't believe any of this. How could Jane possibly help Michael?" Rose gave Logan another sip of water.

"Michael wanted the estate. He was desperate. He has a serious gambling problem. Ran was always bailing him out, paying his debts, but got tired of it. The night of the exhibition he told Michael he wouldn't cover his debts anymore. That man," said Costello, "the one with the missing fingers, is a loan shark. We've been looking for him, and finally tracked him down yesterday. He lawyered up when we pulled him in for questioning, but he led us to Michael after some negotiating."

"Anyway, Michael promised Jane money, lots of it. I think he always intended to do away with her once she served her purpose. She already had animosity toward you for things that happened in college, so she was easy to recruit."

"Poor Jane," said Logan.

"Poor Jane?" said Rose. "She's made your life miserable from the day you started dating Luke. She had him all picked out for herself and you ruined it."

"I know, but she didn't deserve what Michael did to her."

"He used her vulnerabilities and her hatred for you to get what he wanted," said Costello. "He told her that you were trying to steal the estate from Ran."

"Of course," said Rose, "she never questioned what he was saying. In her mind, you were capable of doing it. He convinced her to help him stop you."

"And we found out she was the one who caused your bike accident," said Costello. "A witness got the tag number of the car and we traced it to Jane."

"But why was I a suspect?" she asked, looking directly at Beatty, who'd entered the room a few minutes before.

At least he had the good sense to look sheepish. "The evidence against you was stacking up. You were on the scene of Ran's attack, the weapon had your prints all over it, and there was a matching bookend at your home. You were the last one to see Jimmy alive. Your uncle changed his will and left everything to you."

"Okay, I get it. When you put it like that, I guess I'd suspect me too. But what about Jimmy or even C.J.? Did you even talk to them?"

"We talked to C.J. and she denied any involvement, and we didn't have any evidence against her," said Costello.

"Despite what you think, we did look into this development project and one of the other property owners was holding out too. So it's just possible that the project wouldn't have come to fruition," said Beatty. "And we planned to talk to Jimmy, but by that time he'd disappeared."

"Did you even check his phone records to see who called him that morning?"

"It was a prepaid phone, but when we started to focus on Michael, we checked his phone records and found out the call was from him."

"Of course," said Costello, "that didn't prove anything. We don't know what the conversation was about."

"Who sent that note to Logan?" asked Rose.

"We're not one hundred percent sure, but we think it was probably Michael. According to Mrs. Rosen, Michael was a frequent visitor, usually after Logan left the house. And he's lawyered up.

Claims he's innocent. That he was trying to rescue you," said Costello.

"He can't possibly expect to get away with that, can he? I'll certainly testify that he held me hostage and physically hurt me."

"And he killed five people that we know of, Millicent, Jimmy, Peter, your mother, and Jane, and tried to kill Ran," said Rose.

Logan caught the look that passed between Beatty and Costello. "What's going on?" demanded Logan.

Costello cleared his throat. "We don't have any proof that he killed anyone. There's no evidence. We can't charge him. The only thing we can charge him with is kidnapping you."

"What?" said Logan. "You can't be serious. He confessed."

"It's hearsay. His word against yours. We need evidence. Without it, he'll never stand trial."

"That's ridiculous. Get out there and find some evidence," Rose shouted, pushing Beatty toward the door.

"We're doing our best," he said. "My men are going through every square inch of the rectory and church. If there's anything tying him to those murders, we'll find it and make sure that he's charged."

Costello looked over at Logan and saw that she was sobbing and took her hand. "We're doing everything we can to get evidence."

"He'll never pay for what he did," she said, resigned to the fact that Michael would probably worm his way out of having to pay for his crimes.

"He's not going anywhere. We have him on kidnapping and your attempted murder. The District Attorney's filing the paperwork. He'll be going right from the hospital to jail."

"Will he get bail?" asked Rose.

Costello looked at Logan. "Probably."

"He'll kill me so I can't testify, and then disappear." Logan was as sure of that as she was of the fact that he'd killed her mother.

"I won't let him hurt you."

"You can't protect me twenty-four hours a day, seven days a week."

"I plan to do just that," he said, smiling at her.

Beatty continued. "We found out that all of Michael's discussions with Ran regarding the sale of the property went nowhere. Ran was determined to restore the estate. C.J. told us that she and Michael had what she called an ironclad contract. He was going to sell her the property so she could develop it. Although, I'm not sure how ironclad it was, since Michael didn't own the property. According to the contract, settlement was to take place by the end of May."

"Why would C.J. sign such a contract? And why with Michael and not Ran? She knew Ran owned the property."

"After we found out about the contract, we had another talk with her. She admitted that she was desperate. Her business was virtually bankrupt. Michael told her that Ran was dying; that he had stage four cancer and he wasn't expected to live but a few more weeks. Michael had her sign the contract so that they could save time after Ran died. C.J. hadn't seen Ran in years, that is, until the night of the exhibit. When she confronted Michael about Ran's illness, Michael convinced her that Ran had been feeling better the last week or so and insisted on going to the exhibit, but the prognosis was still the same. He told her that it's common for someone to rally just before the end. C.J. was so desperate that she bought it."

"What about the fact that someone tried to kill Ran? Didn't C.J. think that was odd?"

"She convinced herself that it had nothing to do with the property. That is, until you and Rose went to see her. You really freaked her out. She knew the whole deal wasn't kosher, but..." He shrugged.

Logan's eyes teared up. "All this hatred and violence, for what? A piece of property?"

"That was one reason," said Costello, "but Michael loved the game. He loved manipulating people and watching how they acted and reacted."

"He said something like that to me," said Logan. "Something about loving to watch the animals, and later, the people he captured go from fear to resignation. I just don't understand such evil."

"Most of us don't," said Costello. "He's wired different. He doesn't have a conscience. He can't feel."

"What about Millicent? Why did he kill her?"

"I think I can answer that," said Costello. "Millicent was doing research on the estate, as you already know, and she was very conscientious. Apparently, she found the original blueprints of not only the estate, but the church and rectory. The tunnel between the rectory and the estate was clearly marked."

"Why was there a tunnel between the buildings?"

"Well, as far as we can gather, the church was built by the same family who built the house, the Armstrong family. They were wealthy Irish. Mrs. Armstrong's twin brother was a Catholic priest over in Ireland, and they all immigrated together in the early 1800s. When they built the estate they also built the church so the brother could have his own parish. The church was all for it, of course."

"I had no idea," said Logan. "I never heard anything about any of this. My father never said anything, but maybe he didn't know."

"When Millicent announced that she'd found the original blueprints and that there was something interesting on them, Michael knew that she was about to blow his secret."

Rose spoke up. "Michael found the tunnel accidentally when he was a teen. Apparently, he's known about it for a very long time and has been using it to move back and forth without being seen."

"Does anyone know why the tunnel was there?" asked Logan.

Costello answered, "As near as we can surmise, it was originally for the family to move back and forth, to visit, especially when the weather was bad, but at some point there's evidence that it was used as part of the Underground Railroad. Slaves found their way down the river to the estate and were then moved into the rectory and protected. They could also hide in the tunnel if the house was being searched. Apparently, the authorities were suspicious, but could never find anything."

"Oh my God," said Logan. "I had no idea."

Rose took Logan's hand. Logan looked up at her, but didn't say anything. She knew Rose well enough to know that she wanted to tell her something. Something important. So she just waited. Rose cleared her throat. "I talked to my mother last night, after we found out you were missing," she said. Logan looked up at her and knew. Rose smiled, and patted her hand. "My mother confirmed what we were thinking about Michael. We'll talk about it later, when you get well. It'll be okay."

# CHAPTER 16

"What day is this?" Logan asked.

"Saturday," said Rose.

Logan began to rise, but let out a cry of pain. "Jewel, I have to get out of here. I promised her."

"Relax," said Rose. "I've already taken care of her. I went to her corner and told her what happened. If you're up for it, she's waiting outside."

"She is? Bring her in."

Jewel came in, looking from one person to the other, clearly uncomfortable.

"Jewel, it's so good to see you. You know Rose, and this is Detective Costello."

Jewel's face became pale and she started to back away. Logan immediately realized her mistake. Kids like Jewel didn't trust anyone, especially the police.

Costello saw her reaction. "Call me Frank," he said, extending his hand.

She hesitated, then shook hands. "I'm sorry you got hurt," Jewel said, inching her way closer to the bed.

"Yeah, me too, but it's over now. I haven't gotten a chance to print the shots you took."

"That's okay."

*As loquacious as ever,* thought Logan, smiling. "When I get out of here, if you like, I can show you how to download the pictures to the computer and make contact sheets and prints." Logan saw that spark of interest she'd noticed the first day and continued. "Jewel, I'm starting a visual arts center for young people and would love to have you as a student. Would you be interested?" Logan was pretty sure she would be, but wanted it to be Jewel's decision.

She didn't respond and Logan was puzzled.

"Logan's been getting grant money so she can buy equipment. That way she doesn't have to charge the students," said Costello.

Logan saw some of the tenseness and wariness melt away. "So," she said "what do you say? Are you interested?"

"I guess so."

"I have a lot of work to do getting set up and could use some help. Would you be available? You'd get paid, of course."

Logan detected the slightest smile for an instant and then it was gone, replaced by the emotionless mask, but it was there, if just for an instant, and it warmed Logan's heart. "I should be getting out of here in the next couple of days and we can talk then."

"I have to go now."

"I'll drop you off," said Rose.

"No, I'm fine."

"Goodbye, Jewel," said Costello. "It was nice to meet you."

"Jewel, you take care of yourself. We'll talk in a couple of days."

"Bye," she said without any emotion, and left.

"Thank you, Rose. I suspect she's been let down too many times. I didn't want to be one more person she couldn't depend on."

"Be back shortly. Can I bring you anything?"

"I'm good."

"Costello, we have to talk." She tried to sit up.

"Now, now. You rest," said Costello.

The nurse walked in and went over to the monitors. She checked Logan's blood pressure and pulse and injected something into the IV line. "She needs to rest now," she said.

Logan tried to protest, but the nurse wouldn't hear of it. She had to tell them. She had to let them know. With those thoughts, she began to drift off. When she woke again it was dark. Her heart was pounding and the hospital gown was plastered to her body. A monitor was beeping and the nurse ran into the room and took her blood pressure. She was safe. She started to sit up but the stabbing pain in her side left her unable to breathe. The nurse gently guided her back down.

"Where do you think you're going?" asked a voice. Logan jerked her head around, causing the room to spin, and saw Costello standing in the doorway.

"Ran. I have to see Ran."

"You're not going anywhere," he said, moving to the side of her bed. "Ran's fine." He looked over at the nurse. "I'll make sure she stays put," he told her.

"I'll be at the nurses' station if you need anything."

Logan looked up at Costello. "I need to see him. Please?"

"Not tonight. You need to rest."

"Please?"

"I'll make you a deal. You rest tonight, and no more trying to get up, and I'll take you down to his room first thing in the morning. Okay?"

She agreed, but only because she knew he'd be watching her. "Now, go back to sleep. You won't be any good to him if you're not well."

She closed her eyes and drifted off into a fitful sleep. Images of her mother the day she disappeared flitted through her dreams.

They had been in the yard at Mount Joy, she and her mother, sitting under one of the big oak trees. Logan had forgotten about that. Her mother was reading and Logan was taking pictures of a squirrel playing on the lawn. It was her first camera. She remembered taking pictures of her mother too. She was so beautiful with her wavy auburn hair and green eyes. She remembered that her mother was wearing a light green cotton dress that matched the green of her eyes. They'd laughed at the antics of the squirrel. She had forgotten all of that. She jerked awake. It was still dark outside. "Costello." Her voice was just above a whisper. She looked around the room, but she was alone. She gathered all of her strength and called him, louder this time, and he materialized in the doorway.

"It's okay," he said. "You're safe. Everything's okay." She tried to shake her head, but it hurt too much.

"Where is he?" She was panicked. She didn't have to tell him who.

"Intensive care, with a police guard. I promise you he isn't going anywhere."

"He'll try to escape."

"It'll be okay. We won't let him get away."

He saw the panic on her face.

"He'll escape and he'll kill me."

"Look, I'll go down and make sure he's secure. There's a guard outside your room and Ran's. I have to make some calls, but I'll be back shortly, and I'm going to sit right here in this chair for the rest of the night. You get some rest. We'll talk in the morning and you can tell me everything."

With that, she relaxed some and closed her eyes. The next thing she remembered was the nurse coming into her room to check her vitals. It was daylight and Costello's chair was empty. The nurse saw her looking in the direction of the chair.

"He's been sitting there all night. He's in the hall making phone calls. He didn't want to disturb you and said to tell you he'd be right back. That's a fine man you have there."

Logan smiled and didn't bother to correct her misunderstanding about the nature of their relationship.

He walked back into the room. She took one look at his face and knew.

"You found Peter," she said.

He walked over to her and held her while she wept. "We found something else," he said.

"My mother?"

After a couple of minutes, Logan pushed away from Costello and looked into his face. "How many?" she asked, her voice shaky.

"We're not sure, but so far we found three human skulls and some remains in the tunnel, near where he was holding you."

"Was one of them my mother?"

"We won't know that until the Medical Examiner reviews the remains."

She flinched. "My father always thought she walked away from us. How could he have thought that? Last night, while I was drifting in and out, I remembered our last day together. My mother loved me. Somehow, I forgot all about that. I was so angry that I didn't remember the good times."

"I know. When we're hurting it's easier to remember the bad times and redirect the hurt into anger." He stroked her face and she shivered. These feelings she had for Costello scared her, made her feel disloyal to Luke and his memory. Costello sensed her conflict and stepped back. "I'm having your mother's original missing persons file forwarded to my iPad. I should have it shortly. In the meantime, would you like to go see your uncle?"

She took a deep breath and smiled. "I would. How's he doing?"

He smiled at her. "The doctor said that he stirred once during the night."

"Is that a good sign?"

"They're planning on bringing him out of the coma today."

"Does that mean he's going to be okay?"

"They're cautiously optimistic. The fact that he's stirring is a good thing, but they won't know if there's any brain damage or neurological damage as a result of the injury until he's fully awake and they can run some tests."

"Does Rose know about Michael?"

"She was there, remember? She knows he was shot and had surgery."

Her mind was still muddled. "No, Michael told me that he's her father," she blurted out.

Costello looked at her, speechless. "Are you sure he said that? After all, you did have a head injury and a slight concussion. Maybe you misunderstood."

"No, I didn't. He said he was accused of raping her mother. Rose is his daughter. She talked to her mother. I wonder if she knows."

"If who knows?"

Logan looked toward the door and saw Rose standing there. "Rose, I'm so glad to see you."

"Are you supposed to be sitting up like that? You look like you're going somewhere. I hope they aren't discharging you because of some insurance rules," she said, looking at Costello.

"No, she's just going down to Ran's room. I'll go get a wheelchair," he said, striding out of the room.

"I can walk," Logan protested, but Costello was already gone.

"I know you can, but for once let someone take care of you," said Rose. Logan sighed. Rose planted herself on the bed beside

Logan. "Okay, what were you talking about when I came in? If who knows what?" she asked again.

Logan might have known that she wouldn't forget. "We'll talk about it later. They said Ran stirred some last night. They're bringing him out of the coma. I can't wait to see him." She looked at Rose. "What? Don't you think that's good news?"

"Of course I do." Rose took a deep breath. "I talked to my mother again last night. I wanted to let her know that we were both okay. Everything was all over the news."

"Great," sighed Logan. "How did the media get a hold of it so fast?"

"She told me the whole story about her and Michael."

Logan was pretty sure what Rose was going to say and braced herself.

"She told me about being raped."

"Rose, I'm so sorry."

"She also told me that it was Michael who raped her." She was watching Logan. "You knew that, didn't you?"

"Not until last night. You never liked him. You always said something wasn't right. I wish I had listened to you."

"He never showed that side of himself to you."

"Not until last night. Rose, I've never seen pure evil before then. I'm so sorry that he's your father."

"No, he's not my father. He donated the sperm, but he's definitely not my father. Alan raised me, He's my father." She took a deep breath and turned to Logan and smiled. "But it does make us cousins, and Ran is my uncle too."

Logan hugged her, ignoring the searing pain. When they both stopped crying, they saw Costello standing in the doorway with the wheelchair. He brought it to the side of the bed and helped her get seated, then they all went down the hall to Ran's room. Costello maneuvered the wheelchair next to the bed.

"I'll wait in the hall with Rose."

"No, I want both of you here with me. He's your family too," she said to Rose.

They sat, one on either side of him, and held his hands and talked to him. Costello stood beside Logan with his hand on her shoulder.

Ran's his eyes fluttered, and she heard him whisper. She moved closer to him and heard him say something that sounded like "out."

She responded, "Yes, you are getting well and you'll be getting out soon and going home."

He said it again, and again she assured him that he was recovering.

But then the heart monitor changed. The nurse came running in.

"What's happening?" Logan asked. "Is he okay?"

The nurse asked them to step outside without answering her question. Costello wheeled her into the hallway. Logan started to get out of the wheelchair to see what was happening. Two other nurses joined the first ones, and Logan saw his doctor rushing toward them. He closed the door behind him.

"Please, God, please let him be okay," she prayed. Her heart was racing. "Oh, Rose, he has to be okay. He just has to be."

"They'll take good care of him," she said.

It seemed like they sat in the hall for hours watching for the door to open. The squeaking sound of the rubber soled shoes of the hospital personnel on the linoleum was getting on her nerves. She had Rose wheel her over to the nurses' station, but they couldn't or wouldn't tell her anything. The nurse suggested she might want to go back to her room and get some rest and said she would have the doctor go down to her room when he was finished, but Logan wasn't going anywhere. Rose pushed her closer to the doorway so they could listen for any scrap of information, but all they heard was the low murmuring of the doctor and nurses. The smells of disinfectant, sickness, and death seemed more acute.

"Let's go back to your room," said Costello. "They'll let you know how he is as soon as they're done examining him."

"No, I'll just wait here. I don't care how long it takes."

"At least let me go get you some tea while we wait," said Costello

"No, I don't want anything."

"I'll go down and get you some tea," volunteered Rose. "Do you want anything?" she asked Costello.

"No, I'm good."

"I'll be back in a few minutes," and she turned and started down the hall.

Ran's door opened and Dr. Lawrence stepped into the hallway. Logan pounced on him before he had a chance to say a word, firing one question after another without giving him a chance to reply. Rose raced back down the hallway and joined Logan and Costello.

"Your uncle is okay. There was a spike in his heart rate, but he's calmed down now. We're going to take him down for some brain scans. Why don't you go back to your room and I'll come see you as soon as we get some results." He squeezed her shoulder and nodded at Costello and Rose, who were standing a discreet distance away.

"Is he coming out of the coma?" she asked. "Will he be okay?"

"One thing at a time. Let's get those tests done and I'll come see you later."

Costello released the brake and took her back to her room. "You look tired. Why don't you take a nap and I'll wake you as soon as the doctor comes back."

"So much has happened. How can one person be so evil?" It was a rhetorical question. She wasn't expecting an answer. Then she looked at Rose. "Oh, Rose, I'm so sorry. I didn't mean…"

"It's okay. He is evil."

They arrived at her room and Costello helped her back into her bed. "Now, you get some sleep," he said. "We'll both be right here."

Logan had just begun to drift off when a commotion in the hall woke her. She heard the raised voices and immediately recognized one voice. Costello ran into the hall to see what was going on. Logan started to get out of bed, but Rose gently pushed her back down.

"Costello will take care of it."

Logan groaned. "I don't think even Costello is a match for her."

"You recognized her voice, did you?"

Logan rolled her eyes and Rose laughed. "I'll tell her to come back later. That way you'll have time to prepare."

"I'm not sure postponing the inevitable will help. You might as well let her in."

"Are you sure? You don't have to do this, you know. You can wait until you're stronger."

"Let's get this over with."

"Here, lay back and close your eyes. I'll tell her that she can come in, but she has to be quiet."

Logan laughed out loud, forgetting about the pain that laughing caused.

"Just lay back and look out of it," Rose said as she disappeared into the hallway.

Logan could hear the murmur of voices, but she could hear one voice above all the others. Luke's mother, Vanessa. She sighed and did as Rose told her, which didn't require too much acting. She felt like an avalanche had struck her. She hurt all over and was emotionally drained. She tried not to think of the terrible things Michael did to his family, her mother's last moments, and what Michael did to her. Tears leaked from her closed eyes.

She heard movement by her bed, but didn't open her eyes until Vanessa demanded that everyone leave the room. She said she wanted to talk to Logan. No way did Logan want to be alone with her, especially right now, so she groaned a bit and opened her eyes. Rose and Costello were standing in the background, and Vanessa's face was right in hers.

"You can leave. I want to be alone with her," she repeated. "Logan, what kind of trouble have you gotten into? You know, people are talking. This isn't the kind of publicity you should be attracting."

Logan sighed. "Vanessa, I want them to stay." She motioned for Costello and Rose to come closer. Rose understood. Logan needed a buffer and they were it. Costello wasn't sure who this woman was and what her relationship with Logan was, but took his cue from Rose. Rose moved to the side of the bed that Vanessa was on and positioned herself close to Logan's head, forcing Vanessa to retreat some. Costello stood on Logan's other side. Logan took each of their hands, watching Vanessa's face as she did. For a moment, Vanessa was speechless. Something Logan didn't often see.

"Vanessa, you know Rose, and this is Frank Costello, the detective in charge of the investigation."

She gave Rose a grudging hello, and didn't even bother to acknowledge Costello's presence. After all, he was a public servant.

"They are both responsible for me being rescued." She gave each of them a smile and a quick squeeze of their hands.

"Well, you must have seen the news reports, since you knew where to find Logan," said Rose. "She was kidnapped."

"I've told you that you have to be careful about who you allow into your life. There are a lot of people out there who kidnap people like us for money."

Logan remained quiet. She knew any argument would fall on deaf ears.

Costello spoke up. "Mrs. O'Malley, this had nothing to do with ransom." He was using his controlled, evenly modulated voice, the one you might use when talking to an out-of-touch-with-reality perp.

"This was about someone trying to kill my uncle, and when I started asking questions, he came after me."

"Why did you get involved? You should have let the police take care of it." She shot Costello a look of derision. "That's why we pay taxes. He had no business involving you in this mess."

"He didn't involve me. Someone tried to kill my uncle and frame me. Even if I wasn't a suspect, I would still be involved because I'd want to know who did this to my family."

"When are they going to release you? Of course, you'll come stay with me."

"I don't know when I'm being released," she took a deep breath, "but I'm going to my own home." Logan realized that this was the first time since she'd met Vanessa that she'd stood her ground, and realized that it felt good, darn good. It was as if a weight had been lifted. She wasn't cutting Vanessa out of her life, more like taking charge of it. She hadn't done that in years. Rose smiled and Costello winked.

"Nonsense, you can't go there alone. The media will be all over this. You'll need someone to handle them. You never were very good with knowing what to say and when to say it."

Logan attempted to say something, but Vanessa waved her hand in dismissal. Logan ignored her and told her again that she was going home, this time a little stronger. Then she said, "Vanessa, thank you for coming. I'll let you know when I get discharged," effectively dismissing her. Vanessa was so shocked that she was being dismissed, that she hesitated, not sure what to do, but in the end decided to leave gracefully. She kissed Logan on the cheek and flounced out the door without so much as a look back.

"You were kind of hard on her. She looked upset," said Costello.

"It's a long story, and my being assertive and taking back my life where she's concerned has been a long time coming."

"Well, maybe you can tell me about it over dinner when they spring you," he said.

Logan smiled. "I'd like that."

Rose winked and squeezed her hand. "Now, why don't you get some rest before the doctor comes in," said Rose. "We'll be right here."

# CHAPTER 17

L ogan was dozing off when Costello woke her.
"Dr. Lawrence is here."

She opened her eyes and saw them standing by the bed. His face held an expression that Logan thought doctors must be taught in medical school. "How is he? Is he okay?"

Dr. Lawrence sat down on the side of her bed. "We have the test results and everything looks normal."

Logan didn't realize she had stopped breathing. "So he's going to recover?"

"I think so. He's not fully awake yet, but he's responding appropriately."

"So, he's going to be okay?"

"It looks good. You can go see him now if you like."

Costello helped her into the wheelchair and the three of them went down to Ran's room. He lay against the pillows. His face was pale. The monitors were blinking. She could hear the respirator breathing for him. Costello parked her chair next to him, and she took his hand and squeezed it. He squeezed back.

Tears sprang to her eyes. She looked up at Costello and Rose, and they smiled down at her.

"You're going to be okay," she told him, and he smiled.

Logan refused to leave his bedside and the nurses ignored the visitation rules. Each time he woke, it was for a longer period of time. Over the next few days, Ran continued his slow recovery. He began breathing on his own and was sitting up for longer periods of time. All of the tests were coming back normal and he was responding appropriately. He was even taking a few steps.

"The doctor said that you can probably be discharged soon," Logan told him.

His face brightened. "I can go home?"

"Well," she said, looking down at her feet. "They said you'll have to go to a rehab facility for about a month until you get all of your strength back."

He looked so disappointed. She took his hand. "It'll go by fast and I'll be there every day. Just do what they tell you so you can come home."

"Crank up the bed so I can sit up."

Logan got him sitting and adjusted the pillows so he was comfortable.

"Tell me everything that happened. I've gotten bits and pieces, but still don't have the full story."

"Well, as you know, it started with Millicent's death."

"Poor Millicent. I'm going to miss her."

Logan filled him in on being kidnapped and Michael's confession. When she mentioned Peter, he interrupted.

"Logan," he said, "I remembered everything about the day that Peter disappeared. We were playing outside. Me, Michael, and Peter. Your father was off with his friends somewhere. Michael wanted the truck Peter was playing with. It was Peter's favorite and he wouldn't let Michael have it. Michael grabbed it and ran off toward the outhouse and Peter ran after him, crying. Michael was laughing and waving the truck just out of Peter's reach. Peter was jumping up to grab it and Michael crashed the truck down on his head."

"Oh my God, Ran, I'm so sorry."

"I was almost four at the time. I ran over to Peter, but he didn't move. Of course, at that age I didn't know what that meant. Michael shoved me and I fell in the dirt. He put his hands around my throat and told me if I ever told anybody that he would kill me. I couldn't breathe and I must have passed out. When I woke up, Peter and Michael weren't there. I heard noises coming from the outhouse and went over. Michael was in there throwing sticks and leaves and stuff into the pit. He saw me and punched me in the stomach and told me to forget everything I saw. And I did. I guess I was so terrified that I blocked everything out."

"Ran, you were so little. It's not surprising you would block it all out."

"I saw Peter while I was in the coma." He looked at Logan. "He talked to me. He told me that he was happy and not to worry." He sighed. "I did see him, you know."

"I do believe that you saw him." Logan debated whether or not to tell him about her mother, and decided that he was going to find out anyway. She would rather he hear it from her. She turned and looked at him.

"There are some other things Michael told me while he was holding me hostage." She took a deep breath. "He admitted that he killed my mother and buried her on the estate. They found three skulls and some bones in the tunnel, and are running tests to see if one is my mother."

Ran's face turned ashen. "All those years you thought she left you. I'm sorry he did that to you. I should have protected you. I should have known."

"Nobody knew. He was good, but let's not talk about him right now. How are you doing?" she asked, patting his hand.

"I should be asking you that." He wiped the tears from the corners of her eyes. "Logan, he was evil. I think our mother knew it. She always seemed to be extra hard on him. Always watching him. Now that I look back, a lot of things make sense."

"Do you remember what happened in the attic?"

"No." His eyes were sad. "I was looking through some drawers. I heard a noise, but that's all. I guess he thought he needed to get rid of me. He knew we were digging around in the attic. I think he was afraid that if we found any photographs or records referring to Peter that I would remember what happened that day. I'm not a scared little kid anymore. Michael knew that if I remembered I would report it."

"He knew that if you continued with the restoration it was only a matter of time until we had some archaeologists come in and excavate the outhouse," said Logan.

"I remember that Millicent mentioned something about that in one of our meetings. I guess Michael couldn't take that chance. Of course, I had no idea…"

"He wanted to make sure he got his hands on the estate," said Logan. "He made plans with C.J. to develop it. He was going to take the money and disappear before any excavation could take place. When he realized that Millicent discovered the blueprints showing the tunnel, he knew he had to move fast."

"I'm so sorry he hurt so many people," said Ran.

"I'm sorry C.J. got herself involved with Michael," said Logan. "I heard that she's declaring bankruptcy. I hope it was all worth it. She could have stopped Michael if she'd said something instead of going along with him. Why don't you close your eyes and get some rest?"

Ran was resting when Costello and Rose came in. They chatted in low tones while Ran slept.

A loud voice echoed through the halls and they rushed to the door. Before they got there, someone shouted, "You killed my boy. Hell is too good for you." Shots rang out.

Logan and Rose jumped back into the room. Mass chaos ensued. They heard feet pounding down the hallway, and peeked around the door. Everyone was running, some toward the crumpled body on the floor by the nurses' station, some toward the gunman, and some ran from the scene, ducking into rooms. People were shouting orders and others were screaming.

They watched the activity. Logan's hand flew to her mouth. "It's Michael," she said, looking at the body lying in a pool of blood. "Look, Mrs. Donahue. The police have her on the floor. Oh my God, they're cuffing her."

She heard movement behind her and turned. Ran was trying to get out of bed. "No, you stay where you are," she said. Rose ran to him. "Do not get out of that bed."

"What's going on? I heard you mention Michael."

"Lay back."

"I heard gunshots."

"I know. The gunman isn't going to hurt anyone else. The police have everything under control."

"Was anyone hurt?"

She had to tell him before he heard it from someone else. "Yes, someone was hurt." He watched her, waiting for more.

"What's happening?" he asked, trying to get out of bed again.

She went to his side, nudged him back in bed, and took a deep breath. She saw Rose slip into the hallway. "It was Michael. He was shot. Mrs. Donahue shot him. I'm sure he's dead."

Ran was grey and silent. Logan was just about to get a nurse when he spoke. "It's for the best."

Logan processed his reaction. While his comment sounded uncaring, even cavalier, she knew better. And he was right.

Everyone knew what he had done. A trial would drag on for years because she was sure Michael would do everything he could to remain in the limelight. That is, if he didn't escape. He would file appeal after appeal. His legal machinations would prevent them from putting this nightmare behind them and moving on. But she also knew Ran was grieving, for the loss of his brother, but mostly for Michael's victims.

Rose came back into the room shaking her head, letting Logan know what she already knew. "Mrs. Donahue's in custody, but I think they're going to take her up to the fourth floor."

"Fourth floor?" asked Ran.

"The Psychiatric Ward," said Logan.

When all the excitement died down and they were settled back in Ran's room, Logan reminded him that on the morning he was attacked he had called her to say he had found something.

His face lit up. "Oh, that. I completely forgot about it. I found a letter addressed to the Armstrong family. It was dated 1869 from a Quaker organization. The letter thanked them for their part in assisting slaves to freedom before, during, and after the Civil War, by way of the Underground Railroad."

"Really? We should frame it."

His face clouded over and Logan noticed that his eyes became moist. "Are you okay?"

"He tore it up."

"Tore it up? Who? Michael? But why?"

"He didn't want any documentation that would support Millicent's bid for landmark designation."

"Maybe we can tape it back together. We'll look at it later," she said, patting his hand. "It'll be okay."

The nurse came into the room. "Good news, Mrs. O'Malley. The doctor is completing your discharge papers. You should be able to go home in an hour or so. Do you have someone who can pick you up?"

"I'll take her home," said Costello.

Logan glanced up at him, startled. "That's not necessary. Rose can take me home."

Rose looked from Costello to Logan. "Sorry, Logan, I can't do it. I have something to do," she said, but Logan caught Rose winking at Costello.

*Ah, a conspiracy.* Rose matchmaking again. This time, though, Logan realized she didn't mind. In fact, she was looking forward to spending some time with him. And she didn't feel guilty. Didn't feel like she was betraying Luke.

"I'd better get my stuff packed."

"I'll help you," said Costello.

"I'll stay and visit with Ran," said Rose.

Costello pulled up in front of Logan's house and helped her out of the car. Mrs. Rosen was sweeping as usual, wearing the same black skirt, white starched blouse, and sensible shoes. Logan noticed that her face was softer. Her lips weren't just a thin line, but were parted. Not quite a smile, but close. She stopped sweeping when they got out of the car and came over to Logan.

"Mrs. Rosen, thank you for your help. The information you gave the detectives helped them find me."

"I'm sorry you were hurt. I hope you're getting better."

"I am. Thank you."

The silence stretched into awkwardness until Costello spoke. "Mrs. Rosen, thank you. You were a big help in the investigation."

"That man. Did he go to jail?"

"He's dead, Mrs. Rosen. He won't hurt anyone else."

"Good."

"Well, I need to get Logan in. She still needs her rest."

"Thank you again," said Logan.

Costello made them each a cup of tea and set them down on the coffee table. Logan started to lean forward and winced. "You sit back," he said, handing her the mug.

"Costello."

"Would you call me Frank, please? Costello sounds so impersonal."

"Okay, Frank. Thank you for everything you did. I have to say, I was really worried about getting arrested." She looked directly at him. "Did you really think I was guilty?" He hesitated before answering. Her heart sank. He thought she was guilty, capable of hurting another human. "It's okay, you don't have to answer. I shouldn't have asked."

"No. I want to answer." He took her mug and set it back on the table, and took her hands in his. She tried to pull back, but he held tight. "The evidence was piling up and it looked like you could've done it." She tried again to pull away from him, but he wouldn't let her. "I said the evidence looked bad, but my gut told me that there was no way you did it. I was doing my own investigation, but don't tell Beatty," he said, winking. "He really thought you did it."

"Yeah, and he supposedly has such great instincts."

"Well, I think the fact that your uncle was a priest biased him. He has a real problem with the church."

"Rose told me that her brother went to high school with Beatty and that something happened. Beatty left school. Her brother said after that he was mean."

Costello didn't say anything, but Logan had the sense that he knew something. "So, you really didn't think I did it?"

"No, I didn't. Now, I have a question for you."

"What?"

"Will you have dinner with me?"

Logan didn't know what she was expecting him to ask, but that wasn't it. Without hesitation, she said, "Yes."

"We'll wait for you to mend some, but it's a date."

A date. It had been a long time since she'd been asked out on a date. "I'm looking forward to it."

"I have to get back to the station and fill out paperwork. Will you be okay?"

"I'll be fine. You go do your paperwork. I have a question of my own, though. If you're a psychologist, why are you playing detective?"

"I was a police officer before I was a psychologist. The department wanted me to work full-time as the department psychologist, but I love being a detective. We compromised. I work cases but I also do criminal profiling."

"Why did Beatty react the way he did that day Mrs. Rosen attacked him?"

He sat for the longest time, and Logan thought he wasn't going to answer. He cleared his throat. "Let's just say he doesn't believe in criminal profiling. He's old school."

"Are you building a profile on him? If you're not, you should be. I think he needs help."

Costello laughed. "Don't we all. I really do need to go, and you need to get some rest. You stay there," he said when she started to get up. "I'll let myself out." He leaned down and kissed her on the cheek. "I'll pick you up in the morning. Ten okay?"

"That'll be fine, but Rose can take me."

"Not a problem. Get some rest. I'll see you in the morning." With that he was gone.

Logan was ready and waiting when Frank pulled up at precisely ten. They rode to the hospital in silence. Not an awkward silence, but a companionable one. When they got to Ran's room, he was sitting up having a cup of coffee.

"So, how are you feeling this morning?" Logan asked him. "You're looking much better."

"I'm fine. I was thinking about everything that happened. I know you told me, but some things are still muddled. You know," he said to Costello, "I'm not clear on why Michael did the things he did."

"Michael wanted the property so he could sell it to C.J.," he said. "They'd already made a deal. There were a couple of circumstances that caused Michael to escalate his plans. If the existence of the tunnel came to light, along with its possible link to the Underground Railroad, then all of Michael's plans were for naught. Too many historians would be looking at the property for Michael to quietly get rid of you so that he would inherit. Then, you threw a monkey wrench into his plans when you went to see your attorney. He found out that you changed your will to leave the property to Logan. That's why he kidnapped her."

Ran looked at her. "Logan, I'm so sorry. I wanted to help you, and all I ended up doing was hurting you. I almost lost you." He hugged her.

Logan cleared her throat. "About the property."

Ran held up his hand. "It's yours Logan. And forget about the will. I'm going to transfer the deed to you. You and Luke always wanted to start a visual arts program for disadvantaged kids. The estate is the perfect place. There's plenty of room."

Her eyes teared. "I don't know what to say. That's so generous. There's something else you don't know."

He looked at her expectantly.

"Michael confessed to me that Rose is his daughter."

Ran's mouth dropped open. "How…Are you sure?"

"I'm sure. He raped Rose's mother and Rose was the result."

"Is there no end to all the harm he's done?"

Murder at Mount Joy | 277

"I know."

She gave him a few minutes to compose himself, then he smiled. "She's my niece, and your cousin. Our family has grown a bit."

"I know. And I'm thrilled. I want to put Rose's name on the deed. Split the property."

"Are you sure?"

"Very. She's family too."

He smiled up at her. "That can be arranged," said Ran. "I'll call my attorney tomorrow and have him draw up the papers."

"Ran, I'm so very sorry about Michael."

He took her hand. "It's okay. I've never had any illusions about Michael. He was always selfish and self-centered, but I never realized how evil he was."

"I never had a clue either," said Logan. "To me, he was always kind and caring."

"That was all part of the act," said Ran. "He was a con. People believed in him because he told them what they wanted to hear."

"And, he was a priest," whispered Logan.

"Yes, he was a priest," Ran said.

Logan saw the sadness in his eyes.

Rose came into the room and stopped short, looking at each of them. "I'm sorry. I didn't mean to interrupt."

"No, come in," said Ran, extending his arms to hug her. "You're family too."

Rose smiled. "It'll take some getting used to. I've known you most of my life as a friend, now I have to switch my thinking to include you as family."

"I think Logan has something to tell you." He winked at her, and Rose turned.

"Ran wants to deed Mount Joy over to me to use for the visual arts center."

"Really? I'm so happy for you. It's perfect."

"That's the plan. But there's more."

Rose looked at her. "More? That's pretty big."

"It is, but," she looked at Rose, "and here's the best part, you'll be co-owner."

Rose sat down on the edge of the bed, looking from one to the other. "You're serious? I can't believe it. Are you sure?"

"You're family and deserve it as much as I do." But she was thinking that Rose deserved it even more than she did. "And, it solves your gallery problem. We can have everything under one roof. My students can create and you can exhibit."

Ran took Logan's and Rose's hands in each of his own and squeezed them. Rose turned sharply to Ran. "Wait, where will you live? That's your home."

"No, it belongs to the next generation. I don't want to maintain it, and it's too large for me to live in alone. No, the better use is for the two of you to create something new."

"But what about you?"

"I think the cottage suits me just fine."

"The cottage?" said Rose. "It's falling apart."

"We'll have someone bring it back, or better yet, tear it down and build a new one. It suits me much better. And I can still work on my antique cars and see both of you."

"I'll have an apartment upstairs in the main house and there'll be another one for you if you want," said Logan, looking at Rose.

"I don't know what to say. This is a bit overwhelming."

"Take note, Ran," Logan laughed. "Rose is overwhelmed and speechless. You won't often get to see that," and he laughed along with her.

"This is all going to take some getting used to. I don't mean to seem ungrateful, but can I think about the moving in part?"

"No need to explain. Think about it. And you might just use it when you're preparing for an exhibition. Whatever you want is fine with me."

"What are you going to do with your house?"

"I don't know. Sell it and everything in it, except some personal stuff that I love."

"Everything?"

"Yep, everything. Clothes, jewelry, furniture."

"What about Vanessa?"

"She'll be welcome at Mount Joy anytime."

"Amazing," said Ran and Rose in unison. They all laughed.

"Logan's back." Rose hugged her.

# CHAPTER 18

They spent the next few days discussing renovation plans. In the end it was decided they would raze the old cottage and build a new one. Ran left the details up to Logan. He told her to surprise him, so surprise him she would.

"I'm going to get busy with the plans. We want the cottage ready when you come home."

"I don't need to go to rehab. I feel just fine."

"Now, don't argue. You've had a serious head injury and you were in a coma. Just do it for me. When you come home, everything will be ready." He shrugged. "And don't be arguing with the doctors and nurses. Now, I have some errands to run. I'll be back later." She leaned down and kissed him. "You behave yourself."

She and Costello headed toward the car. "You've got your work cut out for you," he said.

"I know. I have a contractor lined up to build the cottage. I have to meet him this afternoon at the estate."

"I'll go with you, but I was referring to Ran."

She laughed. "He's definitely feeling better. You don't have to go with me. You must have work to do." She felt him withdraw and looked up at him, confused. "What's wrong?"

"Nothing."

"You're upset."

He sighed. "I thought we could spend some time together today."

"Oh."

He waited for more, but that's all she said. They walked in silence to the car. He helped her in, then got in himself. "Where should I drop you?"

"What is your problem? You know I have to take care of these things. And I didn't know you wanted to spend the day together. I don't read minds." She sat staring straight ahead, but could see him watching her.

He took her hand, but she still didn't move or look at him. "Logan."

"What?" she asked, still staring ahead.

He gently turned her head to face him. "I'm sorry. I was hoping to spend some time with you. I was disappointed."

She looked down. "I'm sorry too," she mumbled. "Do you want to go with me to the estate?"

"I do." He started the car and off they went. They drove a few blocks before he spoke again. "What are your plans for the cottage?"

"I have a contractor coming with some floor plans. I told him what I wanted. All I have to do is pick the one that will be best for Ran."

"What time are we meeting this guy?"

"We still have a couple of hours, but I want to start sorting everything. There are some things that we'll want to put into Ran's cottage and keep with the house once it's restored. That stuff we'll put in storage. There are other things that will be auctioned, then the rest will be given to charity or tossed. I have to order a dumpster and a storage pod."

They pulled into the driveway and went directly to the estate. "Well, let's take a look at where to start," he said.

They wandered through the downstairs. "I think we should start down here. Get this floor cleaned out first, then we can begin moving things from upstairs."

"You'll have to wait for the all clear from the crime scene investigators," Frank said.

"Yes, Detective."

They were standing in the dining room. Logan noticed an ornately carved ebony box, roughly fourteen inches wide by nine inches deep and ten inches high. "I wonder how this got here," she said.

"What is it?"

"It's Michael's. He said it belonged to his mother's family. He had it on the bookshelf behind his desk." She opened it and gasped.

"What?"

She lifted the Kodak Brownie camera from the box. Her hands were shaking.

Frank took the camera and set it down. "What's wrong?" he asked, holding her hands.

"My camera," she choked out. "I thought it was lost."

"Are you sure this is yours?"

"Of course I'm sure." She felt the tightness in her chest and the twisting of her stomach. "My mother gave it to me the day she disappeared. I didn't miss it right away. Everything was so confusing. I looked for it about a week later, because it had pictures of my mother. I wanted to get them developed."

Costello put his arm around her shoulder.

"But, how did it get in this box? And why did Michael have it?"

Costello lifted the other items out and placed them on the table. When he held up the locket, Logan's hand went to her throat.

"My God."

Her face was grey. He lowered her into a chair and brought her a glass of water. "Oh my God. Oh my God," she repeated. Her whole body trembled.

"Here, sip this," he said, pressing the glass to her quivering lips. "It's hers."

"Who?"

"My mother. She was wearing it the day she disappeared."

Costello's lips were a thin line. "You're sure?"

"Positive. I saved my allowance and gave it to her a couple of months before she…before that day. It was a birthday present. Look inside. There's a picture of me on one side and my father on the other."

He opened the locket and the two faces stared up at him. He looked at the other items. "Do you recognize anything else?"

She examined each item, shaking her head.

He pulled out his phone and called Beatty. "I'm out at the Ranford estate. I think you should come out." Costello listened. "Yeah. Okay," he said, and hung up.

"What's going on?"

He took a deep breath. "We know there are at least two other bodies in the tunnel. We don't know who they might be, if this is what I think it is, we might be able to identify them."

"I don't understand."

"This looks like a trophy box." She looked at him, brows furrowed. He took her hands. "Serial killers often take something from their victims. A trophy. This box has a locket that belonged to your mother. We know Michael killed your mother."

"You're saying these things are all from other people? That he killed all these people?" Her voice rose a few octaves.

"The archaeologists are excavating at least three bodies."

"Do you think one is my mother?"

"It's too soon to tell. An hour ago I would have been fairly confident that it was. Now," he said, looking at the items laid out on the table, "I'm not so sure."

"Oh, God. I thought this was over and it looks like it's just beginning."

"There was always the possibility that there were other victims."

"I know. I was just hoping there weren't."

"Let's not jump to conclusions."

They heard a car pull up and a door slam.

"Beatty," he said. "I'll talk to him." He met Beatty on the porch. Logan watched them walk around the clearing, talking, gesturing toward the woods before walking to the house.

"You think there are more bodies on the property." It was a statement. Neither detective spoke. That was her answer. "Here's the box."

"I'll take this stuff back to the station and begin searching the missing persons records. See if we can match any of these items to a missing person. If we get any hits, we'll bring out cadaver dogs."

"Talk to Mrs. Donahue. She might know something. Get back to me later," Costello said as Beatty left. "Let's take a walk," he suggested to Logan.

Logan took a deep breath of fresh air, then turned to Costello. "What's up?"

"It's about that photograph you saw on my desk."

"Oh."

"You recognized him."

She was looking down at the ground. Her hands went back to the old habit of cracking her knuckles.

"Logan."

"He hangs out on Market Street." She looked up. "Why are you asking?"

"It's an ongoing investigation."

"What did he do?"

"How well do you know him?"

"I've never met him. I've just seen him around the neighborhood."

He tilted her head up and watched. "You know your friend, Jewel, hangs out with him."

"I know. Is she in trouble?"

"Depends. Do we have anything on her? Not yet."

"But you're looking."

"We're investigating drug trafficking. We know Jimmy was growing the stuff. We know the man in the photograph is a low level dealer. What we don't know is who's in charge."

"I can tell you that."

"What? You know and didn't say anything?"

"I just found out," she said, crossing her arms, "and pardon me if it slipped my mind. What with a couple of murders, Ran in a coma, getting kidnapped and almost murdered, finding out about my mother…"

"I'm sorry. I get it. We've been investigating this for almost a year, and we're still not any closer to shutting it down. None of the low level dealers have any idea who's in charge, but they're scared. I'm not sure they'd tell us even if they knew."

"It was Michael. He confessed it to me in the tunnel."

"Michael. And he's dead."

"He had a journal with names, dates, amounts, etc."

"Great. Where is it?"

"I don't know. He said Jimmy stole it. That's why the cottage was torn apart. Apparently Jimmy told him he hid it."

"So we don't have any idea where he hid it."

"None."

"Well, with Michael dead, maybe some of these guys'll be willing to cut a deal."

"What about Jewel?"

"We don't have anything to connect her with dealing. Smoking? Probably."

The sound of a car approaching stopped the conversation. Logan went to greet Tim Lockhart, the contractor. He brought a half dozen plans and they spent the next few hours evaluating everything. Logan asked Frank for his opinion and together they choose a bungalow that she thought Ran would like and would suit his needs. She made minor changes, showed him the site, and he promised to have his crew out as soon as the investigation was complete.

"Let's see if we can find Jewel. I promised to show her how to download pictures and print them. Maybe she'll talk to me, but I won't push her. She has some serious trust issues."

"Do you think it's a good idea to let her know where you live?"

"It'll be okay."

They found her walking alone toward the park. Logan called to her. "I thought you might want to learn how to print some of the pictures you took the other day."

She saw that flicker of interest again. "Hop in."

Jewel took a step back and examined the car. "You expect me to ride in a cop car?"

"It's unmarked."

"Pleaseeee."

"Yeah, you're right. It might as well have neon lights all over it."

She did a quick survey of her surroundings and jumped in, slamming the door. She slouched down in the seat. *Making sure none of her friends saw her getting into a cop car,* thought Logan. And off they went.

"I have everything downloaded to the computer. We can print them, and if you want later we can play with some of the software, get creative." They pulled up to Logan's house.

"You live here?" she asked, her mouth open, taking in her surroundings.

Logan was almost embarrassed to admit it. She could only imagine where this girl lived and the conditions she lived in.

Mrs. Rosen was out sweeping, but instead of waving her broom at them, she stopped and gave them a smile.

"Hello, Mrs. Rosen."

"How are you feeling?"

"Getting better. Thanks. Mrs. Rosen, this is Jewel. She's my first student at the visual arts center."

"Hello, Jewel."

"Hello," she said, not making eye contact.

"We'll see you later," said Logan, opening the door and ushering Frank and Jewel inside.

"First things first," she said, hanging up her coat. "Something to eat. Are you two hungry?"

"I am," said Frank enthusiastically.

"I guess so," said Jewel.

"There's not much here in the way of groceries. Is pizza okay with everyone?"

"Fine."

"What do you two like?"

"Everything," said Frank.

"Jewel?"

"Whatever," she said, shrugging. Logan rolled her eyes at Frank.

"I'll order," he said, taking out his cell phone.

"Jewel, come on up to my office. We can get started while we're waiting for the pizza."

Jewel climbed the stairs, her head snapping every which way, trying not to miss anything.

"Here we are," she said, switching on the overhead light. "First, do you know anything about computers?"

"No."

"No problem, we'll start at the beginning. You're a quick study. You'll have this down in no time."

Logan gave her a crash course on hardware, software, and how they work together. They'd just finished when the doorbell rang.

"Pizza's here. Let's take a break."

They chatted about everything and nothing. Jewel began to open up and share some minimal personal information. She had four brothers and two sisters. No father. No information about where she lived or her home life. She thought school was boring.

Jewel was exceptionally bright from where Logan stood, with a thirst for learning. The slow pace and constant disruptions of public school education would take their toll on someone like Jewel. School wasn't designed to allow students to be creative. It was all about test scores and memorizing the material to pass the state and federally mandated tests.

Frank offered to clear away the debris if Logan and Jewel wanted to get back to work. Logan quickly agreed. Jewel watched Frank take the dishes over to the sink, fascinated.

They spent hours printing, playing with the software, and printing some more. Jewel's images were spectacular, both the originals and the creatively manipulated images. They went downstairs, amazed to find Frank and Mrs. Rosen sitting in the breakfast nook, sharing a cup of tea.

"Finished?" asked Frank.

"For now. Jewel, show them what you've created."

She had the pictures pressed to her chest and hesitated before laying them out on the counter.

No one said anything for several minutes, and Logan could see Jewel begin to fidget. Then Frank spoke up. "Jewel, I've never seen anything like this." A look of fear passed over her face before being replaced by her usual passive expression. Frank continued, "They're amazing."

Mrs. Rosen's hand went to her throat. "They're beautiful. I've never seen anything like them."

Jewel's eyes shone with pride, and for the first time, she really smiled.

Six weeks later, the contents of the house and outbuildings had been sorted. The police took anything that might be relevant to their investigation. Everything that was going into the restored estate was put in storage, and the rest of the contents were auctioned, donated, or trashed. They also found another closet in the attic which contained a stack of original oil paintings in various sizes, signed by one of the Armstrongs. They depicted the peace of the river and the hustle and bustle of the city. Logan decided she would hang them in prominent places throughout the estate.

But it was the contents of one of the sheds that was the most exciting find of all. In the back of one of the dimly lit sheds they found a large piece of machinery under a tarp. Ran was speechless when he uncovered it. Logan could see enough to know it was an antique car. But apparently Ran recognized the model and was so excited that all he could say was "Oh my God," over and over again. The car looked to Logan like it was in somewhat decent shape. It needed work, but wasn't a pile of rust. The tarp must have given it some protection, she thought.

Ran was gently running his hand over the chrome. "Incredible," he was saying. "Unbelievable."

"Would you like to share what is so incredible and unbelievable with the rest of us," said Logan with a teasing lilt to her voice.

"Oh, Logan. What a find. I can't believe this has been sitting here all this time."

"It looks like an antique car."

"This isn't just any antique car. This is a 1920 Rolls Royce Silver Ghost Pall Mall Touring car. I just can't believe that this car's been right under my nose the whole time."

"Where did it come from. Whose car is it?"

He paused, brow furrowed. "I remember hearing about it when I was little, but of course, I didn't really know what it was they were talking about. I'm pretty sure it originally belonged to my grandparents. But, I seem to remember something else," his brow furrowed.

"Did you ever ride in it?"

"That's it. My father used to take us out on Sunday afternoon for a drive."

Logan saw sadness pass over his face.

"What?"

"Peter loved riding in the car. He used to sit in it and pretend he was driving."

"Maybe that's why it was put away. Like those boxes we found with Peter's photos and clothes."

"That would be just like my mother. It's like she erased Peter from our lives." Logan noted the bitterness in his voice. "I had no idea this car was here the whole time, I just can't believe it."

He got a few of the workers to help him move it outside so he could get a better look at it.

Logan heard someone coming up the lane, and turned to see Jewel. She lingered at the edge of the clearing, looking down at her feet.

"Jewel, it's good to see you," said Logan, walking over.

"I have something for him," she said, nodding toward Frank. Logan waved him over.

"What's up?"

"Jewel says she has something for you."

With that, Jewel opened her backpack and handed him a large manila envelope.

"What's this?" he said, opening it and pulling out a book. He flipped through the pages. "Jewel, where did you get this?"

"What is it?" asked Logan.

"Why don't we go somewhere more private and you can tell us how you came to be in possession of this."

"I didn't do anything wrong." Her eyes darted around like she was looking for an escape route.

"Jewel, we know you didn't," said Logan, leading her down toward Ran's bungalow-in-progress.

"Let's sit here," she said, indicating the steps. Logan, Jewel, and Frank each took a step. "Tell us what happened."

Jewel looked at Frank. "I didn't do anything wrong," she said again.

"I know. Where did you get the book?"

"Jimmy."

"Jimmy gave it to you? You knew him?"

"He was friends with Luis."

"Who's Luis?" asked Logan.

"The guy in the picture," said Frank. "The one who always carries the cane with the skeleton handle." He looked at Jewel. "That's him, right?"

She nodded.

"It's okay. Take your time," said Logan.

"I saw Jimmy give it to Luis and tell him to hide it, that someday soon it would be worth a lot of money, and then Jimmy was dead.

I thought Luis killed him so he could have all the money. So when Luis went out, I snuck in and found the book. Then I heard Luis coming back and he was with some man and they were arguing. I put it back and hid. I didn't have time to get out."

"Do you know who the other man was?" asked Frank.

"He was the man who hurt Logan."

"Michael," said Logan.

"What happened next?" asked Frank.

"The man told Luis that Jimmy stole a book from him and asked if Luis knew anything about it. He said no. Then the other man told him that if he found out he had the book he was dead."

"You must have been terrified," said Logan.

Jewel looked down and shrugged, then continued. "Luis laughed and asked him what was so important about it. The man said that if the wrong people got it then they were all going to jail. Then he left."

"When was this?" asked Frank.

"The day before Logan was in the hospital."

"But you didn't know what was in the book?" he asked.

"I saw a bunch of names and stuff."

"Did you know Jimmy was growing pot and that Luis was one of the distributors?"

She looked down and began picking her cuticles.

"Jewel," Logan said, "you're not in any trouble. Frank needs to know everything you can tell him."

"I heard you two talking. Frank said he wished he knew what Jimmy did with that ledger. I figured that was the book Jimmy gave Luis, so when he was out I snuck in and took it. Then came here."

Frank opened the ledger and ran his finger down the column of names. He looked at Logan and smiled, and Logan breathed a sigh of relief.

"Thank you, God," she said, looking to the sky.

Frank turned back to the first page and scrutinized it. He thumbed through a few more of the pages, a huge smile on his face, then snapped it shut.

"I've got to get to headquarters."

"Jewel, you took a big risk. Thank you, and don't ever do anything like that again. Promise?" Logan said. For all her street smarts, she was still such a child.

"I promise."

Frank gave Logan a quick kiss and squeezed Jewel's shoulder, then practically ran to his car with the ledger tucked under his arm.

A week later, Logan stood back squinting through the scaffolding to see how the restoration was progressing. The company assured them that it would be completed by the end of December. In time for her to open after the holidays. Logan couldn't see how that was possible, but…

"It's coming along," said Frank, draping his greasy arm over her shoulder and looking up at the house.

"How's your restoration going?" she asked, looking over at the garage.

"We're waiting for some parts from England. They should be here in plenty of time to have it ready for the classic car show in Hershey in October. I must say, it's a beauty."

"Thank you for helping Ran."

"Don't thank me. My motives are purely selfish."

She looked up at him. "Oh, and what might those selfish motives be?"

"I've always enjoyed working on cars, and you have to admit this is a once in a lifetime opportunity. A Rolls Royce," he said, shaking his head and laughing at her frown. "Of course, seeing you every day is an added benefit," he said, squeezing her.

"I'm glad you're here. For my uncle and myself."

"Logan," called the site manager.

"Duty calls. Another crisis to avert."

They ironed out some minor details, and he went back to share them with his crew. Logan busied herself with making choices about rugs, paint, etc.

"It's really coming along."

Logan turned to see Rose standing there. "When did you get here? I didn't see you come up."

"I left my car at Ran's bungalow. Didn't want to risk driving over a nail and getting a flat. Where's Frank?"

"Probably in the garage with Ran. The two of them have been glued to that car. I think a couple of Jewel's friends are with them."

"Jewel looks happy," said Rose, looking toward the garden. "It's great to see her smile."

"It is. She has a knack with the garden. It's really taking shape. Frank said her two friends know their way around cars, but I'm not going to speculate how they came by that knowledge," she said, laughing. "Jewel's bringing a friend by this afternoon who wants to learn photography."

"That wall she built to protect herself is slowly disintegrating," said Rose. "She's an amazing young lady. And talented."

"And a hard worker. She pitches in wherever she's needed without any complaints. And she seems to enjoy the work."

"She feels needed. I'm looking forward to displaying her work. I'll have to come up with a unique display that will enhance her themes," said Rose.

"You'll do an extraordinary job, as always," said Logan. "You'll have plenty of time. The grand opening's planned for the first weekend in January,"